FATEFUL
HOPE

Cover design by Ryan Slaven
Layout by www.spiffingcovers.com

Find out more here: www.aleksandrjarid.com

FATEFUL
HOPE

Aleksandr Jarid

"Love has a construct of confusion and clarity that transcends any manner of our intelligence. If you have never been so clearly confused over something, then that is the moment you are in love. Remain confused."

Aleksandr Jarid 2021

Thanks to all to have given me so much love and support in this project.

To Beverley who planted the seed to write thoughts down and started this journey for me.

Dearest Paige, editor and all-round boss, who without your guidance, this would not have been completed.

Ryan for your talent at cover design and bringing my imagination to life. Your visual ideas make me want to write more!

The ever efficient Gabriel and his team at the endless detail in getting this to a presentable state out there for all to have!

Charlie for the dinners, words of wisdom and the gin. Miss you dearly. (Don't say a word!)

The tour guides at St Paul's Cathedral and at The London Mithra Temple. Your knowledge was fundamental here.

The amazing staff at the OXO Tower resturant for the fun times and to be able to create the scene for one of the chapters.

Hollie, my dear friend. Thank you for the inspiration and direction on character building!

All the staff at University College Hospital and St Mungo's doing outstanding work and allowing me to create stories from you all.

Special thanks, forever in my thoughts and heart, always to… (No name needed. You changed my life forever)

"It's easy to see things going wrong now. It's easy to wallow in a sad song… so we might as well dance in the light of the moon…we might as well dance before you kiss me goodbye."

Madeleine Peyroux. *We Might As Well Dance*

PROLOGUE

As he lies there, motionless, she slowly walks up to him. He blinks, his vision maintaining a fuzzy field, though he can just make out the silhouette moving towards him. The outline darkens and the edges blur against the bright light behind her. The weight of his eyelids causes a simple function to take so much effort. The figure blocks out all the light and crouches by his side.

He feels the cold, hard, stone floor against his back, pressing through his perspiration-soaked shirt. He wonders for a moment if his sweat is the only cause, or if it has something to do with the warm, thick liquid trickling down his face.

He does not know how he got here or even whereabouts 'here' is.

He can feel the liquid trickling into his mouth. Around his lips. It's warm. Metallic.

A fall: no, definitely a push – he recalls a push, a struggle and a flash. Was it the sunlight, perhaps? A bolt of lightning? He's unsure.

Pain pierces through his head and he groans at the energy of the disturbance.

Cameron feels a warm droplet on his face, which trickles down into the corner of his mouth. It's salty.

A tear.

Emilie's tears.
Turn back; don't leave.
Then darkness and silence.
The ringing ends as Emilie walks away.

PART ONE

CHAPTER ZERO

London, before

The warmth of the afternoon sun reflected high on the horizon. Buildings mirrored the rays, creating the haze and glow of a perfect day. Emilie walked up the steps, squinting her almond eyes against the brightness. The gentle breeze gracefully moved her hair across her face, coming to rest on her shoulders. The sun's rays gave her a glow with a vivid brilliance of comfort, the type that would magnetise one's soul. A radiant smile crept across her face as she looked up. That entrancing smile could penetrate every aspect of your body, enticing you into her safe invitation.

Emilie wrapped her arms around Cameron and kissed him passionately, drawing him tight into her. As they parted, she held his face with her left hand, looking deep into his eyes. In her right hand, she held a bag containing a jacket. She handed it to him and smiled again... this time an intimate yet shy smile that spoke a thousand hidden words.

"Thank you for bringing the jacket. I hope it didn't take you out of your way... Do you have time for coffee?" He calmly waited for a reply, looking directly into those enthralling eyes.

A slightly choked response flowed from her, "Super busy day today, actually. Let's get coffee another time, if that's OK?" He matched her reply with a simple shrug; however, the answer left him unsettled.

A simple, innocent combination of words, informative, polite, yet said in a tone that was direct and cold in its manner, caused an alarming notion to rise in Cameron. A meaning that perhaps one day it might be discovered. Emilie flashed a casual show of affection as if she knew her intimate feelings might have peaked through the surface. They rubbed noses, yet he felt a sudden rush of uneasiness as she walked away.

"Give me a call later then, when you are free!" Cameron shouted after her, watching her retreating figure hurry down the steps and back onto the street.

There was a slight pause from Emilie. She motioned to turn back and look over her shoulder to face him, but she resisted and carried on her way, getting lost in the busy street.

The afternoon dragged into the evening. The unsettled feeling within Cameron persisted throughout. Checking and rechecking his phone for any messages or calls from Emilie proved to be pointless. It was unlike her to not even send a smiley face – just to let him know she was busy, but still thinking of him. His messages had gone unread so far.

```
Thank you again for the Jacket :) 15.26

Hey how is your busy afternoon going?
17.13

Is everything ok?! 18.57
```

Emilie?! 19.25

Each time he tried calling the phone rang out, eventually reaching her voicemail. Cameron felt his normal inner calmness becoming replaced by an uncertainty that grew and grew like a tight band around his chest, almost to the point of physical pain.

Hey, listen, not sure if you are home and just shattered, but I'm nearby and was going to pop round to say hi. Be there in 25 mins xx. Cameron sent the text at 20.18.

Then, he made his way to her apartment, his spare key to the building clutched firmly in the palm of his hand. They both had each other's apartment keys and it was a comforting feeling that each of them could stay over any time they wanted. But, on this occasion, Cameron felt like an outsider, an intruder – uninvited and perhaps even unwanted.

One last look at his phone as he stood outside her front door. Wishing and hoping there were missed calls or a message from Emilie to say she was stuck in a meeting or that she had totally forgot that she'd made plans with friends for the evening. He lingered at the door, watching the blank screen until the next minute passed. Still, none of his messages were read. His eyes narrowed and he let out a sigh as he put the key in the lock and twisted.

"Emilie?" he called out as he slowly and gently pushed open the apartment door. It was dark in the hallway as Cameron stepped in. "Emilie? You in?" He flicked the switch to get some light in the hall. Glancing to the coat pegs on the wall, he noticed that all her jackets were missing. He frowned and took slow, deliberate steps, looking over to the master bedroom door. It was slightly ajar with what seemed to be a shirt on the floor just behind it. Cameron pushed the bedroom door open. As he stepped inside, he was met with a chaotic scene of disordered disruption. The wardrobes were open and empty hangers were cluttered around the floor. There were a few items of clothes scattered around the room. Generic items like t-shirts and jeans. The dresser had the contents of the drawers spread all over the surface. Cameron's eyes were wide with fear and confusion. He stood in the middle of the room, transfixed. He called out once again, "Emilie!" This time it came out more as a strangled cry rather than a call with purpose.

It was a cool evening as they sat on the balcony of Somerset House overlooking the busy Embankment road below. Across the river, to the right, the London Eye was slowly rotating with its carriages full of spectators. Cameron allowed Emilie to nestle into him as he watched the slow-moving Ferris wheel. He could feel her breath tickling his neck. "I want us to be a team, Emilie. It's important to me, well, to us, to be able to share not only the good times but also the stressors we face."

There was silence from Emilie. Cameron could feel that their breaths were matched in sequence. Chests rising and falling in unison.

She let out a slight sigh and replied, "We *are* a team. But sometimes, I just need to deal with things alone. It's not me hiding anything. It's just how I process things at times."

"Well, that could risk me thinking all sorts of things and getting the wrong end of the stick. You know how my imagination can work overtime at times!"

"Umm," Emilie hummed. "Don't you trust me?"

Cameron moved Emilie away from him and forced her to sit upright in her chair and untangled his legs from her own. "I didn't say anything about trust, did I? That's you jumping and making your own interpretation again." He got up and took his drink in his hand and walked over to the edge of the balcony and leant against it. "You work a lot, just like I do. But, at times, I feel like you don't want to share your work with me because you think I wouldn't be interested or that..." He trailed off.

"Or what?" Emilie asked, folding her arms across her chest.

He sipped his drink, looking towards the London Eye. "That I would disapprove of your research work?"

CHAPTER ONE

London, now

The restaurant overlooked the London skyline of towering buildings. The structures were illuminated with office lights creating a bed of warmth floating in the night sky. Floor to ceiling windows allowed the restaurant-goers to focus on the outside world while waiting for their exclusive menu of starters and cosmopolitan cocktails. The diners ranged from romantic couples to groups of friends out for a refined evening, all creating memories and mischief. The table staff were methodical in ensuring a smooth experience for their clientele, gliding around with effortless composure.

The Oxo Tower had a distinctive character to its location and history. Overlooking the river on the south aspect of the Embankment, it was a common destination for people to enjoy an elegant evening. The history of this building dated back to the early 1900s when it was a power station, providing electricity to the Royal Mail and Post Office services. Subsequently, it became a meat factory in the 1920s, producing stock cubes called Oxo.

Cameron glanced at his tourbillon watch as he ascended in the lift towards the twelfth floor of the Oxo Tower for the reception of the restaurant. As he leant on the far wall, he caught the eye of the other two female passengers. They smiled covertly to each other upon seeing him, however, they were not at all subtle in how they assessed the attractive gentleman, from head to toe. Both took in his smart, freshly cut and groomed hair, his well-fitted blazer, the tailored shirt underneath and pristine black shoes that were complemented by symmetrically tied laces. The light stubble on his face highlighted his sharp facial features, which, with the slightly deliberate rough look, combined with elegant clothing, made him seem even more irresistible to those women in the lift. They wanted him to take note that he commanded their attention.

Cameron directed a polite, rather thin, non-committal smile at the women, making it clear that he was uninterested in conversation. He kept both hands in his pockets, patiently waiting for them to arrive at their designated floor. This restaurant was one of his personal spaces where he could attend without a reservation – he always managed to secure a table for his dinner date for one. It had been some time now since he had been accompanied and it was obvious that he had no intention of diverting from this practice tonight.

Over time he had become friends with the staff and appreciated that no attempt was ever made to elicit any personal information from him. Cameron did not intend for these two women to break that code of his. He allowed himself to be kind and gentleman-like, however, he ensured he didn't give off any further signals of attention towards them. As the lift doors opened upon their arrival to the twelfth floor, he waited while the ladies approached the reception desk where they were greeted by the concierge who looked over and held his finger up to Cameron.

"I will be with you in one moment, Sir."

Cameron nodded, patient and poised.

When a waiter returned, he led Cameron to his usual seat, where Cameron crossed his legs and leaned back in his chair. His trousers were the perfect length when seated to expose just enough of his black socks neatly resting in his shoes. As he calmly went about adjusting his shirt cuffs so that they made just a slight appearance from underneath his blazer, the waiter took note of Cameron's order of his usual glass of wine, before departing.

On his next return, he set down the glass of red wine on the table for Cameron. He nodded at the waiter with a smile and gracefully moved to pick the glass up gently from the stem between the tips of his fingers and thumb, as one would imagine picking the petals off a delicate rose.

Cameron took his time to savour the wine as it slowly coated his tongue and moved down his palate. Sitting there to just be at one and take in his surroundings. Upon finishing his drink, Cameron stood from his chair, smoothed down the front of his suit and made his way toward the exit; however, the gaze of the two women from the lift drew his attention. He smiled to himself and shook his head before making a beeline for the waiter, where he pulled him close and whispered in his ear.

"You see those ladies over there?"

The waiter nodded.

"Put their bill on my tab and tell them I apologise for not being able to entertain; I have an early morning."

The waiter nodded, "Yes, Sir, of course."

Cameron gave a brief smile to the women and then stepped into the elevator.

***

The local gym is a sanctum for self-inflicted punishment; the physical for Cameron is his form of therapy, both mental and emotional. It was Wednesday morning and the training session was, as always, an intense boxing interlude with no respite in sight. The punching bag resonated with elegant movements, resembling a work of art, yet the energetic tone suggested an intense battle raging deep within and beyond the various layers, to shield his emotions.

The spirited atmosphere could have been mistaken for a nightclub, with the neon-lit room blasting a music theme fit for a raging war with gladiators. Yet, the handsome young athlete was far from warrior status, even though his heart carried the passion.

Sweat poured from his face onto the gloves below that pounded the bag. With each hit, Cameron's face displayed intense concentration. Teeth gritted with his jawline aching from the constant pressure. A combination of right hooks followed the left jabs to the bag. Each time, Cameron twisted from the hip, drawing all of his power. The timer rang on the clock that indicated the end of a four-minute round. Cameron's total concentration remained un-displaced by the piercing ringing of the timer. Everyone around him stopped, panting away; some were holding their hands over the back of their heads to catch some air, others collapsing to rest on the floor. Following a forceful upper cut to the bag, it swung back towards Cameron and he ducked his left shoulder, easily weaving past the object.

"That's time!" The shout from the back of the room hit Cameron's ears, but he ignored them.

"Yo!"

On this occasion, Cameron stopped. He turned to notice the rest of the class watching him, those accusing eyes focusing on him. Without breaking the look in his face, the muscles tight around his neck and jawline tensed and he shook the sweat from his forehead and reached for his towel lying on the floor next to him.

For the past year, Cameron had been searching for an outlet that would calm those tumultuous battles raging inside him. He went through all the usual rituals of partying, women and self-defeating behaviour, but the practices only served to further escalate the emotions he had tried so hard to suppress. It was only after the suffering nearly killed him that he turned to drilling his body with energy-sucking physical workouts. He could leave the gym silently, confident the battle in his head was calming, even just for the present moment. The persecution gave him the strength to command the attention his fame deserved. Admirers gravitated to his energy, yearning to learn more about this modern-day enigma. It was a strange relationship; they fed their hunger to satisfy their emptiness, while Cameron found solace in the attention.

At no time did Cameron's presence go unnoticed. The prying eyes pierced his soul while he walked to the sleek luxury vehicle in front of the gym.

Goram, his driver, stood by the car and took his gym bag as Cameron approached. "Hello, Sir... how was the workout?"

"Pleasant, thank you," replied Cameron.

While climbing into the back seat, taking care to duck his head, Cameron felt his apprehensions ease once he was safely behind the dark tinted windows. A puff of his cheeks with a sigh, slumming back into the seat.

Goram noticed a reluctant nature about his boss today. "Sir… is—"

"Yes, Goram..?" Cameron interrupted.

"Fine, Sir. Where are we headed?"

"The bespoke menswear shop in St Christopher's Place."

"Of course, Sir."

The atmosphere inside the car silenced, Cameron's reluctant nature seeping to the surface. Goram knew his boss well and it was not an unusual circumstance. City traffic was light at that time of day, shortening the drive. Goram pulled up to the curb, parking in an allocated bay before climbing out and opening the back passenger door.

"Sir," he motioned. Cameron hesitated before exposing himself to the world once more. He paused to scan the streets in hope of finding a friendly face. A face that somehow would at least try to help resolve some unanswered questions.

When no such face presented itself, Cameron took long strides and entered the shop where he was greeted by Darren, the proprietor, an English menswear designer with family roots in Italy.

"Cameron… my friend, it has been a while; how are you doing? You have perfect timing as we have our new collection just in. You will love the pieces." He smiled with relaxed shoulders.

The shop was a neat, exclusive store hidden away in the passages of St Christopher's Place behind the hustle of Oxford Street. As Cameron walked through the entrance, he scanned all the displays of shirts and blazers on show and the clever placement of accessories of ties and scarves that complemented the main garments, to entice the consumer to purchase more than they came for. Cameron felt encapsulated with the surroundings and obvious calmness within Darren, whom he regarded as his friend.

"It seems your collections get better and better!" Cameron remarked with a smile as he rifled through some of the blazers on the rack, which were highlighted to his attention by the spotlights overhead. "How are your sons getting on in the new school? I remember last time I came in the move was concerning you."

Darren moved from behind the counter where he was going through the takings and matching the stock items with what was projected as needed for the coming weeks, toward where Cameron was standing and admiring the clothes.

"Thanks for asking, mate. They settled in eventually. Obviously found it difficult to start with, but all turned out well. Much better school for them in the long run."

Cameron acknowledged this with a nod as he gradually moved around the shirt counter in the middle of the store. His movements stayed smooth and calm, which was common for him when he felt distracted from the daily thoughts of his previous battles and scars.

Darren looked over to Cameron. "Is everything OK, Cameron? You seem like you have a lot on your mind."

Cameron tried to contemplate a response; he felt his heart pounding. His sweaty palms drew his attention and he slowly rubbed them on his thigh. His eyes narrowed slightly with a focus on his false smile as he looked up at Darren. "Today marks exactly one year, Darren."

The room stayed silent for a short time. Darren knew

of his previous loss. "I'm sorry, mate, I didn't realise. I still cannot get my head around it. To just disappear with no trace. Nothing. It's like she never existed!"

Cameron paused before giving Darren a response, to check for other patrons in the shop. Cameron opened his mouth, ready to speak, trying to form the sentences, but nothing was coming out. He closed his mouth, bit the inside of his lip, breathed in deeply and let out a deep sigh. The quick shift of body language prompted a change in style and focus. No words were needed; just the action was enough. "So… Darren, what do you have for me? Let's spend some money!"

"A number of fitted blazers should suit your body frame perfectly," Darren remarked as he clearly got the hint that Cameron did not want to discuss the matter any further.

The blazer was Cameron's style, tapered at the back with two pleats. The smooth fitting over the shoulders with two buttons in the centre at the front would take advantage of Cameron's sculptured mid-section. Cameron took the garment, posing in front of the mirror, admiring his physique.

Darren commented, "With a few adjustments in the shoulders, it will be a perfect fit."

"Where's Lee today? Out with the ladies again, no doubt? We arranged to do some training, but I haven't heard anything from him. He is such a ladies' man and a tart," Cameron chuckled, "but you know, I wouldn't change it. It's good entertainment to let us know what we old farts are missing out on!"

"You know him, Cameron." Darren left the room towards the back of the store where the stock was kept. "Always out and about. He's a pretty boy, not serious about anything, but he is great at what he does here."

"Please tell him I said hi." As Darren finished putting the final pins on the sleeves of the blazer, Cameron felt an urge to get on with his day. "Are we done here? I will have these picked up next week, if that's OK with you, Darren? And we really need to do dinner some time; it's long overdue. But let's look at what works for us both and message over a few dates?"

Darren moved to the back of the room and hung up the clothing once Cameron had taken care to remove the blazer. "Yes, we need to do that again soon. Just let me know what works."

There was no reply from Cameron and, as Darren glanced back into the main shop floor, he caught sight of Cameron walking towards the door. The shop doorbell chimed as Cameron left the building and he glanced up to see his driver waiting with the car door open.

"Goram, I'm going to walk; meet me on the walkway at the South Bank near the Shell Centre. I'll ring when I am ready."

It was one of those rare sunny days and Cameron felt the warming rays radiating against his face. A cool breeze scented the air with fresh wild flowers. To many, this would be a day to enjoy. To others, this was far from an ordinary day. For Cameron, his subconscious was transfixed by a memory that contained a combination of pain and comfort, nostalgic reminiscence. The painful memories swirling around in his head all centred around one name – Emilie.

CHAPTER TWO

London, before

"Do you think we should try Italy this year?" Emilie asked. "It would be a fun road trip; we can even do the coast." There was a slight wavering nervousness to her voice.

Cameron watched closely as she sipped at her drink.

"Sounds like a plan; just need to be careful with the sun along the coast. As you know, the sun does not get on with me, but it sounds like fun!"

"Perfect! What dates work for you? Maybe we should look at other parts of Italy as well?"

She seemed slightly more relaxed after his response to the request for a holiday. It was time to take advantage of his mood. Emilie went in for the kill. "The wine tasting in Tuscany is supposed to be amazing." She had obviously picked appropriately as Cameron had a love for red wine.

"I think that sounds wonderful. Do you remember our trip to Santorini when we became fine wine experts?" Cameron smiled and they both chuckled.

When her smile faltered, Cameron leaned forward, eyeing her carefully.

"Emilie? Is everything OK? You seem a little, well, on edge today?"

"I'm fine, honey. It's just work; it's been a bit busy and

stressful recently." She sighed and looked past Cameron's shoulder.

He gently placed his hand on her face and brought her gaze back to his. "You know you can talk to me about anything, right?" His question hung in the air. Cameron tilted his head and raised his eyebrow while looking directly at Emilie.

"I know. It's nothing. Just same old issues, being short-staffed and not enough resources for what I need to do." Emilie's words came out a little too rushed from her. "It's just that there is…" She paused.

"There is what?" Cameron did not let his hand leave Emilie's face.

She placed her palm over the back of his hand resting on her face and interlocked their fingers together. Pulling his hand off, she took it and kissed his fingers.

"Nothing, hun. It's sweet how you care, but it's just boring work and research stuff. It will all pan out OK in the end."

"Wow, now that's not fair. I may not be a smart arse like you and understand all that medical and science stuff you do, but I can still be a voice of reason and an ear of concern for you, can't I?"

Cameron sat back in his chair and studied Emilie, trying to now understand the root of her anxiety. "Go on. Try me. I may surprise you with just how logical I can think a problem through."

"Seriously, it's nothing to worry your little head about!" Emilie got up from her chair and dragged it round to place it next to Cameron's and sat down again. She placed her head gently onto his shoulder and put her legs over his so that they were interlocked around the knees.

Emilie let out a loud bout of laughter, which took Cameron off guard, and he spun to face her.

"What is that supposed to mean?" she demanded. "Disapprove? I mean, yes, my research work *is* cutting edge and it does push some established norms and boundaries, but come on, hun, do you really think I need anyone's approval?"

"Maybe a poor choice of words from me," Cameron conceded.

CHAPTER THREE

London, now

A cyclist dashed past Cameron, disrupting his recollections while he walked along the South Bank riverside of London. As the daylight began to wane and the evening drew into night, the event caught him off-guard momentarily. In the fading light, he caught sight of a figure walking towards him. It was that of a tall, attractive female with a commanding look. Their eyes met as they moved closer together, but her expression remained blank. Cameron struggled to figure out if he knew her, but before her gaze drew him in close, he felt his own divert at the last moment. A concerning anxiousness was settling within Cameron's mind. Why would he notice this woman if it were not someone he had interacted with in the past?

This feeling made Cameron move to a more defensive stance. The woman turned to face him head-on and spoke in a direct tone.

"You took from us and you knew we would have taken back from you, Cameron." She stood defiantly. "Did you think we would turn a blind eye? Did you think you could walk away and invent a new life? A new life in a city like London? Come now, Cameron, how very disappointing; I would have expected more of a complex challenge from one with a reputation such as yours."

Hearing the words, Cameron moved slowly towards the wall of the riverbank. He felt his heartbeat quicken and felt the adrenaline swim throughout his body to create the fright response. Looking into the water below, the reality and concern festered in him that this person was here to inflict torment and pain.

"Why have you come now? What do you want now from me?" Cameron asked without gazing in her direction, his voice holding back the quiver inside him.

The fear rose like a flame within and overcame him. It suddenly occurred to him that this woman had showed up on the very day his world had shattered one year ago.

"Where is she—" Cameron demanded. "She had nothing to do with this... What have you done with her?" Cameron glanced around to verify they were alone before grabbing her arm. His posture remained tense. "Where is she?"

It was obvious she was resisting any form of struggle to free herself and, in fact, moving in ever closer to him.

The fading light kept their encounter somewhat covert, so it did not draw attention at all to passers-by. It was a busy, crowded place in the evenings; couples on an evening stroll, tourists taking in the sights, joggers exercising after a long day at work and street performers playing for tips on each building corner. However, their interaction remained unnoticed. They appeared to be two people having a conversation – perhaps friends or lovers.

Cameron's gaze never faltered, while his opponent grinned. With a slow, intentional gesture from her, she moved close to caress his jaw delicately, ostensibly portraying a show of affection and trust. Cameron understood the eyes are the windows to the soul. The only reflection he saw in her was that of evil, a dispassionate coldness of a hunter sizing up its prey. She continued by placing a hand on his face softly, just as a lover would do.

She whispered, "My love... you took from us, we took from you. I can see the love you carry for her; it's unquestionable, unattainable. The more you wish for it, the harder it becomes to capture. Oh, how I envy that feeling." In a final gesture, Cameron felt her lips glide across his face, embracing him with a deliberate kiss.

Cameron found the interaction strangely unnerving yet maintained his concentration, despite her attempts to rattle him. The conversation remained intense; Cameron fought back his emotions as the woman came close to straighten his tie.

"And so it begins, my dear," she said, pulling a small box from her pocket and placing it in Cameron's hand.

Cameron's grasp was forceful, yet she elegantly slipped out of his fingers and disappeared into the midst of human bodies walking the Embankment. Cameron felt the pain envelop his body; the closest link he'd had to Emilie in the past year had just walked away from him. He stood there alone fighting to understand if this was reality or if he'd slipped into a dream-like state.

While struggling to regain his composure, the mystery of the box aroused his curiosity. By this time, his survival instincts had taken over and Cameron turned around before engrossing himself in the contents of the package to be sure no one was now watching him. It was obvious: someone wanted to get his attention. The plan had worked. He could feel his heart pounding while he fought to open the box. His normal calm demeanour had at this moment abandoned him and left him gasping for breath as his eyes focused on the contents. A necklace lay delicately across a piece of velvet.

CHAPTER FOUR

London, before

"So, Cameron. We have been invited on a date with a couple of my friends; they have been looking forward to finally meeting you." Emilie sprung the rendezvous on him, hoping he'd agree.

The walk along the river was on a perfect evening, which Cameron never failed to enjoy, especially when it was beside the woman he loved. Their walks had no plans, no pressure and no clock-watching. The conversation would range from informative current events to deep discussions in relation to Renaissance art history. And to anything in-between.

Cameron nodded his agreement to the suggested date with Emilie and her friends. He couldn't help himself when she was near him. Her smile melted his heart and it was always easy for her to get her way. At times, the allure made it hard to breathe; he felt his knees weaken and everything would go blank.

"Now I know why my ears have been burning! What exactly have you been saying?" Cameron stated in jest.

Emilie poked at his ribs. "Oi, you! It's all good! They're obviously interested to know about the mystery man I've been spending so much time with over the last few months, especially since I can't stop smiling whenever I talk about you."

He paused while she snuggled in close. "Obviously, I know how busy you are and so we can arrange it when you have the time, of course."

Cameron turned to face Emilie, taking her cheeks in his hands. "You are important to me. Of course, I will make time. It's essential your friends have faith in me. They should be protective over you and have your best interests at heart, just as I should. Besides, I want to learn more about them and hear whatever stories about you they have to tell." Emilie looked up into his eyes and he saw his love reflected in them. It was like a dream, meeting someone who was truly capable of offering unconditional companionship.

"Thank you," she whispered. A gentle, tender kiss followed.

Cameron held Emilie close. She responded by bringing her arms up around his neck and firmly, but gently, pulling him even closer. "It feels like we are as one. I cannot get over this feeling," Emilie said breathlessly. She held his gaze and felt a rush of heat rise from her neck to her face. "What are we supposed to be doing this evening? I am totally lost if we had any plans," she smiled and chuckled.

Cameron raised a brow and smirked. "I am sure it was your turn to be in charge of the dinner plans this evening?"

"Crap!" Emilie took Cameron's hand and interlocked her fingers. "I didn't book anything!" She glanced at her watch. "Do you think it's too late to try and book somewhere to eat?"

"There's always peanut butter and bread at home!"

"Seriously, you must be starving."

"Emilie, stop! Don't worry, let's just see what we come across and if we can't find anything, let's just go to the shop and make something at home."

The breeze from the river drifted along over the Embankment, rustling the leaves. Emilie kept her hair out of her eyes with her free hand. The trees along the Embankment were illuminated with beautiful blue lights interspersed on the branches. Cameron came to a sudden stop beneath one and tugged on Emilie's arm.

"What's up?" Emilie spun around to face him, moving her hair back over her neck.

"Nothing. I just wanted to see your face."

Emilie softly stroked Cameron's cheek with her thumb. Her smile was one of contentment and safety. "You are one strange man, Cameron Hope," she said, "but a strangeness that I would never want to change, ever."

Cameron took a step back from Emilie and pulled a small box from his jacket pocket. A dark navy box, with a smooth, velvety texture. Emilie's eyes were drawn to it; they widened and she went to speak, but no words came out. Cameron opened the box slowly and turned it around.

"It's beautiful, it's just so…" Her words fell away. "I don't know what to say… Why? I don't need anything."

Cameron took the necklace from the box. The elegant dainty freshwater pearl swung from the diamond's round bezel station peg attached to the silver chain. He undid the clasp and placed it around Emilie's neck.

"I am so—" Emilie was not allowed to finish the sentence as Cameron moved in to kiss her lips.

CHAPTER FIVE

London, now

It was late when Cameron finally made it to his destination. Goram waited patiently as always.

"Sir, are you ready?"

Cameron nodded as he slid into the back seat. The day wasn't ending as Cameron had been expecting. Certainly, he was yet to feel if this was going to end in even greater pain than what had already occurred in the previous year of torment. Goram drove Cameron home in silence.

Cameron stood by the window overlooking the river from his apartment. The London skyline covered the horizon, granting Cameron a warm, mystical feeling. His mind raced with thoughts as the necklace lay across his hand. The outside world disappeared as he struggled to process the day's events.

Then, in an instant, interrupting his concentration, the phone rang. A withheld number flashed up on the screen. Cameron paused for a moment watching the phone and then hesitated with his hand as he reached over and answered it.

A deep voice on the other end stated, "I am sorry you have to hear my voice once again. We need to begin."

It was obvious the call was an order; the line went dead

and he placed the phone back onto the table like it was an object of surprise to him. He poured a glass of red wine, placed it on the table and walked over to a wardrobe. Inside was a navy zip jacket; the one Emilie had given to him the last time they met. While reminiscing, he heard the phone alert him with a message and an address in London popped up on the screen. The message meant he must endure a journey of a test. Only this time, it was not of his free will. However, the fact that he was being forced to act may ease the burden just a bit.

As he turned, Cameron noticed a face in the mirror staring back at him. An image that brought his rage to the surface; nothing could prepare him for the experience. A face that he so detested to recognise, a face that made him feel guilt, anger, remorse, hate and vengeance all at once. Not even a thousand washes could erase the figure from his mind, because how does one erase oneself?

Cameron paged Goram; it seemed they had another trip to make. Walking down the hallway to the door, he looked back into the apartment. He let out a sigh and closed his eyes to remember the time Emilie shared this space with him. "I'm so sorry." A whisper from him in an attempt to have forgiveness from Emilie. One final look around the place and he ever so gently pulled the door to a close and locked it secure. Resting his hand on the door as he felt this would be the last time he would be here, he then entered the lift down to the car park below.

Goram arrived, unquestioning of their late-night adventure.

"You will need to take good care of the car while I am away. No messy parties in the back, OK?" Cameron said with forced humour and caught the eyes of Goram looking back at him from the rear-view mirror.

"Of course, Sir. Obviously, I will await your return home and always stay loyal."

The two had a sense of understanding between them. No further explanation was necessary as Goram had been faithful ever since Cameron's life in London had begun, without questioning some of the stranger aspects to his life. Cameron relayed the destination and Goram obliged. It was an address that would be burned into Cameron's mind forever.

The traffic was light in London, which suited the situation, as time was not on Cameron's side. These matters now had a time-sensitive urgency to him. The possible scenarios played out in his mind as he tried to ascertain which path and route to take. He hadn't been here before: in the past he always had selfish motivation and was focused on his own gain. Now, it was a different story altogether. He had to be mindful of his skill, his attributes for this task. He had to remain focused as this was no longer for his own gain. Never before did someone's life hang in the balance due to him. Never before had he needed to think for his own family's survival. This was not something he had ever thought he would need to deal with.

As the battle within his head raged on, he told Goram, "We have time; drive over to St Paul's Cathedral – it will not take us long."

"Yes, Sir."

Cameron grabbed his phone, searching the contact list, before pausing at one name: Heather. After a slight delay, he pushed the call button. "Hi, Heather, how are you?"

CHAPTER SIX

London, before

"You need to get that book you're eyeing up! It is really good; I could not put it down." Cameron turned to see the face of a naturally beautiful lady with porcelain skin and a shy smile, with a hint of mischief.

"Thank you, it looks like a light read. I'm after something light-hearted as the last book was a bit full-on; I need the balance." The lady smiled at his response. They were in a cosy bookshop on the corner of Tottenham Court Road and Oxford Street, a popular place for people to gravitate to, as there was a large reading area on the basement floor with coffee and snacks.

As Cameron approached the counter, the woman gently touched his arm. "I just came to grab a coffee, hidden away from the hectic lunch hour of London. Would you like to join me?"

Right, thought Cameron, here was this beautiful woman in a bookshop, coming up to him and asking him to join her for coffee. What was the catch?

Should he roll with it or politely decline and bring his walls up? He quickly glanced at her left hand, noting the naked ring finger, although he wondered whether that would stop him anyway. It was just a coffee, he told himself, not an audition for a soulmate, trial, judge, jury and sentence. "Cameron. Nice to meet you..." He held his hand out.

"Heather," she smiled shyly with a raised eyebrow and she took his hand.

That cold, grey Monday afternoon in February was the start of a friendship that Cameron would value for many years to come. At that bookshop, the two settled on a table with their book purchases to discuss literature over a cappuccino for Cameron and a latte for Heather.

As the years unfolded, Heather would become more intertwined with Cameron's life than he thought possible at that first meeting. Something that may have a more sinister tone than that of just innocent coffee and books.

CHAPTER SEVEN

London, now

"Cameron… is that you? It has been so long. Are you travelling or just up to no good, as always?"

The attempt at humour was enticing, but he had more pressing matters on his mind. "Listen, Heather, are you still working in the St Paul's area? I am not too far and wondered if you had time for a coffee? I know it is late in the day, but from what I remember, you worked long into the night, in any case?" He struggled to balance his tone.

"Cameron, is everything alright?" Heather asked carefully. "I… am not sure that is a good idea. Yes, I am in the area, but honestly…. I have moved on and it's wonderful to find real joy. I was hoping that had happened for you as well."

Cameron fought hard to explain himself. "Heather, please, I can explain. Will you come and meet me? It is not to disrupt your life, I promise. I just need your counsel."

"I can spare a few minutes with the short notice; you do seem rattled. Meet me at the Coppa Club; it's opposite the cathedral."

"On my way; be there in a few minutes."

Cameron leaned forward. "Goram, pick up the pace, please."

CHAPTER EIGHT

London, before

The streets of London are like many others around the globe – populations of the underprivileged and the needy people Cameron saw in his own distress, forever searching for just a glimmer of light. Being able to empathize with the unfortunate gave this man promise so that he may live up to his name, Cameron Hope. However, it is the vulnerable people who hold the empathy. It is they who see past the masks he so desperately struggles to hide behind.

Since he'd returned to London, Cameron found a calming sensation that overcame his soul when he frequently visited charity institutions such as St Mungo's. He offered his help to the clients who sought shelter and helped run some of the group activities with key worker sessions to facilitate client rehabilitation.

One afternoon on a sunny spring day, Cameron attended to a couple of clients who had long-term rooms at St Mungo's.

The client, Sally, was in her fifties, with a dual diagnosis of substance misuse and paranoid schizophrenia. Throughout the past, her behaviour had been destructive, hence the reason she must stay in the care facilities. On this visit, Cameron was told that she was not mobilizing as normal and had been in her room for most of the day.

As a dutiful servant, Cameron wanted to brighten the client's mood. "I hear you have been in your room all day. No walk in the sunshine today?"

"Well," she began, "today my tea kettle was the wrong kind and left a pain in my ankle. Why did they get me to use that kettle today?" She just stared blankly over to Cameron without any further explanation.

Her room was always kept tidy, a little too tidy for most, reflecting her OCD nature, something that Cameron could relate to with his compulsive nature. His rationale was that clear surroundings allow the mind to breathe.

"I don't believe that would be true. Did you twist your ankle recently? It looks a bit swollen. Would you like me to have a look?"

She nodded in response.

The rapport between them was obvious; another skill he had cultivated to maturity. Cameron bent down to have a closer inspection. Gently, he placed his hands on either side of the ankle, taking care not to move it. Slight pressure to the swelling was applied and Sally responded by withdrawing the foot from him.

"I think we ought to get it looked at by a doctor; would that be alright?" Cameron asked calmly.

"Yes, I suppose so."

"Are you ready?" Cameron asked. "I'd like to make sure you get there safely." Sally agreed reluctantly, but replied with, "As long as you get me a packet of cigarettes afterwards."

On arrival, Cameron was surprised at how quiet the emergency department was, with only a scattering of patients in the waiting room.

A nurse in her late twenties sat in the small, tight cubicle at the front desk. Cameron left Sally sat in a chair closest to the counter, ensuring to remain in sight to create a familiar, safe environment for her.

"Hello! What brings you both here today?" the nurse asked as she looked up from her computer.

Sally, face screwed up in pain, blurted out, "I came to get a bloody ice cream! What do you think I have come for? Can't you see my ankle? It's bloody broken and you just want to ask stupid questions!"

It was clear that public places were an unfamiliar environment to Sally and made her quite nervous. Cameron turned to her. "Sally, it's alright. I will have this taken care of in a few minutes," he said, with a reassuring wink. Sally nodded stiffly and folded her arms, subdued for now.

"I truly apologise for the outburst," Cameron smiled, glancing at the nurse's name tag. "Ciara… I believe Sally may have broken her ankle and will need to see the doctor and possibly have an X-ray."

As Cameron waited for the nurse's reply, a woman walked past the cubicle dressed in green surgical scrubs. Her hair rested just below her shoulders, brunette with light brown highlights. Her skin was kissed golden by the sun. Cameron was instantly entranced by her eyes: they were inviting and warm yet carried a fire inside which he found appealing. A sudden calm came over him, a feeling that he had not felt in quite some time now.

"Excuse me, Sir…" Cameron was lost in thought. "We can get an X-ray done, but the wait time is approximately two hours to see the doctor. Hello… are you still here?"

Ciara sighed heavily.

Sally blurted out once again, "I don't want to wait and I'm going home!"

"Sally! Wait… I am sorry." Cameron saw how agitated Sally was becoming. "Alright, let's go. We can keep the ankle packed with ice. If there is no improvement, we can come back another time." The last thing Cameron wanted was to deal with a scene here. He chose the damage limitation option and let Sally leave. He looked back into the cubicle, past the nurse's shoulder, but could not see the person any longer that had captivated his attention.

The afternoon situation provoked a strange sensation within Cameron. Why did this woman, a complete stranger, who'd had no interaction with him, shift his thoughts in such a manner? He had a growing uneasy feeling, however, it was one of elation. After hours of deliberating over the situation, he found himself back in the hospital.

The emergency room was filled with patients waiting for medical attention. He glanced around the room, searching for the nurse he'd saw earlier that day. Cameron thought there should be a better way of dealing with the demand of ill health in society. It is an ever growing demand, placing the system on the verge of collapse. The reception staff seemed pressured with waves of patient demands and there was Cameron, wanting to get information on how best to play his plan to find this woman. He felt a slight notion of guilt within him.

While he contemplated the next course of action, the answer came to him. "Excuse me, madam, I was hoping to see if a nurse called Ciara is still working. I was here earlier with a patient and I forgot to ask her about the treatment plan in detail."

The receptionist looked uninterested, especially at the term 'madam', but agreed reluctantly that she would have a look and find out.

Cameron tried to use this to his advantage. "I remember she was in the triage cubicles. You are busy and I don't want to take you from your duties." He flicked his eyes to her neck. "Oh my, that pendant on your necklace is so special. I got the same one for my daughter last year on her birthday. It's her birthstone."

Cameron had learned that if you build a rapport using the right body language and words, it becomes much easier to get what you're looking for – a skill set that came to him as easily as breathing. It worked like a charm; she fell for the compliment and let him through the doors, right past security.

"Go through those doors and see if you can find her," she instructed.

Cameron walked into the working section of the hospital; he noticed the rows of cubicles with patients' beds, nurses gathering information from various machines attached to each bedside, doctors discussing management plans and peering at computer screens. The demands on the staff left him free to roam unnoticed. He looked around at the sea of bodies wearing surgical scrubs, all rushing from place to place.

He did not have to think any further as the woman who had mesmerized him was standing behind the nurses' station by the computer terminal. He was instantly taken aback once again. In seconds, every portion of her charisma transfixed his attention.

She stood with elegance to her character, so beautiful,

yet grace and humility enveloped her presence. Cameron watched how she moved her fingers across the screen on her phone while checking messages. Even the brilliant burgundy colour of her nail polish caused a stir: the shade reminded him of fine red wine from the slopes of east-central France. It was her effortless, yet perfectly coiffed hairstyle nesting alongside her neck and shoulders that he found to be the most appealing. It was breath-taking.

It took a few moments for him to gather his thoughts and proceed with the plan that he was making up as he went along. While she was typing a message, he noticed with relief that her ring finger was empty. Cameron made a quick scan of the room and proceeded to the nurses' desk, flashing his most engaging smile. His gaze wandered down to her full lips and he wondered how they must feel.

Upon his approach, she noticed him as well and their eyes met. Cameron realised there was no turning back; he had to look at this like any other mission. "Hello, may I help you?" She had a delicate, slightly accented voice, but spoke decisively.

Cameron could not quite place her accent; not European, perhaps Welsh, but not strong enough to confuse an untrained person.

"I was here earlier with a patient; we were seen in the triage rooms up the front and I noticed you walk past. Due to my circumstances, I was unable to speak with you, so I decided to come back later and see if I could find you. And so here I am."

Cameron waited patiently while she contemplated her response. In their close proximity, he could feel the electricity flowing.

She tilted her head, tucking long strands of hair behind

her ear. "Well, is it in relation to a patient? Have we met before?" she replied with a curious tone to her voice.

Cameron struggled to pay attention while scanning for a name tag. *Just do it,* Cameron thought to himself. "Do you have a pen and paper, please?"

She smiled. "Sure. Just a second." She handed Cameron a piece of paper and a pen from the chest pocket of her scrubs. Cameron took the paper. He let his grip linger slightly as he took the pen from her also. He noted down his phone number on the paper and handed it back to her.

They were lost in the middle of a busy department: all around them was a stream of people on missions to check on patients, give medications, interpret test results, report to seniors and relay information to families. They were two strangers about to embark on an emotional journey in this busy environment. "This is a mobile number?" she hazarded. Cameron smiled.

"Yes… No wonder you are a medical professional – very intelligent! That's my number and I wanted to ask if you would like to join me for coffee or dinner at some point?"

"You are an absolute idiot, whoever you are," she said, turning away from Cameron while clutching the paper in her hand.

"Emilie – that's my name in case you were wondering and, for future reference, it's normally better to introduce yourself before offering your number," she remarked, with a smile that stretched across her face, eyes shining.

Cameron responded in a shy, schoolboy manner. "Cameron. Nice to meet you, Emilie." Emilie responded by smiling shyly and turned to leave. Cameron watched her walk away, completely mesmerized.

He heard a voice to his right shout to him as he walked past the reception desk. "Did you manage to find the nurse you were after?" It was the receptionist that had let him in earlier.

"Oh. Yes, thank you so much, I managed to get what I needed and much more."

Cameron was a keen judge of character; his sixth sense was rarely wrong. He'd learned many years ago that nothing happened by accident and he knew something special was about to transpire. A childlike excitement sparked. The memory of Emilie's eyes, her brilliant smile, the burgundy painted nails, the long locks of hair resting on her shoulders, the sweet voice with a touch of command from her in a playful, yet independent manner and her slightly tanned skin would remain forever embedded in his mind, to grow and nourish his heart. *It is amazing how a split moment in time, a little glance and whisper of emotion can alter someone's path so dramatically,* Cameron thought to himself.

CHAPTER NINE

London, now

Cameron stared at the beautiful architecture of St Paul's Cathedral while he awaited Heather's arrival. He once again regretted the decision of trying to hide in plain sight, especially in a city like London. How could he have been so foolish? There was history with Cameron and the cathedral, unfinished business from a time long ago. Around 1717, when Sir Christopher Wren was the Master Mason for the lodge at St Paul's churchyard, little did he know that, centuries later, a man would be responsible for a potential breach of hidden secrets the brotherhood were kept under oath to protect. Cameron began to feel an air of uneasiness while he stood there, the weight of guilt bearing down on him.

Outside the Coppa Club, an elegant woman walked towards him. "Well, I honestly didn't expect my day to go like this. You look well, Cameron." The soft voice of Heather gave Cameron a slight smile.

Once inside, Cameron led her to a slightly secluded booth. Even after all this time, he still held a special place for Heather in his thoughts. What an incredible portrayal of exquisite attributes she carried: the sharp features with her high cheekbones accentuated by her brown hair pulled tightly into a ponytail. Cameron is always captivated when in her presence.

Cameron began to pull out a chair on the opposite side of the table for Heather. "I take it you still like to drink lattes? If my memory serves correct, that was a favourite." He looked at Heather's facial expression and it was obvious she was in no mood for pleasantries. He paused and spoke in a more serious tone. "Thank you for meeting me, Heather; I know it's unexpected and out of the blue."

In the silence that followed, Cameron tried to analyse Heather's body language, but she was always so good at playing it calm and controlled. Even in very stressful situations, she maintained an air of control around her. The surroundings of the booth had an intimate but tense setting. Perhaps it subconsciously matched the situation at present. The lighting was dim to create an illusion of a smoky environment. Just the slight glow from the table lamp and the overhead lighting at a distance near the counter. On the wall were chronological pictures of the construction stages of St Paul's Cathedral.

Cameron smiled from the corner of his mouth while reaching for his warm drink and eyed Heather. With a slight tilt of her head, she returned a calm, controlled smile. "I don't have long, Cameron. Tell me. What's on your mind?" There was a slight edge to her voice. "That is if you feel you want to tell me."

At that moment, Heather withdrew her gaze from Cameron and seemed to shuffle anxiously. With her voice maintaining a hushed tone, steady and with purpose, she prompted Cameron. "You sounded a little stressed on the phone wanting to meet. Not normally your style."

"I, uh… it was always wonderful that you respected me

enough to not ask about my past, especially the specific aspects of my professional career. It would seem as though it has caught up with me and perhaps put people in danger." Cameron was aware of the anxious tension increasing within him.

Heather raised an eyebrow as she sat up straighter. "Danger? What do you mean? What kind of danger?"

"Emilie." He sighed and looked away from Heather. "Emilie is the one I am talking about; I think she may be in danger."

"Wait… I thought she left some time ago because you weren't spending enough time with her, not focused on the relationship. Somewhat took her for granted!" Heather's voice now rushed.

"I thought that as well. I mean, she hinted more than once to me to play a better part in the relationship with making meaningful time. After she left and there was no contact, I assumed it was over. When I tried to reach out, she never responded. I just hoped she went travelling like she always planned. Plus, even her close friends broke any contact with me. However, considering recent events, it seems that may not be the case." There was a bead of sweat forming on the neck of Cameron.

"OK, you are kind of freaking me out. What have you done, or do I not want to know?" Her voice had a weary tone to it. "And why have you come to talk to me? If you are worried over the safety of Emilie, shouldn't you be talking to the police or something?" Heather placed her drink back on the table, without taking a sip.

"I had to speak with you first, face to face. I thought that my past, which basically created my present, was long behind me. My actions were not always acceptable in society, but—"

Heather interrupted. "Do I really need to hear this, Cameron?"

"Yes – you do. You see, my previous employer is a very powerful organisation and they use their influence to get what they want. My job was to, well, locate and acquire certain artefacts and knowledge for them."

"Oh my God, you're a thief!" Heather exclaimed, moving as if to stand up. "You *do* remember I work in the legal industry, right? The very fact that I am here, listening to this, puts me in a very difficult position that I don't wish to be in."

Cameron reached for Heather's hand. "Please… let me explain."

Heather sat back down with a slight blush creeping across her face. "Go on then, what do I need to know?" In an instant, Cameron felt his mood starting to settle; she could always calm him.

"Heather, if I am correct, these individuals have got to Emilie. I'm not sure if it happened a year ago, or recently, however, they could be calling my bluff. Either way, I cannot take the risk. A short time ago, they contacted me and hinted that Emilie's safety might be in jeopardy if I did not go on another quest." Cameron allowed the words to sink and sit with Heather for a while.

"Alright; *do* continue. What type of quest, Cameron? And… where do I fit in with all this?" Heather's frustration level festered in the tone of her voice as the conversation continued.

"I can see this is bothering you, so let me get to the point. The very fact that they have located me and made contact shows that they can get to anyone I know personally. It's obvious these people have been watching me for years. It means that anyone, including you, Heather, could be in danger. Please don't get upset or worried: I am sure you will not be affected, but you need to be aware." Heather's mouth opened slightly, she rubbed her fingers anxiously together and he noticed the red, raw skin around her nail bed. "They will not come for you; I will make sure of that. I need to know, Heather, is there anything about me, my life, what I did, that you ever suspected or came to learn without me knowing? Has there been anything that you saw, experienced or have since concluded about what I did or who I was and am?"

Heather took a deep sigh. "I have a life of my own now, Cameron, and I don't want or need any of these issues. Your life has always been a secret. I never questioned it or pushed you to tell me. It was a mystery and still is. Yes, I wondered where all the money came from and the lifestyle you showed me. I mean, come on, who eats out at fancy restaurants every night for dinner? But I never thought it was any of my concern or my business. I trusted you to always keep my safety a high priority. Have I been wrong?" The conversation fell into silence with Heather's gaze firmly fixed on Cameron for a response.

Cameron ran his fingers through his hair and puffed out his cheeks. "Heather, yes, I kept things from you for a reason: to keep you safe. As I look back on the whole situation, I regret ever allowing myself to get close to you. It has put you in jeopardy and, for that, I am truly sorry. By the time I was ready to move on with my life and put the past behind me, you had already moved on and were happy."

There was a slight reaction from Heather and Cameron

could see her expression soften as perhaps there was some sadness coming through.

"Heather, for Emilie's sake, right now, I have to go back to those dark days and put an end to this once and for all."

Cameron's direct tone subtly converted the conversation into an interrogation. "I will end this mess once and for all. I will be sure this time, but I need the truth: is there anything else about me that you are aware of which may put you at risk?"

"Cameron, you never told me the truth, yet you never lied. I know that sounds crazy, but I have always trusted you and knew it was for a specific reason." Her voice sounded strained and exhausted.

The light was fading outside fast and the lamp seemed to gain brightness at the table. The glow on Heather's face reminded Cameron of her natural beauty and he wondered how she could have such a direct, cold side to her at times like this. "All I know is that I had feelings for you a long time ago and was willing to do almost anything to hold onto that. But… time waits for no-one and we all gain what we need from that moment in time. I was no different. I made use of the situation back then. Today, my feelings for you are gone. I feel nothing. Don't take that wrong, we will always have history. However, you need to leave me out of this! Do you understand, Cameron?"

The words 'I made use of the situation back then' weighed on Cameron's mind. He pondered why she'd chosen them. Was there something *she* was hiding from *him*? She was blunt and to the point. In a manner that seemed she had been saving up all this energy for years in a jar. She stood up and walked quickly away and out into the night, never looking back. Cameron watched her closely from the window. Heather held her head high as she strode away, facial expression as calm as her walk. At that moment, a slightly unsettled feeling came over Cameron about her.

Cameron left a twenty-pound note on the table, then held back just long enough for Heather to gain some distance. It was time to take back his life. A passionate man with a zest for life walked into that coffee shop, albeit wearing a mask to hide behind, but a hardened, emotionless man left it without the shield of the mask.

Goram was waiting as Cameron walked out of the coffee shop, the strained situation weighing heavily on his mind.

Cameron glanced back at the cathedral once more; he knew his time in this place was far from over. A dangerous game was unfolding that had to play out perfectly. He only wished that the instructions were written prior to the hunt.

The shadow of the cathedral towered in front of Cameron; he felt it was whispering to him. Cameron had stood in front of this historical masterpiece many times in the past and taken it in with ease, with no guilt to darken his demeanour. The thrill of the chase always made him hunger for more. It was an unrelenting drive that he desperately wanted to forget. Yet now was the time to force those emotions out of his mind and to burn through the evil to understand how to make Emilie safe once again.

Cameron's life ran by the clock and his inner alarm was screaming. Everything in the past was always about finding things, solving puzzles and using the clues to locate artefacts all on a tight timeline. Now, it was that time again.

The car door was opened as he approached. "All set, Sir?" Goram asked.

Cameron paused at the car and placed his hand on Goram's shoulder. "You have been a loyal, good friend. Thank you for your unquestionable commitment and service."

"Thank you, Sir. You make it easy. I am sure today's trip is not the last time I will have the pleasure of driving you." Cameron nodded. Goram's unspoken discretion helped Cameron to focus wholly on his need to hide his actions.

The blacked out car sped off through the streets of London. Cameron pressed to erase all remnants of his present life by removing his watch, necklace and phone from his jacket pocket. Under his seat was a small black box with dark purple velvet lining. As he placed the objects in the box, Cameron's eyes fixed on the jewellery. It had a ring weaved in the necklace. He reached to rub his finger around the ring. Feeling the intricate symbols that made up the circumference of the ring. He sighed and closed the lid of the box. Goram knew the routine: he would take its contents to the vault and await any instructions one day on how to deal with the contents. Cameron felt the horrible reality of an evil he once ran toward, now chasing him.

A sudden sorrow came over his soul. He had started to come to peace and be at one with the person he had become in London. Will he ever see this person again? How many people will be involved in his destruction this time? Where is Emilie? Is she caught in this web? Is it too late? These questions burned through his mind; questions too faint to even whisper.

The day was drawing to a close and evening settled in fast. Traffic in town picked up as the commuters headed home, a long day's work completed. This was an unfamiliar notion to Cameron – the day-to-day routine, a commitment that controlled every ounce of life. He had never been satisfied with society's perceived 'normal'. The burning desire living inside was to become something different, to achieve seemingly unattainable aspects. However, this need comes with a sacrifice that has also become too familiar.

Goram followed the car navigation system to the predefined address that matched the one that pinged on Cameron's phone back in the apartment. It led them to one of the most expensive residential and commercial areas in the world. The Mayfair district dated back to the 1660s when it became the home of the Grosvenor family, one of the most powerful and influential families in Europe at the time. Now this exclusive part of London is home to many restaurants, financial hubs, art galleries, trendy clubs and members' bars. What many do not see is the powerful history and secrets buried deep within its buildings and artefacts. The mysterious enigmas that hide amongst the normal, day-to-day busy streets. As with many things, there are secrets hiding in plain sight.

Goram pulled up to one of the buildings and parked the car. "I believe we have arrived, Sir." Cameron left the car without saying a word, yet inside he whispered, "Thank you, Goram. Please take care of yourself."

CHAPTER TEN

Cameron watched the car drive away, knowing it may very well be the last time he saw his exceptional driver. Nonetheless, he had more pressing matters to attend to. The address on his message belonged to a large building just ahead. He looked up at a black door, which had nothing but the number five at its centre, with a five-pointed star below. Cameron knew the meaning of this figure all too well. A quick chill dashed down his spine as he reached to knock.

Cameron prepped for battle and he knocked in three timely spans. The three knocks that were a code to enter such premises guarded by secret establishments. As usual, his training kicked in; it was his craft, his skill. He used it to gain the trust of aging establishments, to infiltrate those sacred traditions and to gain an audience amongst those who lived within these walls. He knew the ritual needed to gain entry here.

Cameron could hear the echo as his knocks sounded throughout the building. His summons was answered by a man dressed in a bespoke black suit and tie complemented by a tightly pressed, crisp white shirt and fitted white gloves.

"Mr Hope…" he says in a monotone voice. "Follow me. I trust your preparation is satisfactory? It is important to have established this procedure before you step over this threshold." Cameron knew this was more of a warning statement rather than a question.

Cameron knew there was no need for full body searches or security checks on entry to this building. It was protected by a much bigger entity.

"Indeed, it is," he stated smoothly.

Cameron followed this monotonic individual down a long hallway. It appeared much different from the outside; it had a seemingly impossible square footage. They entered a large, perfect nonagon room. Nine walls with nine corridors leading off in the distance. Cameron recognised many of the artefacts in his eye line. To the untrained eye, these would be a priceless collection, but Cameron felt no desire to inspect any of the wonderful structures. His mind and thoughts focused on the task ahead. There was no time to deviate his attention and no time to have his train of thought distracted by meaningless dead ends.

Cameron was led into another corridor leading off the main room. In silence, he followed. There were no further doors there, ending in a bare room with nothing but a desk in the middle. A small square box lie waiting on the desk for Cameron. A single table lamp illuminated the room, creating a halo-like glow around the box. The man leading the way came to a stop at the threshold and stepped aside, allowing Cameron to enter. As he entered, a sense of dread came over him. How many times in the past had he seen such a box and opened it with pleasure? His sweaty palms clutched by his side. Mouth dry and with slight vertigo setting in, Cameron took a moment to gather his concentration again as he felt the walls closing in on him.

Cameron's hands were shaking as he reached for the box. It was the first time in his life he had ever felt as anxious as this for such a task. He felt an unnerving anxiousness. He took a deep breath and opened the lid; he removed the items one by one and placed them on the desk in front of him. What seemed to be everyday objects he knew had deeper meanings. A car key, a burner phone and two envelopes, both sealed.

Once he gathered the items, his minder stood at the door, waiting for him to exit. "Good luck, Brother, on your quest." Cameron ignored the words and kept his head down with his gaze to the floor.

By the time they reached the exit, the sun had set and the day into the early night, with darkness reaching out to Cameron as he stepped back out onto the street. In the driveway ahead of him was a car that had no business being there. He grabbed the key from his pocket, one of the objects from the box. The whole incident had a familiar, unnerving feeling. *A dangerous spiral*, Cameron thought to himself. The situation unfolding for him seemed to be awakening a past that he thought was over. All to save a woman that he thought he had already lost.

CHAPTER ELEVEN

London, now

Sofia

The room was an architect's visionary masterpiece, gracefully illuminated by gilded chandeliers predating the 1870s, which hung elegantly from the lofted ceiling. The floors were covered with African blackwood, the finest of all rare wood. It had been flown in and specially crafted to add to the building's ambience. At the far end sat a grand desk with a solitary chair that played host to a shadowy figure. A low voice with strong character captured Sofia's attention and she approached the desk.

The room echoed as Sofia strode effortlessly across the polished wooden flooring. An air of confidence followed the seductive, yet commanding, walk. Her dark hair moved to the co-ordinated pattern of her pace, falling below her shoulders. She wore a bespoke blazer with black fitted trousers, giving an air of being sexy in a sophisticated, elegant manner. The opening of her jacket exposed a silky white blouse and the outline of her clothing revealed a toned, strong body that she worked hard to maintain. Nevertheless, the most alluring aspect of Sofia's presence was her piercing grey-green eyes. They had the ability to create several various illusions to anyone who looked into them – anything from kindness to a cunning assignation, perhaps – the same eyes that were used to pull Cameron into a spiral during their meeting on the river embankment.

Sofia had not officially met Cameron until that day, yet she had studied every aspect about him: his life, his actions, his strengths, his powers, his weaknesses and his love. As the clock ticked, Sofia developed a voracious appetite for it, wanting to engross herself in Cameron's very essence. Now she had been let loose to play the game.

"Sofia, when you first laid eyes on Cameron… what did you feel?" The question emanating from the shadowy figure caught her off-guard.

Sofia stopped behind the chair; she couldn't see his face as he sat facing away from her. "He is in love – he longs for a woman to return to him. He is torn with guilt, anger and bitterness over how his choices have hurt the woman he loved so much, yet he clearly does not know what has happened to her." Sofia's eyes became accustomed to the darkness in the room, yet she still struggled to make out any aspect of the facial features of the individual she addressed. "Our chemistry was strong; I wanted him. It would allow me to show how much I care. I can help ease his fears. It would be easy to taste his love and fulfil my insatiable thirst for that love."

A glass of wine sat on the desk, the brilliant crystal glinted in the dim lighting from the desk lamp. As the figure reached out for the glass, Sofia took note of a unique ring on the man's left fifth finger.

As he sipped from the glass, a gradual smile crept across his face. "Wine, in its simplest form, has the ability to change the perception of the human mind and emotions with such ease. We as a species are weak when under the influence of a simple processed fruit." A priceless wooden box rested on the edge of the desk. "These are wine storage vessels from the Shang dynasty dating back from 1600–1046 BC. Much to the surprise of many, wine was first used for its mind-altering properties in China. Most find it hard to believe that it was not first used in Greece. It has taken me years to acquire these artefacts. My purchase has caused much chaos; the blood spilt is enough to populate a small village." The mysterious man leaned into the light slightly. "Balance needs to be restored. Humanity has lost faith within itself; it is out of sync with the universe. We must be protected at all costs with whatever it takes. Cameron is the key; you must keep him close. He was foolish enough to think one man was bigger than humanity. Do you understand this, Sofia?"

"Yes," she replied softly. Sofia was strong with deep inner focus, but the overwhelming importance of the task had her feeling uncertain. The potential ramifications if Cameron failed to comply could be catastrophic and she had to be sure that this man in front of her was convinced that she thought that. She relaxed her mind, a training technique she'd learned many years ago. "I will ensure Cameron adheres to his part of the plan; he will not deviate. I am aware that too much is at stake."

"We were charged with this task in a time long forgotten." The man continued to speak while slowly rubbing his fingers around the rim of the wine glass. "The power balance was employed to keep humankind's faith in place. Its meaning granted us the ability to believe in ourselves. To accept that a higher power is here to protect us. We must protect and carry these secrets throughout time. No one person, artefact or emotion is bigger than protecting what we have been given. Your father was a great man who understood the power of what we were charged to defend. As a child he taught you well; however, he also blamed himself for his failure of Cameron. Sofia, it is time to avenge the sacrifice, but... not before Cameron restores the balance."

The conversation reminded Sofia of a time long ago and she subconsciously reached for her necklace. As her fingers coursed the circular green pendant, tears threatened to flow from her eyes, but she held them back. The necklace had been a gift from her father on her sixteenth birthday.

To the man sitting in front of her now, she had to let the pretence of anger held towards Cameron come through in a controlled, believable manner. She wanted the intolerable sense of revenge towards Cameron to be known, yet she was aware that the situation demanded that it was imperative Cameron needed to survive and remain alive.

"Sofia. Cameron will suffer in the end. Just as Emilie was made to suffer once we got what we needed; he will face the same fate. But we need to be sure we have everything from him first."

"My father taught me well and I know what needs to be done." This was a statement from Sofia intended more for her own reassurance. She continued, "Cameron still believes Emilie is alive and we have her. He also does not know of the child as of yet."

The communication was mutually understood. "Are you ready? We must begin and concentrate. We enter now to unite the Freemasons and the Illuminati to protect the very nature of humankind once again. Through our quest to restore balance, the world will once again be at peace. Both Cameron and Emilie must never be allowed to put this at risk again. Be sure Cameron disappears for good once the tasks are complete. Am I clear?"

Sofia agreed with a tilt of her head.

Taking deep breaths and calming her mind, Sofia forced her conflicting thoughts away to allow her to focus on the current task. It would be a struggle to maintain self-control, but she whispered to herself, "Not long now, just hold on a bit more."

CHAPTER TWELVE

London, now

Cameron

An elegant, powerful car raced through the streets of London with Cameron at the wheel. He'd always had an affinity for formidable cars and his previous employers did not disappoint when providing him with one. It was the one aspect of his previous job, which excited some portion of his mind. They never spared any expense. The navigation system had been pre-programmed with co-ordinates as Cameron started the car for this trip. All preset by the organisations to maintain control. As Cameron glanced at the clock face on the dashboard, he thought about how his world had been torn apart in just a matter of a few hours. He could not help but think of all the mistakes he had made over the years and how he had played right into their hands. However, Cameron knew the past needed to be kept locked away at that moment, as he needed focus for what he had been charged with. On the passenger seat were the contents of the box – the two sealed envelopes and the burner phone – which he had now switched on, waiting for whatever instruction came next.

The navigation system took him to an upmarket area

of London, Kensington, and the car pulled up next to the Royal Albert Hall. At this time of night, the only witnesses were passers-by – tourists stopping to take pictures of this iconic site. There were no performances taking place this evening.

Cameron continued to drive slowly past the entrance and parked in a side street next to the Hall. At that precise moment, the burner phone rang.

"You have arrived, I see." Sofia's voice was unmistakable.

"I should have known the car would be tracked. Yes, I have arrived and have the contents of the box."

"Good. Bring the envelopes with you and come to the third doorway. Make your way to the Coda restaurant; I will be waiting there for you." The phone cut off.

As Cameron entered the building, it seemed oddly empty.

Sofia was seated inside the restaurant. "Sit down, Cameron – where are the envelopes?" Sofia was surrounded by an empty, elegant dining room. The tables were made ready for evening dinners to be served. The dim lighting in this high ceilinged room added to the dramatic atmosphere present.

"Right here." He felt the need to whisper in such an intimate setting. Cameron placed the envelopes on the table. On the back was an embossed seal on each of the envelopes. A seal that Cameron knew all too well.

Sofia clutched one of the envelopes. The slightly smaller envelope of the two. "Cameron, within this envelope, you will find the exact details of how to find Emilie."

Cameron sensed the ulterior motive; *go find Emilie, but...* He knew their games all too well. But he had to maintain his calm demeanour, as reflex actions would not gain any ground here in this situation.

"What do you need?" Cameron remained steady; he wanted answers.

Sofia laughed. "Oh, my dear, how can you be so confused about the role you play here? Come now; do not disappoint me. I have held you in such high regard for you are an intelligent individual. You should be able to figure it out."

Cameron pulled his eyes from the envelope that was in his grasp just a few moments ago and sat back, sizing Sofia up in a glance and replied.

"You kissed me as if you knew me. Not a great kiss, by the way; felt a bit desperate." Sofia's ears reddened, but her composure remained unchanged. Cameron continued, "It resembled familiarity. Have we met previously? It is obvious they know who I am and you have been sent to track me down. I am also aware that I disappointed some very important people, but what does this have to do with Emilie?"

"Cameron… you have worked for two of the most powerful organisations in the world. Either directly or indirectly. Knowingly or unknowingly. They have lived in harmony and peace, protecting artefacts to maintain the safety of the human race. They must preserve our faith. Do you really not know what you have done? All they want is to restore the balance. The scales put back into a state of unity before all hope is lost."

As he studied her, he noticed the pendant around her neck. The image struck a chord. "Who are you? How did you obtain that pendant?" he demanded.

Sofia's hand flew protectively to her neck. "You arrogant– How dare you question me? If I had my way, you would be suffering right now for all the damage you've caused. It is because of you I lost the only constant stability in my life. It is taking everything I have to focus my attention on something else but vengeance–"

"Sofia," Cameron interrupted. "I don't know what you have been told, but this cannot be true." Cameron reached for her hand. She pulled it away. "They have lied to you. Your father was–"

"Enough!" she shouted, her eyes flashing furiously. "Your selfishness cost my father his life; it tore apart my world. Does that sound familiar? It seems to be your trademark. Now you have done the same for Emilie. If you really want redemption, maybe you can salvage something in all this."

Her voice wavered slightly with anger and she turned her head to the clock, composing herself once again. "You are wasting time… If you want to save the precious life you once had, then do as you are told. I am merely a messenger."

"Please, just tell me where Emilie is… I need to know!" He leaned across the table towards Sofia.

"Is that all you took from this? Is Emilie safe? Well, guess what? You will find out soon enough. Just remember one thing; some things are best kept hidden." Sofia glared at Cameron and then moved her eyes down to look at the other envelope resting on the table.

"Cameron… I will make this very clear. You will die when this mission is over. But you may get a chance to protect Emilie and the child."

Cameron jolted with shock. "Child? What do you mean? *What* child?"

Cameron gritted his teeth at the silence that followed.

"Speak to me; what child?"

"Do you really think I am going to tell you anything? If they wanted you to know, it would have been part of this mission. Please concentrate… there is a lot at stake here. Now, shall we get down to business? We have had enough foreplay, don't you think?" She pushed the second envelope towards him. "In this envelope, you will find the task you need to complete to restore the faith that you came close to destroying. Both the Freemasons and the Illuminati need these secrets restored by you. They have contemplated various ways to regain the balance – however, to this day, neither one has harmed you and both have protected you. Nonetheless, time is running out and you must put back what was taken."

Cameron shook his head furiously. "Sofia, please… if something happens to me, no-one will know the truth. Eventually, the secrets will be exposed, so there is no point in these empty threats. They know this; I was not protected by them. They need me alive to ensure the cover-up stays intact. The fear they command over the world is based on lies. They are afraid of the damage I can do," his voice struggling to maintain calmness to it.

"Cameron, you are mistaken." Sofia's eyes narrowed and she glared at him. "I feel for you that you have missed out on one of the most important aspects of your life."

Cameron felt slightly puzzled. "I would not say that this adventure is an important aspect of my life. Concerning and unfortunate, but my life has more to come, Sofia."

Sofia let out a non-committal laugh. "You really do have no idea, do you? Poor you. She hid it so well. Emilie may be stronger than what I have given her credit for."

Cameron lent forward and allowed his shoulders to

hunch into his chest. He waited and just allowed Sofia to watch him.

"Do not let them pay for your mistakes, Cameron."

Cameron clenched his jaw. "They?" he questioned.

Sofia sat up straighter. "You will learn soon enough how it feels to lose family, to lose your own blood, Cameron. A daughter you have never met and never spoken to and you have never felt the soft skin of her face or the whisper of her hair. You don't have much of a choice, but they may survive if you do as you are told." She pushed the envelope further across the table.

The walls of the room started to close in on Cameron. He felt a wave of nausea with vertigo come over him. His forehead developed a bead of sweat; he could feel the uncomfortable warm dampness on his back with the shirt starting to stick to his skin.

"What evil nonsense and lies are you trying to spin here? How dare you play on my emotions to be a father to get what you want from me!" The rage in his voice now resonating clearly for Sofia to know that she had rattled him.

"I agree. It *is* evil to pull on the love of family as a threat, but…" Sofia sighed, "this evil I speak of is *not* a threat."

Cameron pushed back his chair forcefully and stood up. The clamorous sound of the chair echoed around the room. Leaning down onto the table with his palms, he was close to Sofia's face. In return, Sofia did not move, but smiled. "Siena. Such a beautiful and precious name for a daughter." The mention of the name from Sofia crushed Cameron. His legs became weak and nearly gave away.

"I…" Cameron was unable to form the words. Sofia

pushed him back down into his chair with her hands on his shoulders.

"You should know by now, Cameron, that the purest things in life are never planned. And what is more pure and innocent than a newborn child?"

There was no use in Cameron thinking he could understand what the truth here was with Sofia. He needed to remain calm and not give into her. With more composure, he managed to think clearer. "By what you are saying, you are suggesting I have a daughter that I have been unaware of. And you use that to threaten me now!"

"You have both envelopes. The order in which you open them is your own choice. Please, choose wisely for everyone's sake. Selfishness will get people killed."

Cameron stared at the table; two white envelopes sat in front of him. He was still trying to process the facts and was fighting to order his thoughts. Sofia bent down and whispered, "The great Cameron lost for words?"

Cameron turned as Sofia leaned in and gently kissed his cheek. Then she gradually moved toward his lips and he responded as their lips touched. Sofia felt him tense and she sensuously bit his bottom lip. "How does this kiss feel?" She ran her finger down his cheek and stroked his mouth gently.

Cameron smiled, remaining relaxed, as he knew she was willing him to react and lose his composure. As Sofia headed for the door, he called after, "Your father was a good man. His death was not my doing and you must understand that."

She stopped at the door, turning back and looked at him in the eye. "Save your child, Cameron, while you still can." The door closed behind her and her heels rapped on the floor as she walked purposefully down the corridor.

CHAPTER THIRTEEN

Vienna, before

In Cameron's first few months of working with the organisation, he was introduced to a mild-mannered, intellectual man named Maynard, an unassuming individual utterly dedicated to his work. Maynard began and ended his days dedicated to his craft. He was a passionate history major with a PhD in theology. His education had gained him a good reputation, attracting the attention of many organisations that wanted to utilise his knowledge. His intellect, coupled with outstanding skills in the field, made him the envy of numerous colleagues.

With his blue eyes and silver short hair, Maynard always seemed to have the look of being deep in thought, especially when giving detailed lectures on complex theories to a lecture hall full of students. Over the years he had become weathered in his look, an effect of his dedication and addiction to his work. The constant and one source of energy in his world was his beloved daughter, Sofia, who became his world after losing his wife to breast cancer.

Maynard was based at the University of Vienna as the lead lecturer and head of historical artefact studies. The department was funded by the organisations that also allowed him to carry out his research with a generous salary, as well as fully funded accommodation and a healthy retirement package. In return, he was to advise the benefactors on the locations of certain artefacts of interest. Of course, it was highly confidential; nothing could ever be disclosed. Violators were dealt with swiftly.

Cameron was earmarked and his working relationship with Maynard was engineered in a covert way by the organisations. Maynard was unaware of Cameron's role in the bigger scheme of things; however, they immediately took a liking to each other. They were both dedicated to their work and maintained a strong code of ethics while perfecting their crafts. Maynard would teach Cameron the various techniques of handling and preserving historical artefacts to enable their safe transportation. Under Maynard's guidance, he learned the science of handling objects, which were precious, sometimes dating back thousands of years.

As Cameron's knowledge grew, he learned the minute details of natural elements and how they could affect the artefact, such as temperature, humidity, pH levels in the environment and even the salt content on one's skin or the composition of glove fibres worn to handle the piece. The process led Cameron down a road that had only been travelled by a few select people.

Cameron's home for the immediate future at that point was itself a prominent object from the past – the Kempinski Hotel in Vienna, an imposing structure in the famous Ringstrasse, Vienna's circular grand boulevard. Built in 1873, it's a grand listed building that is a shining example of how history and modern imagination gracefully coincide. The lobby brought guests the gentle sounds of loose jazz on the piano while they sipped their tea to the rustle of newspapers. The high ceilings with original columns and wrought iron staircase banisters underpinned the past of this building. The architect of this establishment was Theophil Edvard von Hansen, and the hotel had a Michelin star restaurant named after him, The Edvard. It was a place Cameron often patronized for evening supper. At times he was joined by Maynard, as he was on that particular Wednesday evening.

"Tell me, Cameron, why is a young man like you learning the craft of handling such artefacts in this non-conventional manner? Not that I have any right to ask such a question or raise my concerns, I am just curious! I have never had a direct apprentice in the past assigned to me." Maynard's voice low and tired from the day's lectures.

The restaurant was unusually busy for a Wednesday evening, so the waiter sat the two men in a small corner booth closer to the kitchen. A dividing wall had been built to block the sight of the entrance. As with any Michelin star restaurant, especially in Vienna, it was customary to order from the wine list before the main meal was served. Maynard ordered his favourite, a bottle of Mörwald Merlot, interrupting Cameron when the waiter came back.

Cameron smiled. "I guess you are the best at your craft, Maynard, and my bosses felt I needed to be close to you to learn as much as I could in the time I have around you. You should be proud that your reputation has been noted. And since my reimbursement is highly generous, learning about these objects is fine with me."

Maynard raised one eyebrow, unimpressed.

"Maynard, do you have family in Vienna, if you don't mind my asking?" Cameron leaned back, projecting a relaxed, unthreatening demeanour.

It was something that had played on Cameron's mind ever since his arrival. Maynard had always seemed dedicated to his craft. He was meticulous in every detail – a perfectionist. Cameron pondered if this was reflected in his personal life. Did he even *have* a personal life?

These questions reflected on Cameron's own existence; a personal life was something he found difficult. Any form of attachment forced uncomfortable relationships. Cameron knew all too well how to wear a mask to hide secrets, yet he hoped that maybe Maynard was someone with whom he could develop a bond based on personal experience. The idea gave him hope that he could someday feel 'normal'.

Maynard replied, "I have a beautiful daughter who is eminently more intelligent than her father. She does not live in Vienna but does visit me often. She has her mother's eyes, so as you can tell, she sees things more clearly than this old fool!" There was a shift in Maynard's face when he mentioned his daughter's mother, from delight and fatherly pride to an air of sadness.

"Well, if she has her father's brain, then she will be very successful as her genetics have blessed her with an unwavering resolve to achieve her goals."

"My dear friend," Maynard turned to face Cameron, "Sofia, my daughter, will be a handful in years to come; I wouldn't envy anyone who dares to stand in her way."

Maynard reached across to the next chair for his jacket with a smile creeping across his face. Then he pulled out a picture and paused for a moment, the smile morphing to a saddened regret, darkening his face.

"She was sixteen when this was taken. We had a nice fishing trip on her birthday. I had to be the mother and father at the same time. But she made it so easy. At times, I was not sure if she was the one parenting *me*. She just took hold of the challenges we faced head-on and with a strong will and she remains a strong force in my life."

Cameron studied the picture from afar; he felt he would violate the atmospheric emotion if he tried to handle the picture while Maynard was talking. Cameron could tell how much the following years must have taken their toll on Maynard. Compared to the picture, Maynard seemed a worn man sitting there before him. To Cameron, the idea of raising a child alone seemed impossible. He sensed that it was more than just Maynard being mother and father to the child, though; something external had taken its toll, something that had kept him hostage from the start, Cameron thought to himself.

"I can see many resemblances in the two of you, especially your smile. However, I do hope she didn't inherit your taste in clothes. It is a… how can I put this gently, a very distinctive, acquired taste?" The snarky tone caught Maynard off-guard. It lightened the mood and both men sat and giggled for several minutes.

Maynard stashed the picture back in his jacket and proceeded to forget his previous lifetime. The men enjoyed an evening of non-committal conversation; it was the beginning of a friendship for them both and perhaps each of them had a missing void within that the other filled.

Maynard's research facility was a complex interconnected building, with laboratory-like clinical cleanliness and adjoining library room offices. In one of the rooms there were atmospheric pressure-sensitive vaults, displaying cabinets that housed several precious artefacts. The items ranged from ceramic vases to ancient texts on delicate parchments.

Although it seemed strange to have this cache on campus, there were intensive security protocols and this section was off limits to most staff and students. In some areas, even security guards were not permitted access. Any access required an ID check and entrance through a few ports with fingerprint recognition, iris scanning, passwords and pin entry, followed by random phrase recognition, which was set by the individual each time they gained access for entry.

Alongside the academic facility in Vienna, there was the CryoSat-2 project, which had been set up by the European Space Agency. They were involved in satellite research to provide detailed data in relation to the polar region and, in particular, tracking variations in the thickness of ice caps. This multimillion-pound project aimed to study the effects of global warming in relation to the Arctic Circle density changes and the risks it posed to land mass and ocean ratio.

As a globally commissioned department, the project was funded by the organisation's plans to build, launch and maintain the satellite. Maynard was commissioned into a special unit for this project. His brief, however, was not centred on the polar cap density; he was to use the data from the satellite to help identify hidden artefacts and historical sites buried long ago out of the memory and reach of current mankind.

Maynard would spend hours looking over aperture radar data from the CryoSat-2 images to ascertain the location and identity of areas of interest. Cameron would also sit in on these sessions to learn the meanings of those coloured charts of green, blue and red. As time went on, the two of them would move the location and target of the satellite using the data they'd gathered to track areas of interest. The programme was completed under the supervision of those above them both.

Early one afternoon, Maynard approached Cameron and seemed very concerned. "Cameron, may I speak to you in confidence? It is imperative that I can trust you."

"Sure, Maynard. Is everything alright?' Cameron enquired.

Maynard looked around the room cautiously. "For the life of me, I can't figure out who would build and launch a satellite costing millions to study the effects of global warming on polar caps, yet at the same time, use this toy for other projects. Granted, we are researching data, but it's not about polar ice cap density."

Cameron frowned in confusion, struggling to answer. He walked over to the desk, which was piled high with charts, graphs and figures. In the middle of the pile was a date-stamped density chart with certain points of map co-ordinates as references.

"What's this?" Cameron pulled the sheet from underneath the pencils and measuring tools. "It looks like data sets from London, England. Last I was aware, there were no polar caps in London. It doesn't make sense why these would be plotted and recorded like this."

Maynard agreed: the images of the River Thames had distinctive charts showing heat signatures and outlines of well-defined areas that appeared to be walls on the north embankment of the river. There were multiple shots of this area, with various degrees of zoom and colour changes indicating density patterns.

From one of the many bookcases, Maynard pulled out a modern-day map of London. He opened the page that corresponded to the location of the heat signatures.

"Look at this area of London surrounding Bank underground station. From what I recall, it's full of buildings dedicated to legal and financial institutions. You know, the self-absorbed individuals of the corporate machine world!" he said in a sardonic aside.

Cameron smiled; he understood. "Can I have a look? If we superimpose the heat signature map over the map of London, it is concentrated in one particular area. Let's do the intersection of Queen Victoria and Walbrook Streets." He was surprised by a sudden reaction from Maynard and, looking at him, noticed an uneasy expression. "What is it, Maynard? What have you seen?"

Maynard's volume lowered. "The site; its location is very historical. On the face of it, it is nothing but modern-day, concrete, vulgar buildings; however…" Cameron waited anxiously for him to continue.

At this point, Maynard walked over to the door that had been left slightly ajar and closed it before continuing. "It is believed that the Temple of Mithras is at this very location. It was built in the third century and many believers feel this was the first Christian church."

"Professor, I am not a man of religion; however, wasn't the first Christian church built in Jordan, not London? Even I remember that from my history lessons at school."

"Well… my dear friend, that is what history teaches us, what the world has accepted to be the truth. Yet, with matters of religion comes power, and history has taught us time and time again that with power comes hidden truths." Maynard's eyes started to glow with purpose. "The church, as we all know, has been the route of all power as it is the world's biggest religion. We've had many people come up with alternative views on the original foundation of religion. One by one, these ideas are dismissed as pure conjecture or, more concerning, such individuals and ideas go missing. I once attended a lecture by a leading professor and symbologist on religious iconology at Harvard University. We don't know what happened for sure, but some powerful and dangerous entities tried to suppress the professor's work. His discoveries begged to shed light on the real meaning of the modern-day church and its function. He, to this day, has not published any further work and he has not been heard of in public. He's vanished."

"What is this temple and who or what are the Mithras?" Cameron asked while tracing the outline of the heat signatures with his finger on the map.

"Cameron, be mindful that there has been a lot written about the Mithras in history; however, not many know of their existence. This is partly due to powerful control and censorship; nevertheless, some people just don't want to consider alternatives to society's long accepted beliefs. The temple structure, in essence, was believed to have been found at many locations around the world, across parts of Europe, Greece, Egypt and Syria. Many artefacts that date from the same periods with similar physical structures have been found around parts of Iran and India and also in the far eastern areas of China."

Cameron couldn't help but smile a little as he was reminded that he was in the presence of a professor, an intellect, and so he hadn't expected a simple, straightforward answer.

"Alright, I understand all of that information, but… Professor, *what* or *who* is the Mithras?"

Maynard stopped the conversation immediately and began to file the papers covering his desk. "We must finish for this evening, Cameron. Actually, why don't you take a few days off? Go see the sights of Vienna; we have been working around the clock. Besides, I have a trip planned and will be gone for several days. We will resume our work upon my return." Maynard visually distressed and flushed in the face.

Cameron didn't move. He was awaiting an honest response. Maynard sighed. "It is not just the ideology of the first church that is held in the dark secrets of the Mithras – it's something much more powerful, much more sinister that has been kept from view. It is not something that can be discussed in a simple context, Cameron. We don't have time right now, so let's please just finish for the evening, dear friend." Cameron waited and let the silence fill the air for a while. He studied the anxious disposition of Maynard. He was clearly rattled and Cameron was mindful not to push, but this unnerved him. Maynard scrambled to clear the papers from the desk, not looking up at Cameron. As Cameron moved closer to help, Maynard lashed out. "Go… go, my friend! I am alright. Please, let an old man be alone."

CHAPTER FOURTEEN

London, now

Cameron could feel the horrible anxiety rising within him as he recalled his childhood. The notion of him being a father ignited the very childhood memories that he buried deep down within himself. His trauma interwoven with those same childhood memories that burdened him to this day.

He felt claustrophobic sitting in the car and opened the passenger window to allow some air in. Shaking his head, he so wanted to block these intrusive thoughts. Yet, he struggled to maintain that calm concentration he had trained himself to do. He was under no illusion and understood he was at risk of living what he'd wanted as a childhood through his own child. Through Siena. He wanted to protect and shield her from the evils of the world. To give her the safety and love of a parent. The unconditional bond that should go without question or hesitation. He sighed deeply and rubbed his tired eyes in the hope to snap out of this transfixed state. His jaw clenched and his knuckles turned white as he gripped the steering wheel. There were no happy memories for him as a child. There was no unconditional bond from his father. He closed his eyes and concentrated on his breathing pattern. To force a state of calmness.

Cameron had never truly felt ready to be a parent. In his wild and crazy lifestyle, being tied down and raising a child seemed impossible. In most cases, children have their own childhoods to rely on for answers, but how do you seek solutions from something you never had? Yet, once he heard the news that he had a child, he felt overwhelming shame. All the small moments he'd missed in his daughter's life; her birth, perhaps even her first steps. It was a dream that was to be shared with Emilie – now it was only Emilie's dream that she had conjured herself.

Cameron was well aware of how Maynard had raised Sofia alone, amongst all the turmoil, and they had developed their own routine of being father and daughter. Maynard had shared many moments with Cameron about the love a parent has for their child. *"It cannot be described in words, but the love will last all of eternity"*. Cameron recalled his words.

Cameron found a sense of peace while daydreaming about his daughter. It shocked him that a person he had never met and didn't know could have such a profound effect on his life. As the past continued to haunt him, he found himself needing something to clutch onto and keep him sane. Cameron prayed one day that his daughter would know she'd kept her father from going crazy. Just the knowledge of her presence gave him the hope to push forward. Emilie had shared his hopes for the future and, soon enough, he would make them all come true. Or at least, that was the alternative reality he tried to focus on. However, there was no time for sentimentalities – Cameron knew that all too well. He had a job to do, a task to complete.

Cameron's attention was awoken again as he stared at the two envelopes that were placed on the seat next to him. His mind tried to mull over some kind of solution; one held details about the love of his life, his child, maybe their location or both, perhaps? In the second envelope was the task that needed to be undertaken in order to maintain safety for his unknown family. Then, suddenly, a brief thought flooded his mind: what if this was just a plot, an act of deception? An idea that was completely viable – if the organisation could get their bidding done and blackmail Cameron by using a precious love as leverage at the same time, it was something that they would do.

Did they kidnap Emilie to make her divulge intimate facts to leverage his loyalty? Did they spy on them for all those years, just to strike when the time was right? "Damn it!" Cameron slammed the steering wheel; his head was feeling so cluttered. Reality was blurring and there were more questions than answers. *Alright...* He thought hard. Cameron knew the only way to solve this mess was to start with what he knew. Pulling together all the facts and then working forward from that point.

Cameron grabbed the phone and opened the notepad to jot down any facts that he knew right then. 'They had Maynard. Killed him and got to Emilie. Who else might have connections with them? Were Heather or other people Maynard knew in danger?'

After Maynard's disappearance, Cameron's work continued under several different professors. The years passed with not a hint of details in relation to Maynard's untimely death. Cameron was sent on various assignments for which he was still handsomely rewarded. The knowledge Cameron gained was due to Maynard, and it almost broke him when he disappeared. Since his choice of career kept him isolated, finding one person to connect with had kept him sane. Cameron had come to look upon Maynard as a father figure; they developed a deep connection over the years. Although Cameron portrayed a rough exterior, he carried a deep passion for helping people. In that respect, he became highly attached to the ones he let inside. Once they became part of his inner circle, it was his responsibility to protect them. But he'd failed with Maynard.

As part of Cameron's training, he'd developed a sixth sense, if you will. A subconscious voice that kept him safe, and he had learned to listen to nagging perceptions as if they were written in stone. In numerous cases, they had saved his life. Over the last several weeks, Cameron had started to develop feelings that something was brewing behind the scenes. He tried to maintain some type of routine until he could ascertain the reason behind these jitters. At first, he put it down to the upcoming anniversary of Emilie's disappearance, but now it was clear that he'd had good reason for his cautious thoughts.

While Cameron sat in the car, he knew time was not on his side; however, he needed to just take a moment to think back to those days with Maynard and the work being undertaken in Vienna. He sat reminding himself of how Maynard was meticulous in his work and study. How he knew historical facts like no other individual on the planet and how his skill at locating artefacts around the globe was second to none. Cameron knew this all related to where he found himself that day, worrying over the safety of Emilie.

His concentration was diverted to someone walking past the car carrying a cardboard cup of coffee. That made Cameron's memory drift to the morning of

Maynard's disappearance and the coffee shop they'd sat at for morning discussions before the day ahead of research. Nothing seemed out of the ordinary on that day. Cameron opened the notepad on the phone again and noted down the memory of Maynard's desk on that last day. He noted down 'maps of London'. As he closed his eyes while sitting in the car to recreate the image of the desk that day, all those years ago, he tried to recall the exact details. There were maps of London detailing locations of artefacts, yet he also remembered that he was never sent to retrieve them.

The reasoning gave him an unnerving sensation. Whenever he'd asked about the maps, Maynard had always given him some kind of excuse as to why those items were to be left alone. He knew there was a connection. Now, here he was, in London, bringing up all those memories that had made him so uneasy at the time.

The new twist was Maynard's daughter, Sofia. Cameron couldn't find any clues that had led her here. From what Maynard had told him, he and Sofia were always very close. As Cameron sat there in the car, trying to make sense of everything, he knew that there was an unsettling power at work. The slight feeling of anxiety that had been within him all this time was not in vain. A certain part of him felt vindicated that there had been a reason for all those years of torment. And where there was a reason, there were answers, even if those answers were ugly to uncover. One such truth was that the woman that held him to blame and account for Maynard's death was the same girl he saw in that photograph all those years ago at that dinner table in Vienna. The smiling, innocent girl in the presence of her loving father on her birthday.

Finding the time to be slipping by, Cameron grew more frustrated with the situation and knew it was time to act. The decision was made rapidly in a subconscious manner, yet he knew it was the right one. Cameron grabbed one of the envelopes from the seat beside him. He gently peeled back the flap, so as not to tear it, treating it as a delicate artefact. Inside was a card, deep cream in colour with a texture he recognised and which presumed the weight of a well-established, bespoke printer that had an exclusive command to the production. Not just any printers were used to create this card.

It was difficult to read the message. *'The redeemer will be the saviour for us all. A God born from rock bearing light will define beginning for us all. Become the redeemer to maintain the work of the disciples. Return the truth.'* Cameron found the words unsettling.

The passage struck a chord; it was not a riddle that needed any further explanation. To the untrained eye, this combination of words could mean several different intended communications. However, Cameron knew the passage well. It pointed to the very reason he had fled the organisation. It bore resemblance to the last mission he did before he saw reality, the reason for his abrupt departure. It was the same motivation that kept him in a city he thought would protect him. By his reasoning, as he was living so close to the truth it would be the last place anyone would search.

"I know this passage," Cameron said out loud. The words all indicated the myth and stories from centuries ago. The 'God born from rock' extract let Cameron know that this was all in relation to the God, Mithras. Texts depicted him being born and raised from a rock. *'The redeemer will be the saviour for us all.'* "Not much pressure on me then!" Cameron sarcastically jested to himself. There was only one place, one location and one structure that this was all pointing to. Back to that desk in Vienna with the maps and heat signatures that both Maynard and Cameron studied. That street intersection in London, of Queen Victoria and Walbrook Streets. Cameron held his phone at the notepad tab and slowly and carefully studied the words as he typed. He noted: '*The location of the Temple of Mithras*'.

CHAPTER FIFTEEN

As Cameron drove through London once again, he quickly glanced at the dashboard clock and saw that the new day had already begun with the clock hands creeping past midnight. The streets were empty; his car seemed like the only vehicle with purpose to its journey. A journey of urgency.

He stopped at the deserted intersection at Trafalgar Square. Stopped at red traffic lights, he had the Strand leading off to the left, Northumberland Avenue ahead and Whitehall to the far right. Taking a glance in the rear-view mirror, Cameron took note of a car about 100 metres behind him slowing down and coming to a stop. He thought it was a strange place to come to a stop at that time of night. Cameron moved off slowly at the green light and headed south onto Northumberland Avenue. As he drew round the curve of the road, he lost sight of the car behind him.

Driving cautiously, as he passed the Corinthia Hotel on his right, the Union Jack flags at the entrance flowed in the breeze and the lights up the side of the building gave it a grand, somewhat ethereal bearing. Glancing in the rear-view mirror again, he saw the car approaching once more from behind. He could recognise a tail; someone was definitely trying to follow him but making a bad job of hiding it.

Cameron decided to continue to the location. Knowing this car was following him he did not head straight there, instead tried to tease out whoever it was. The car kept its distance behind Cameron as they both passed the empty streets adjacent to Temple and Blackfriars stations. Cameron took a sudden left turn onto Upper Thames Street, coming to a stop on a side street called Skinners Lane. He took the key out of the ignition and turned the lights off, waiting to see if anyone approached from either side of the road. The cooling of the engine made a sound like rainwater dripping on a tin roof. Five minutes went by with no sign of anyone. Cameron left the car to continue on foot to the location of the temple.

A few streets away from his intended destination, Cameron noticed the figure – this time on foot, following him. By that point, he was sure he had been followed ever since he left Sofia at the Royal Albert Hall. He turned to look more closely directly at this mysterious figure and he was sure their eyes met for a second. Cameron thought it was out of protocol that the organisation would have someone there watching him – their ransom of Emilie meant that his interest was already strongly focused on the task. So, who was this figure? What was their purpose?

The air seemed still. For a moment, Cameron had the awareness of déjà vu, the sensation of something that wasn't really occurring in conscious awareness. But that moment came and went. The streets seemed empty; nothing was stirring and yet this individual just stood watching with absolute stillness to them with no physical expression on show at all.

Along the street, warm and lonely office lights

illuminated the empty buildings. It left an alluring impression on Cameron's mind. He tried to place a face to the silhouette, yet none came to mind. Were they a friend or foe? He determined certainly not a friend; how could someone, apart from the organisation, know of his business at this location? They did not need anyone to follow him as they had supplied him with a tracked car to inform them of his movements. So why waste resources by having someone follow him also in this manner? This made him wonder whether perhaps it was someone else not connected to them.

Indeed, the organisations needed to keep absolute anonymity to their work. They already had Sofia wrapped into their web, being their face and conduit to Cameron, if you will. From what Cameron could make out from this dark silhouette, it was not Sofia.

As he peered at the nameless figure, Cameron tried to recall a memory, watching for some signal, a clue. The idea that someone had been physically following him was even more unsettling than the instructive meeting with Sofia earlier. The situation left a dilemma: on the one hand, if Cameron carried on to his destination, he would surely lead the person right to his assignment and potentially hand them what they wanted before he could learn of Emilie's welfare. On the other hand, *not* going to the location would risk him failing the task, ultimately jeopardizing the outcome with Emilie. Although the night was still, it wasn't warm: the encounter had elevated Cameron's senses and he could feel the sweat trickling down his forehead, the uncomfortable dampness around his hairline with the coldness of the night snapping at him, cooling those damp sweat areas. A stress response that Cameron had hoped to never feel again. In that moment, he decided to take the bait and confront this person head-on, but the figure moved silently out of plain sight. Cameron edged closer. As the distance reduced between them, the figure seemed shorter than the illusions of the night's lighting. From across the street, the individual was about five foot six to five foot eight inches in height, wearing dark clothing: a jacket zipped up to the neck and a hooded top poking out of the jacket. Under the hood was a baseball cap to further hide their identity. Cameron instantly recognised the classic tricks used. Not only did a cap act as deflection to keep light away from the face, it also concealed hair colour, lay and texture. Black bottoms made it difficult to ascertain an accurate height, and flat shoes were useful in pursuit situations.

Cameron had closed the distance within speaking range and he saw how the person did not make any effort to retreat. "I thought trust was important? Now I get a guardian watching over me?"

"You have no idea of the work you are about to undo with your acts this evening."

He stopped short. The reply having caught him off-guard. He knew that voice. Heather.

"What the hell are you doing here? What is this?"

Heather stepped forward into the light and raised her arms to uncover her face from the shadow of her hood. Her eyes were as cold and concentrated as steel at that moment, gazing right at Cameron with urgency.

"Wait! Not here, Cameron... We need to talk." Heather's words with a pressured tone. "We need to discuss a few things and you need to understand the wider picture. You may destroy an eternity of work, risking more than you are aware of at present."

Cameron froze at that moment. In an instant, as he heard the sincerity in her voice, he felt disorientated and dazed, halting his pace of concentration and leaving him utterly perplexed.

He had to listen – this was Heather, someone he trusted. Well, at least he thought so in any case. A person who knew him outside of this life, yet in that moment, that evening, that crossroad of time, all that he thought he knew was not as it seemed. "Do not worry, Emilie will be safe, but you need to trust me and act fast. I know there is a lot to take in and it is alarming, I understand that. But the truth will be told in due time, trust me." Heather edged forward slightly and tried to give a reassuring, comforting smile. She noticed the hesitation in Cameron's face and reached out to hold his arm.

In the past, Heather reaching out to hold Cameron's arm would be a gesture of friendship and safety. But this time it felt like a touch of betrayal. "Heather, where is Emilie? How do you know? What is this all about?"

"Please, Cameron, come with me." She stood there, still, looking directly up at Cameron. His eye's narrowed and he sighed. He was about to open his mouth to speak, but he could not fashion any words. Heather turned away and started to walk into the darkness and looked back over her shoulder to see Cameron slowly creeping forward to follow her.

They walked behind Cannon Street station, along the small passageways towards the river. As Cameron's confidence grew and was able to shake off the questions of doubt he had in his mind, he decided he had no choice but to see what Heather had to say. He picked up the pace and they both walked swiftly, with urgency, and with Cameron allowing her to take the lead.

Heather pulled his arm to take an abrupt turn down yet another dark side street of London. They left the open streets of Cannon Street, Bank and Monument behind them as Heather slowed down along Hanseatic Walk right along the river. In silence, they walked along the river and Cameron looked out over the familiar sights of London, which felt like looming omens of fate. Across the river was the shining glass tower of The Shard, an imposing structure overlooking the Embankment. The Thames glimmered with the night lights of London, cloaking the murky depths that lay below the surface. The street was eerily quiet; it felt so far from the bustling nightlife just a few streets away. The cold wind caught Cameron and he felt a tingling sensation down his back. Heather's feet effortlessly navigated the cobbled streets until she pulled him close to her under a beautiful Victorian streetlamp.

"We can talk here; it is as safe as can be away from anyone that may have also been following you. Cameron, listen, this will be difficult to understand and you may even think it is impossible, but I will try to be as direct as I can." Her voice rushed in nature.

There was no acknowledgment to her statement; Cameron stood still with just a slight clench of his jaw, awaiting Heather's explanation.

"Whatever you thought about this situation, it is not exactly the truth. Cameron, nothing is what it may seem. You and I met not by chance or by some twist of fate. You're an extremely talented individual, Cameron, one that possesses a unique set of skills – attributes that we needed."

"'We'? Who exactly is 'we'?" Cameron took a step closer to her.

"Over the past hundred years, there has been unrest within the world and it is finally coming to a head. Humanity and the human species, as we know it, is not what it seems. There is a small sector of people and organisations whose sole purpose is to protect the very essence of what makes us human: our faith and beliefs. The belief in a better alternative. I work for such an organisation. The work you did in Vienna with Maynard brought you to our attention."

Cameron shook his head. Confused if this was reality or a terrible dream. All these names – Heather, Emilie and Maynard – all being mentioned in one scenario. *How could this be?* he thought to himself.

"We knew it would just be a matter of time until you came to London after Maynard's disappearance. It gave us time to contact you. Cameron, it wasn't intentional to have us become so intimate, but some emotions are difficult to fake or suppress. My role was simply to befriend you and gain your trust so I could understand the work you had done in Vienna."

"Heather, you tell me exactly who you are right now and where Emilie is, otherwise I will introduce you to the lovely River Thames that flows behind you!" Cameron wrapped his fingers around Heather's arm in a steel grip and pulled her closer to him. His eyes wide with emotion. She composed herself and spoke softly. "My name *is* Heather, I work for an organisation that has no name. We have been in existence since time first began and our remit, if that is what you want to call it – our mission – is to maintain belief in humanity and to allow faith to mean something. It is our work that keeps people directed, otherwise they would be lost… We have created meaning, by protecting that which is most sacred. You and Maynard worked to maintain this direction of our work."

"This is all in relation to the work Maynard and I were doing in Vienna?" Cameron eased his grip on Heather, but not releasing it.

"Yes, Cameron, that is exactly what I'm saying. The organisation who contracted you for your services – gathering information, doing research, collecting and acquiring artefacts from around the globe – that very same organisation is on the brink of destroying human belief along with life, if we do not act quickly."

Cameron's voice was heavy with emotion. "When I came back to London, there was an unfinished sense in my soul. After Maynard's death, I knew I had to leave Vienna, but it was too soon to run at that time. I had to be sure no-one suspected that I knew there was something else hidden beneath all this. I knew we were on the edge of discovery; something was seriously wrong. I knew it was going to put everyone, along with me, at risk. Emilie was dragged into danger, caught in this web of deceit because of me."

Heather tilted her head at the sound of Emilie's name; she seemed moved by his confession. "Cameron…" She turned away and got out of Cameron's grip, looking at the river, her face displaying conflicting emotions.

"Tell me…" Cameron stated.

She turned back to face him. "When you made your discovery, in the Temple of Mithras, you uncovered something that no-one ever has. What you have done, Cameron, puts everything in danger – it risks our very survival."

The pieces started to fall into place in Cameron's mind.

"You know about the Temple," he sighed. "I was lied to and left in the dark by you all these years – now, how do you expect me to build trust in you?" Heather looked down, away from Cameron.

Cameron continued. "So, if I understand this correctly, Maynard was killed because of his work, by the same organisation that is now holding Emilie and you expect me to do your bidding? And in return, I get Emilie back?"

"Cameron… Emilie is safe with us. We can keep her completely secure and therefore know we can rely on your compliance. She is safe for now, but I can't tell you how long she will stay that way. Although we know where she is at this time, we are unable to bring her back because the risks are just too great. You need to tell me what you know… We must work together; time is running out. It's hours at the most we have."

Cameron felt his fury boiling beneath his skin. "I am not doing anything until you take me to Emilie."

"It's not that simple, Cameron. We must make things right again before that can happen."

"Heather, do I have a daughter? Is that true?" There was no response from Heather. "Answer the question!" Cameron's voice stern.

"Cameron…" Heather sighed, looking away to face the river. "Siena, yes, she is your daughter, yours and Emilie's daughter. She is nine months old; Emilie was pregnant when you last saw her."

"How is that possible? I would have known! I would have noticed something, she would have told me!"

Heather shook her head sadly. "She wasn't showing the

last time you met. That's why they left her alone until the very last moment. You were never supposed to know about the baby."

Hurt coursed through Cameron, almost causing him to buckle over from the pain. He could feel his heart racing, pounding away in his chest. "I was never supposed to know – why?" Cameron moved away from Heather, turning furiously towards the water, asking with a tremulous voice, "Why did she leave and not reach out?"

"You're not going to like this answer, so I will be blunt."

Cameron interrupted, whirling his head in her direction. "Oh, now you're going to be blunt... You should have never lied from the beginning. You, of all people. I should have known you could not have been trusted."

"Cameron." She reached out to touch his arm.

"Don't!" He snatched his arm away as though her touch would burn. "Just say what you have to say!"

"Fine. We used you to get to Emilie. Her research was the key to everything – then, when you discovered the secrets of the Temple, the final missing pieces of the puzzle were at your fingertips and it was only a matter of time before your discovery became others' knowledge. We had to act, to protect both of you. There was no time to explain, we had to act and take Emilie out of the equation, then wait until your past haunted you. It just happened to take an entire year. Understand this: if we hadn't protected Emilie, she would not be alive, nor would Siena."

"What research?" Heather hesitated; she seemed uncertain of what to say. "Heather..." Cameron pressed.

"We have to go... I will give you the hard facts." She glanced at her watch, aware that there was such little time to hand. How much should she tell him? What should she leave out?

Cameron's stare was always disconcerting, but tonight, it was as if his rage was burning a hole into her very soul.

Heather succumbed to his question. "Emilie was doing ground-breaking research into the viability of being able to reproduce without conception, i.e., without the need to have a partner."

He frowned. "You mean artificial insemination?"

"No, I mean the divine moment of creation, the start and the creation of mankind."

Cameron's eyes widened in the darkness. He took a step closer to the embankment wall and used it to support himself. "I…" he stuttered.

This idea shouldn't have stunned him so much; in most cases he would just laugh off such a ridiculous notion, except as his recollections flooded back, their evidence was damning. The block wall served as a support while he gathered his thoughts.

"Creazione di Adamo," Cameron managed to verbalize. "Michelangelo's Sistine Chapel masterpiece. Emilie and I spent hours there, studying it in silent enthrallment. She had an extraordinary understanding of the painting. There was a certain science to how she explained aspects of the painting, its meaning and how it related to the current timeline. At the time, we debated the meaning of modern faith and religion and I introduced her to the Mithraic mysteries. I tried to explain the alternative parallel that existed in history based on the god, Mithras, who was recognised many years before any form of religion. But it was just intellectual dalliance at the time."

"Yes, Cameron… you do see the link. You and Emilie had the missing link of the same chain. The amalgamation of your discovery with Emilie's research had the potential to overthrow any argument of any faith and religion that man has concocted. Do you understand why we must protect the research now?"

Cameron had been waiting to hear the truth for years; however, to hear such a stark reality was alarming. He was nothing more than a pawn, caught in dissolution at someone else's expense. It was now noticeably clear to Cameron how this web had been in the making for much longer than he expected. How, now, was the naked truth that the woman he loves is part of this great deception?

"So, this was all a game at peoples' expense, including Emilie and me; it was all manufactured? Everything? Every touch, every tear, every laugh? They were all a lie?" His tone was a tortured mixture of emotion.

"Cameron, no words could ever make this right, but you must trust me as you always have. Please…" Cameron looked down as Heather extended her hand in an urgent gesture.

Cameron squared his shoulders and, taking a breath, asked steadily, "So, how do I get Emilie back?"

Heather sighed. "Thank you, Cameron… I can't even imagine how hard this must be for you, but we have to focus on the task at hand. Come with me and I can tell you everything."

"You have no right or idea how I feel right now." Cameron nodded to the path behind Heather. "Move and let's get this over with." Amid darkness, the two walked along the riverbanks of London, disappearing into the evening fog.

CHAPTER SIXTEEN

Rome, before

It was an April evening in Rome, with the waning sun hanging low over the horizon. The sky was ablaze with a mix of colours, with flame-red streaks merging into a burning yellow haze, which eventually sank into the depths of a deep, midnight-blue sky and a befringe of cottony purple clouds. It resembled a rippling sheet of silky velvet, with its ruffled edges wrapping around the night. As the sunrays faded for the day, Rome's ancient structures were illuminated against the skyline by the night lights. It transformed the busy city into a romantic, mysterious destination that held an allure for tourists from all over the world – a breath-taking adventure that the Romans lived on a regular basis.

A few hundred feet just outside the Via Vittorio Veneto was the Mirabelle restaurant, perched on top of the Hotel Splendid Royal, where Cameron and Emilie found themselves on that memorable night.

"Cameron… you didn't need to book such an expensive restaurant!" Emilie protested, excitement in her voice as she took in the beautiful scenery around them.

He felt a rush of emotion as he looked at her. "Emilie, you look absolutely stunning! I don't think any woman could be more beautiful right now." Emilie blushed. She glowed with radiance, dressed in the black evening dress that was cinched around her waist and fitted to flare over her hips, before falling just below her knees, accentuating her toned, yet curvy figure. Delicately interwoven lace gently overlaid her shoulders, coming down to the middle of her chest. The dress was etched with studded embroidery throughout the lower thigh area. Slightly nude silhouettes finished the ensemble perfectly.

"It's not every day you turn sixty-four now, is it?" Cameron laughed with a cheeky smile. Emilie responded to his impudence with a playful clap around his head.

"If today's birthday is my sixty-fourth, then I dread to think how old that makes *you*, darling! Oh, sorry, do you need me to speak up? Did you get that, dear? Or has your advanced age started to affect your hearing now?" Emilie grinned playfully.

An evening spent at Mirabelle could calm any apprehensions one might have about life. Rome was an incredible spectacle from its terrace and brought forth delighted smiles from both Emilie and Cameron. Their table suited the mood of the night, separated from the main dining area, leaving room to share intimate moments between any couple. All that could be seen were the silhouetted movements of lovers.

"Cameron, look! It's St Peter's Basilica. It is so alive at night. I can't believe I'm here for my birthday, in such a magnificent setting." Emilie turned to him, her hand on his arm, eyes shining with contentment. "Can we stay here? I don't want to go back to London."

"Oh, I'm sure your patients would just love me for keeping you here all to myself, never to return," Cameron laughed.

"Cameron, don't forget – *you* are the workaholic here, not me." Emilie shifted her focus slightly. "Speaking of work, have you studied any of Michelangelo's work in your antique research?"

Cameron fidgeted in his seat uneasily. "Michelangelo di Lodovico Buonarroti Simoni; try saying his full name after a glass of wine. Personally, I think he was the greatest poet and architect ever to walk this earth. Not many people recognise him for his skills in architecture. I mean, just look at that structure!" Cameron gesticulated towards St Peter's Basilica. "What a magnificent feat of engineering. An incredible accomplishment, standing strong since 1546. He finished the work that so many before him could not complete, by completely transforming the plans in an exceptionally innovative way."

Emilie smiled. "Impressive, darling, you really know your Renaissance history." She took his hand. "Walk with me to the balcony; let's get a closer view of Rome as it descends into the night."

The flowering scent of spring in Rome filled the air; the lavender and rose bushes growing along the terrace exuded an intoxicating aroma. Cameron whispered in Emilie's ear, "Rome's beauty is eclipsed with you standing silhouetted against the skyline."

The Basilica dominated the skyline beneath while the lovers explored every essence being released within them. "Our starters are probably getting cold," Emilie said in a soft, breathless voice.

Cameron smiled and placed his hand on her cheek. Their foreheads pressed against each other as their noses delicately touched. The moment brought their passion for one another to new heights; breathless, the couple kissed deeply, their bodies moving in rhythm with each other, aching for more.

"Cameron, this moment is perfect," Emilie said tenderly as they pulled apart. The couple leaned in again, this time for a gentle, intimate kiss. A perfect end to the day for them.

***

The following morning, Emilie relaxed on the veranda of their hotel, sipping a hot cup of coffee while watching the sunrise. The streets of Rome start busier than other cities around the world. Tourists line the routes towards the ancient architecture that dominates the cobbled roads. Coffee houses open to accommodate busybodies performing their daily ritual of reading the morning papers with their requisite espressos. The small, boutique hotel booked by Emilie provided a perfect setting for her and Cameron to enjoy an immersive experience of Rome. What seemed to be an exclusive hotel, in fact, was a newly opened and only partially finished establishment. However, it served its purpose and could even be described as 'cute'. Their morning plans were to visit St Peter's Basilica within the Vatican City walls.

Their tour guide brought them to a stop outside the chapel and spoke in a reverential tone: "An architectural masterpiece, the Chapel is the official residence of the Pope in Vatican City. It has served as the foundation of the Catholic religion for hundreds of years. Many great contemporary artists of the day painted stunning depictions of Biblical stories. However, these pale into insignificance in the light of the awe-inspiring centrepiece, *Creazione di Adamo,* meaning *'The Creation of Adam',* which Michelangelo painted over the course of four years, finally completing it in 1512."

"Cameron…" Emilie whispered, "it would be impossible to fathom the magnificent beauty of one man's creation until you have seen it with your own eyes."

"Emilie, you disappoint me by using the word 'man'. I thought you would have been all for equality and said 'individual' instead?" Cameron teased.

"They are not *my* words. They are the words of Johann Wolfgang von Goethe, who was probably the best poet, novelist and playwright that ever came out of Europe. My dearest Cameron, you have much history and literature yet to learn," Emilie said, patting his arm mockingly. Cameron smiled at her as the tour guide led them into the chapel.

The moment they entered the chapel, all sounds of the real world vanished. Life seemed to stand still for a moment. Visitors' previous thoughts disappeared as the intense beauty enveloped their minds. It was a vast room with high-beamed ceilings and arched windows, six on either side and two on the end. The flooring was made of marbled coloured stone, which was difficult to fully appreciate due to the number of tourists filling the room. However, it wasn't the flooring that drew the crowds, but the decorative frescos that millions flocked to see.

The southern wall was home to the stories of Moses depicted by Botticelli. Along the northern wall were stories of Jesus, including the famous Last Supper. On the eastern side was the Resurrection of Christ. Both Cameron and Emilie were lost in contemplation; the beauty within this building could consume anyone willing to let the intense nature of faith fill their soul.

At opposite ends of the room, Cameron and Emile stood frozen studying the *Creazione di Adamo*. An iconic symbol of humanity, which emitted combinations of colour in giving the semblance of carved stone, perfectly merged with wood, as well as clever illusions of paper and ink. These elements were all intentionally amalgamated to evoke powerful feelings of spiritual faith. The meaning behind the masterpiece altered anyone who visited such an incredible place. Emilie and Cameron had their own personal reasons for visiting the chapel, but at that moment, transfixed by the splendour before them, any differences vanished. They didn't know it then, but the bond created by *The Creation of Adam* would cause a ripple effect they wouldn't understand until it was too late.

As Emilie admired the images, an elderly woman standing in the far corner caught her attention. She was dressed in plain black trousers, a blue floral blouse and a white shawl covering her head. The woman stood with her eyes closed and her lips silently moving in what seemed to be prayer. In her weathered hands, she held a beaded necklace, rolling the beads as she prayed. In her left hand, she also held a black and white photograph of a baby. Emilie felt strangely drawn to her intense presence and she gradually moved closer. As she drew near, she saw a tear roll down the woman's cheek. It was apparent that she was in torment; the pain radiated from her soul.

Emilie wanted to reach out and comfort the woman, to say a few words of reassurance, maybe help her find some peace. But as she started to form a dialogue, the elderly lady opened her dark brown eyes and stared directly at

Emilie. A sense of apprehension filtered through her mind and she felt uncomfortable, as if she was invading someone's personal space. The experience gave Emilie an anxious feeling, but it was difficult to pinpoint the reason.

Cameron noticed Emilie's attention on the elderly woman. He watched as Emilie stepped toward her before halting, her shoulders slightly slumped.

Cameron went to her. "Emilie…" She flinched as she turned back to face Cameron. Her face was pale and ashen. "Are you okay?" She smiled nervously and took his hand, gesturing for him to follow her. As they walked away from the woman, Cameron sensed something was wrong and wrapped his arm around Emilie in a gesture of security. She responded by kissing the back of his hand.

CHAPTER SEVENTEEN

London, now

Every day, the citizens of London walk on a labyrinth of city streets that keep hidden undiscovered mysteries, unknowing of the magic beneath the surface. The legal professionals of London work amongst the enriched architectural traditions every day, blind to the secrets that lie in this quarter of the city around Lincoln's Inn and Temple, the centre of the legal trade for many years in London. Instead, they balance duty at one end of the spectrum with social media and Instagram hashtags at the other end. They are unaware of the mystery that unfolds around them. Such individuals would rather consume bespoke cocktails on a rooftop terrace bar that matched their mediocre life.

An unassuming stone building stood with black double doors and brilliant white bricks, merging with the other terraced buildings on the street. The ironwork on the metal door resembled reefed leaves. There was no apparent street number or plaque to indicate a private residence. It took Heather and Cameron almost thirty minutes on foot to arrive. In the dark stillness of the night, the neighbourhood houses seemed to whisper to each other; in the silence they were quietly alive. Cameron and Heather moved in sequential motion. "Where are we? What building is this?" he whispered.

"Come inside; we can't talk out here." She ushered him onto the front garden, a short couple of steps to the front door. Heather pulled out a key, turned the lock on the door and pushed it ajar, gesturing to Cameron to walk through. The hallway was wide and dark. Cameron took note of how deceptively wide it was once he stepped through the front door. Stairs ascended to his right and to his left; a doorway led into another room.

"Through there, Cameron. The door is open." Heather pointed to a doorway to the room on Cameron's left as she turned to close and lock the front door. Leaving the lights off, the hallway descended into darkness without the brightness of the street to shine through the open door.

A large set of Victorian sash windows allowed the moonlight to illuminate the room as he walked in. He surveyed his surroundings while Heather took to her mobile phone, fingers frantically tapping away. In one corner was a grand Chesterfield leather captain's chair upholstered in ox-blood red, allowing the brass buttons to shine out in an authoritarian manner. It sat imposingly beside a captain's wooden desk, complete with green leather inlay. Bookshelves lined the far wall, with volumes of law references categorized by case law. A clear writing pad sat in the middle of the desk; Cameron rifled through the pad on his first pass of the room. He found it strange that there were no pens in sight and the pad was blank. It was obviously not a functional room.

"Have a seat, Cameron," Heather announced, placing her phone back in her jacket pocket.

"I prefer to stand; besides, if you don't start explaining

what we are doing here, I am leaving."

In the illuminated room, Cameron watched Heather closely as she moved over to the window. The glistening moonlight lit up her cheekbones. Her pale skin seemed to have an ashen colour in this light.

She spoke as she blew out her cheeks. "Cameron, I cannot believe you didn't know of Emilie's research. It came to our attention many years ago, before we met and before you knew her."

"Heather, you and I didn't meet, remember? Your so-called organisation had me as a pet project for you to play with." She ignored the agitation in his voice and continued.

"You came to our attention much later, once you were working closely with Maynard in Vienna. He was impressed by your ability to acquire new skills and apply them with what seemed like no effort at all to his work."

Cameron squinted his eyes and his mouth curled at the edges. "Excuse me – *Maynard* was in contact with you..?"

She nodded. "Yes, we had a covert operation with Maynard while you were under his wing towards the time he disappeared."

"Are you telling me he was a spy and working with you all this time?"

"No, Cameron. He was and still is a brilliant, intelligent man who unfortunately is cursed with knowledge. This knowledge caused him to attract the attention of powerful people who wanted to steal it and they would harm anyone in their way in order to get at it."

Cameron ran a furious hand through his hair. "Why didn't you save him, for God's sake? If your so-called friends are all-powerful then why not get him to safety, just like you say you did with Emilie?"

"What makes you think we have not done that, Cameron? You assume his disappearance means he is no longer with us."

"I met his daughter earlier. A few hours ago – Sofia. She told me he was dead; in fact, she blames me for it. She also claimed, as *you* do, that she has Emilie."

The night's confessions had him baffled. "Heather, how can I trust you?"

Heather looked down, pulled a small key from her trouser pocket and slowly walked over to a small wine cabinet that was barely visible in the opposite corner of the room. Cameron followed the path of her walk and saw the moonlight creeping onto the glass doors of the cabinet. She used the key to gently open the glass door and she pulled a bottle from the middle shelf. "Cameron… come here."

With a roll of his eyes, he wandered over. "Yeah, so what – it's a wine bottle?"

"Look at it, Cameron," Heather said, while turning the bottle slightly and gesturing for him to hold it.

He picked up the bottle and used the moonlight to highlight the label. His expression changed from one of frustration to one of surprise. "How did you get this?" he demanded.

"Do you believe me now? Cameron, I am not lying."

"I…" Cameron paused.

He couldn't form the words as his mind wandered back to Tuscany, lost in a memory pulled from deep within him by the sight of the bottle he now held, and then to a memory with Emilie back in London discussing that very bottle of wine.

CHAPTER EIGHTEEN

London, before

"So, honey, do you think the bottles of wine from Santorini and Tuscany will taste the same as they did when we were there?" Emilie posed the question to Cameron as they walked hand in hand, enjoying a gentle, leisurely walk around Covent Garden. It was warm in London, but nothing compared to the Italian heat they had just returned from.

"Well, remember what we said? The flavour of the wine is a combination of taste and the surrounding atmosphere when the wine was drunk. So, we should experiment on a day when it's raining and we are stressed out with work, to test out the theory?" was Cameron's reply.

"Ummm, so that's pretty much every day for you, right?" Emilie dug her elbow into Cameron's side. He glanced down to see her cheeky smile. The moment caught him off-guard, seeing those incredible pools of passion staring back. He thought to himself in that instant that he couldn't resist the warmth and love from a woman that he found more beautiful in every sense the more he learnt of her.

CHAPTER NINETEEN

London, now

"Cameron…" Heather shook his arm. "Where are you? Come on, we need to fast-forward to today, not memories…"

Cameron shook his head. "We had two bottles, Heather. Both red. On our rare holidays, we brought back one bottle of red from Tuscany and another from Santorini. Santorini was our first time away together. We always called the bottles sisters and promised to only open them later in our life. We wanted to see if the taste of each was as good as we remembered."

"Cameron…" she took his arm. "Emilie told me. She took this bottle when she left. She said you would know about the meaning of it and would be able to trust me when I showed it to you."

Still staring at the bottle in disbelief, Cameron used the moonlight to highlight the label. He could see the handwritten passage on the label as he turned the bottle. *'We ran in the hills and watched the sunrise in the east suites. Trust her.'* Cameron recognised the Santorini bottle; the sentence written matched Emilie's handwriting.

The news shook Cameron to the core and he grabbed the chair for balance. "Tell me Heather… tell me everything. I'm listening."

Heather closed the glass door to the cabinet and walked around the desk to stand opposite Cameron. With a deep breath, she started. "Just as you were, Cameron, I was also approached. The organisations – a number of these covert organisations, some with names, others without – approached people after years of vetting with surveillance until it was a hundred per cent safe to approach them. Until they know every detail of that person's life to that moment. When they feel confident, they approach and offer the chance to live 'off-grid'. No NI number, tax implications, financial woes, voting rights or criminal blueprint. It is utter freedom as an individual. In return, the research and work that is carried out is done so with absolute precision and discretion. However, that perceived freedom is, in some ways, like being imprisoned under the rules of a secret establishment. One that is not held to account by any government or society. One that makes you live in fear of them."

Heather continued, "The real war and politics aren't played out under a microscope. Governments, society and religion are the three interlaced building blocks of order; they are the smokescreens. They've been created to maintain order and enforce the lies humans see as truth. But… what underpins these rules to maintain structure is our job, Cameron, including you. We are the protectors of the truth. The more we uncover and try to protect, the more we risk getting to a place where the balance will alter the future of humanity."

He shook his head again. "Heather, you are speaking in riddles. How is all this relevant to what we are doing right now? How do these dots connect to help me get to

Emilie and my daughter?"

"Emilie came to our attention when she wrote a paper on the merits of artificial insemination and how it compared to real-world auto-insemination in plant species. The paper was part of her master's during her studies at University College London. It was very impressive work and the theories she presented, we came to know by chance. One of our field operatives, whose main role was to keep abreast of published work in areas of interest, came across the article. But, as we came to learn of her work, so did the other organisations."

Cameron nodded this time, finally understanding something. "I remember her mentioning this paper and how she was going on to develop the ideas pertaining to the solution. I didn't realise that she'd actually continued her research to the next stage. She had published that paper before I met her."

"Oh, Cameron, she did far more than continue her research. She opened Pandora's box. Over the years, we've kept a close eye on her progress while Maynard, in parallel, worked with the other organisations to help discover various historical sites around the world. Such sites that needed protecting. The problem started when the organisation began using the discoveries for its own power, to position itself to dismantle order, as we know it. At that point, we weren't sure how strong the connection was between Emilie's work and what Maynard was uncovering; however, we knew it was important. We also didn't know what the other organisations were planning for Emilie and her work, so we needed to get Maynard's attention so we could protect him and his discoveries before it was too late."

"These other organisations, you can name them. I have been to them, the Freemasons and Illuminati. They are all beads of the same spectrum. Heather, it appears both are threatening me."

"Yes, Cameron, in that respect you are correct. You are missing one important link, however. They are real organisations, very powerful establishments and yes, part of the same brotherhood. The issue is that they are claiming that their work and purpose is to maintain order and humanity, but they seek to destroy everything." Heather's phone chimed and, as she took a seat on the window ledge, she took it out and clicked open the message.

Cameron placed the wine bottle gently back onto the desk as he spoke. "What was her work?"

Heather glanced up at him. "Emilie practiced the theories written in her paper. She used examples of cross-pollination in flowers to grow new flowers without the two types of plants ever being in contact. In this part of the experiment, it was easy to reproduce using bees as the transport vector. The second step was more challenging, but it was the stepping stone for artificial insemination. Again, no amazing breakthrough there, as we have established proven techniques for IVF. In vitro fertilization has been around for quite some time. But Emilie continued stretching the ready proven theories. In essence, her work was looking backward to how the building blocks of a specie's creation came about in the first place. The one thing we all have been missing."

"So, this medical research is some sort of new wonder drug or medical technique?"

"Well, no. It is new knowledge. Undiscovered real theories that change the meaning of life for us all," Heather replied.

"And all this links to Maynard, how? Why were Emilie and I 'accidentally' introduced?" Cameron voiced in one long breath.

"Civilization, Cameron. The human species and how it came to be. As I said, the meaning of life – that is the link. The work you were doing with Maynard was encroaching on uncovering how humanity had preserved the knowledge. It had to be protected. The secret clues left behind over generations were almost exposed. The essence of faith and every religion has been charged with protecting the truth, hiding it from society. Although it goes much deeper, it is also about finding new ways to keep the secrets hidden."

"And Emilie's work – did she use the information we discovered to complete this picture?"

"Oh, no… we couldn't let that happen. Emilie found *you*, Cameron. A tall, dark mysterious stranger, who captivated her heart. She talks about you all the time; you are the love of her life. Why can't you see that? She cracked the code of life all on her own. The only things missing were a few key pieces of the puzzle. All she needed was the keys to open the door. You had those keys all along."

Cameron's eyes lit up. Suddenly, the early hours of the morning, lack of sleep and running on fumes all faded away at that moment of realization by Cameron. "Michelangelo's the *Creation of Adam* and the mysteries of the Mithras."

Heather continued. "Emilie recreated acts of history without any knowledge of the past, without understanding the power behind her results. Your actions were completely separate; you found the path to the past as well. But you, with Maynard's work, uncovered truths that history has tried desperately to keep hidden. Now the events are in line to truly ignite the clash between science, religion and history. Things between supernatural fact and manufactured fact are but a whisker away and you are both creators of the foundation."

"Heather..." Cameron paused.

"Yes, Cameron, now you understand the dilemma."

"We must not fail," Cameron said firmly.

"I am aware of that fact, which is why there's the urgency to stop any interference, especially from you. This is why we were pushing so hard to find you and explain the gravity of the situation to you."

Cameron turned to Heather, displaying urgency in his movements. Then, at that moment, he noticed a fleeting shadow moving across the wall alongside the desk. In the darkened room, Cameron was already on high alert. Heather grabbed his arm and calmly whispered, "It's okay, Cameron. Relax. Look."

"Hello, Cameron." The tired, rough voice of Maynard came across the room as he moved into the moonlight, glinting on his greying face.

CHAPTER TWENTY

London, now

The dark room closed in on Cameron and the silence was deafening as he faced various unfolding truths in front of him. He was just coming round to the revelations that Heather had unravelled for him. He was also coming to terms with the anger and betrayal because of the deception he'd faced from people whom he'd cared for in the past. What still troubled him, as he could not concentrate on that at this moment, was that Heather was explaining all this to him. She also mentioned working for 'others', yet he was not sure who these 'others' were. His concentration was focused now on the ghost of Maynard who stood in front of him in that shadowy room.

"Cameron –" Maynard's tired voice.

"Stop…– don't! How dare you! First Emilie and then you. I was trusted to find your precious treasures, but not enough to be told the truth? How dare you–" Cameron's voice trailed off, his face a mixture of hurt and disbelief.

The moonlight cast an eerie shadow on half of Maynard's face. Cameron recognised it as pale and lifeless.

Cameron turned away from Maynard and focused on Heather. "How did you get the bottle of wine?" he demanded.

Cameron waited patiently for a reply while Maynard sheepishly entered the room. Now more visible in the moon's lighting, Cameron glanced over and noticed the aged skin on his worn face; life hadn't been good to Maynard. Maynard's voice was less confident – less dominant from what Cameron recalled it to be. "I know you feel betrayed. Anyone in your position would be beside themselves. You have heard some dangerous truths tonight. Such truths that will cost people's lives. The last few years have been a nightmare, my dear friend, but Cameron, my life and yours are in grave danger. I had to leave and it was the only way it could work. Everyone had to think I was dead, including you."

As much as Cameron wanted to put his hands around Maynard's neck for all those days, weeks and months of pain he'd been through because he thought he was dead, he contained his emotions within himself.

"Don't…" Cameron paused and crossed his arms before continuing, "…make me regret standing here and being accountable for my actions, Maynard, as you may not like what I have to say or what I might do."

Maynard flopped in the chair, nodding solemnly.

"Go ahead, get it out," Maynard said. Cameron shook his head and rubbed the back of his neck with his hand, applying slightly more pressure than he'd intended, with his eyes narrowing at Maynard. "Please sit then… I will tell you everything." Cameron acceded to his request while Heather moved to sit on the edge of the desk beside Maynard.

"Tell me."

Maynard sighed. "There is no easy way to condense thousands of years of history into a matter of minutes.

Time, as always, is against us, Cameron."

Maynard glanced over to Heather, who nodded. "The Mithras is why I disappeared. It is the same reason that Emilie had to be hidden. We don't have time, my boy… if humanity is to be saved, time is of the essence now."

"The Mithras?" Cameron took notice. "The Temple in London that we researched in Vienna, just before you apparently disappeared?"

"Mithraism, yes, the ancient religion that worshipped the Persian god, Mithra. It was long before the Roman Empire – before civilization as we know it, Cameron. We were remarkably close to uncovering something that was hidden by many others before us. Those aspects were hidden for an exceptionally good reason."

Cameron stammered as he tried to stretch his neck out. "What does a washed-up religion have to do with anything? With me? With Emilie?"

Heather sighed under her breath. "Cameron! Mithraism has to do with *every*thing. It is the reason for humanity. You came to London after Maynard went into hiding because you wanted to finish what you both started in Vienna. You were curious and you found something, didn't you?"

Maynard swayed slightly in his chair. Cameron glanced as the two shared knowing looks and secret nods of agreement before Heather continued.

"Mithraism started to disappear into the underground around the fourth century. At that time, it was a rival to Christianity. Its supporters were suppressed and persecuted. Nevertheless, when the Roman Empire started to gain strength, both in numbers and reach, it began using any means necessary to have people believe of the new world. Mithraism was pushed further into the darkness; but it continued to survive underground." Heather allowed her words to hang in the air between them all.

With a stern voice, Cameron replied, breaking the deafness in the atmosphere. "How did it continue to survive?"

Heather's eyes lit up as she started to reply, but Maynard held his hand up, silencing her. He cleared his throat. "In light of the situation, the Mithraism hierarchy felt it imperative to work behind the scenes if they were to survive. The Temple's parishioners moved everything underground. Their temples are called Mithraeum and most of them still exist today. Some of them are hidden amongst cities we now live in. Others hide in caves. They're magnificent structures, Cameron. The architecture and design are quite marvellous considering their working environment. Their temples are quite different, but still rival most Roman cathedrals that were built much later in the Empire."

"You forget, Maynard, that I've been to such a temple. The one here, right in London – we discovered the site. The heat maps we analysed in Vienna."

With a nod, Maynard continues. "The followers of Mithras swore an oath of secrecy before they were initiated. They met in shadows before Christianity; why would you think a religion would want to do that?"

Cameron remained silent and resolute in his motion to get Maynard to explain himself.

Maynard sighed. "The god, Mithras, was said to have been born on December twenty-fifth – year and century unknown at the time. Time, as we know it today, did not exist. Tell me, Cameron, why do you think so many religions use December twenty-fifth to celebrate the birth of their deity?"

"Pagan ghost stories," Cameron said flippantly.

Heather let out a chuckle. "Back then, everyone who wasn't Christian was pagan. So, which religion did December twenty-fifth come from, and why do so many other religions use it?"

"I'm guessing you're about to tell me… it has something to do with your friend Mithras, right?"

Heather glared at Cameron through piercing eyes. "Can you not see the reason for the tussle between religions? History has taught humanity to fuss over our faith. We have learned to fight for survival. Why was it their way or death? Why have so many wars been fought over religion?"

Cameron remained distant.

Maynard took over. "History has taught us that it is all centred around greedy, power-hungry humanity. What else? It is not from some outlandish notion of pleasing a higher power. History has proven that civilization is based on greedy, power-hungry humans racing to beat each other into submission. Scripture allows them to justify their actions."

The room stayed quiet before Maynard looked directly at Cameron and asked:

"What if I told you those scriptures say that for a reason?"

Cameron looked between them. "It wouldn't surprise me and nothing does after the events over the last few hours."

"Not the reason you are thinking, Cameron. I can see that you aren't understanding how Mithraism is connected to all the research. So, I'll ask you again. Why would a religion swear its followers to secrecy and build their temples underground, if every other religion that came after them had a mission to spread the word and convert people? What secrets do you think they were hiding underground, and why were their followers not allowed to speak about their religion?"

"They were primitive and paranoid?"

"How do you think life began, Cameron?" Maynard pressed.

"*Oh*, please just tell me, and get this nightmare over with. We don't have time for you to play professor right now!" Cameron growing more frustrated at the riddles that Maynard was posing.

"What if I told you the followers of Mithraism were the answer?"

Cameron frowned. "I don't follow. How are the followers of Mithraism the answer to where Emilie is?"

"The answer is why everything was kept in the shadows. It's exactly why the followers were sworn to secrecy. Christianity and every other religion on the planet were formed to deflect us from the truth of our origins. The idea of the truth being exposed was forbidden; millions of humans have died because of power and knowledge. It's all about greed and a few maintaining the power and holding on to the rest."

The conversation had Cameron boiling inside. He was losing his patience. The only thing he cared about was finding Emilie and his daughter.

"Unless you have proof, this sounds like some nutty conspiracy theory to me." Cameron felt for his phone in his trouser pocket.

"Ah, but, Cameron, the research… the proof has been

right in front of you this entire time. What do you think we were doing? Emilie's research tied directly into many of the artefacts and texts we found at the Temple of Mithras and most of the other such sites we studied around the globe during those painstaking hours in Vienna. We were close, Cameron. When pressure from our enemies began to show, it was time for us to leave. The organisation knew we were close – I had to be sure no one could finish what we'd started. I had to take what was most important and flee. It was only at that point I understood that the organisations *wanted* us to discover the hidden secrets so that they could destroy them and hide them for eternity. I couldn't let this happen. Once they were sure all was destroyed, they would have killed us both too."

The exhaustion presented itself as Maynard continued, "Tell me, Cameron. You left the organisation once I disappeared. You came to London and visited the very site we were looking into, the temple. Did you take anything from the temple? Did you discover anything that made sense of what we started back then?"

"Maynard... the answer is more about what I know. I am tired of all these secrets. Yes, after I thought you'd died, the curiosity got the better of me and I needed to find the truth about that site. I knew it was important and held some part of the answer, if not the actual answer to your disappearance and the discovery that you had made or were about to make. But little did I know that what I would discover would lead us to where we are now, with all these people affected. Perhaps I should have just burnt everything to ashes while I had the chance."

This was the first time that Cameron had confessed to discovering something. Maynard knew the importance of having that admission out in the open.

Heather took a sharp intake of breath. "We need those artefacts, Cameron. Or whatever it is you discovered."

In an instant, the odds seemed to be turning towards Cameron's advantage. Heather sounded desperate.

"Really… Heather, after all these years, do you not know me better than that? If I give you the artefacts, the knowledge, what leverage do I have left to get Emilie and my child back?"

"Damn it, Cameron!" Heather yelled. "I get it. I understand why you're so upset, but you're still refusing to look at the bigger picture. The secret of life is in those artefacts and Emilie's research. What we are telling you is real danger. A war that has been raging for thousands of years. Do you have any idea of the black cloud you pulled over our heads by disturbing aspects that have been left hidden for centuries? You have not only put our lives in danger, but your family's lives too." She started pacing, pressing her fingertips to her temple.

"Heather…" Maynard stated calmly, "Please sit. Cameron. If anyone understands what you must be feeling right now, it is me; but please trust us. They are masters at smoke screens – everything you see is fabricated by the organisations. The establishment that paid us both so handsomely at that time was to blind us. The Freemasons and the Illuminati – their goal was to wipe and eliminate Mithraism and keep the true secret of life hidden forever, all through a combination of cultures and religions and communities."

Now it was Cameron's turn to raise his voice. His veins were pulsating in his temple area and a bead of sweat had formed on his forehead. "You two keep talking about the secret of life, but not one of you has bothered to share that information with me. Why did I go through the heartache to hide what I found and lose my family?"

Maynard pulled his hand over his eyes and used his forefinger and thumb to massage his own temples as he spoke. "Legend has it that the Mithra god was the first to self-fertilise; to create life without a partner. Imagine the power if humans could create life without a partner. What would that do to hope? To belief? To prayer? Power would be lost. It means, Cameron, that believing in a higher power or deity would be pointless. The world is run on fear, using power to control humanity because of death. The anxiety of dying. That alone is why the Freemasons and Illuminati went on a mission to keep these secrets buried. Our research, Cameron, uncovered the truth; do you understand the depth of the situation now? Under the direct vision of the organisations, it was all a way to keep the truth hidden. And Emilie..." Maynard hesitated.

Cameron's eyes lit up, "What about her?"

"Emilie, being as bright and intelligent as she is, found a way through without studying and looking back at history to teach her. That was why everyone that you have a connection with had to disappear. But it doesn't have to stay this way, Cameron. We can work together to piece the puzzle together..."

Heather sighed. "Please trust us. Someone in your position would have a right to be filled with anger toward anyone connected to all this. But you must understand and believe that we are here and we have been here trying to protect Emilie and your child. But we need your help."

"The Freemasons and Illuminati have both the resources and reach to get to Emilie and her research.

If she's given the chance to complete, test and publish her results, the cascade of events would be catastrophic. Imagine civilisation learning that faith was a way of controlling the population. Yet her research also needs to be completed and protected, away from the evil of this world, as it's the first time anyone has come close to unlocking the secret of life!"

The room fell silent.

Cameron had ached for Emilie for an entire year and he now ached for the unknown in Siena.

Maynard and Heather – two faces he trusted once, oh so long ago – what options did he have at that moment but to trust and have faith in them again? But he also knew there is never truly anyone you can fully trust other than your own inner self.

The unsettled feeling in the room increased as the early morning dawned. All three were sleep deprived and hungry, and it was evident that thoughts of reality and his subconscious were being merged into one – but none more so than for Cameron. It was as though the hypnotic state kept playing tricks on his mind, with his subconscious trying to evoke a wakefulness of certainty for the truth.

The thoughts had Cameron perplexed and torn all at once. He wanted to cast doubt on a situation that he struggled to believe. It wasn't the tireless acts of insanity that were playing out in front of him; it was dealing with so many unknown variables that changed as the seconds passed. Disbelief was coupled with the purple hazy moonlight of shadows outside the windows; it was like a psychedelic trace, coming down from self-induced intoxication.

On the ornate mantelpiece was a mahogany mechanical

timepiece, in working order, that caught Cameron's eye. He recognised the era style instantly; '*Strange*,' he thought to himself. How could he recall an innocuous fact while such a chaotic event was unfolding? The clock was a highly elaborately decorative, yet understated, piece in the room. "Obviously French Empire in style," he said to himself, "circa 1860." The warm colour of the wood helped calm his apprehensions. Along the front were columns of bronze-based fittings housed for protection, like a guardsman on the face of the clock. Its silvery-black Roman numerals with a pendulum hanging down created a perfect balance in the structure. Cameron's intense thought paused at the idea of balance; it struck a chord. It was an immediate reflection of his current surroundings; however, his mind was so preoccupied that he had not even noticed it showed just past two am.

Eventually, Cameron turned to Maynard and broke the silence. "Sofia has no idea you're alive. Do you know that she blames me for your death? Which means she's working against me, and it seems – all of us. Are you also aware she tracked me down and threatened my life? Your daughter is working for the very organisations you went into hiding from in order to stay alive. Her eyes, when I saw her eyes – the vengeance they portrayed would have killed me, given the chance." Cameron paused to let Maynard take in what he was saying, keeping his eyes shifting from Maynard to Heather and back to Maynard to look for any signs of emotion. He continued, "It is a look I have seen many times. If I don't do what she wants, they will kill Emilie and my child. Tell me…" Cameron glanced to Heather now, "tell me; you haven't shown me irrefutable evidence that proves all of you are not on the same side. What is there to stop me from walking back out of that door now and going to give Sofia what she wants?"

Maynard's face contorted in pain.

Heather rested her hand on Maynard's shoulder. "You couldn't have predicted the future; it wasn't your fault and you have to believe that. When the time is right, she will see the truth." Cameron remained unfazed by Heather's words.

Cameron mulled over the conversation and knew the weakness in Maynard in relation to Sofia and saw that as his chance. "It's imperative that I can trust both of you. Maynard, you spoke of your daughter with love and compassion – I saw that in Vienna. Sofia's safety was a major concern then, and as far I can see, that hasn't changed. However, she holds me responsible for your death. If… we are on the same side, why can you not pull Sofia inside alongside Emilie and Siena?"

"Cameron, think about that plan. You don't understand," Maynard stated.

Heather raised an eyebrow. "The myths modern society has about these organisations are important. Generally, people disappear when the possibility of the truth being exposed becomes reality. Sofia is working for them, which means she is embedded in the lies – it makes her a marked person. We cannot…" Heather turned to look at Maynard, "…risk getting emotional over a loved one. I know that's harsh, but we must think of the bigger picture. If we fail, there will be nothing to live for anyway."

The words cut deep. Cameron looked away past the windows into the dark abyss outside. He despised the premise; nonetheless, he knew Heather was right. "I understand the statement, although you didn't hear the pain in her voice. Yes, she is angry and capable of anything, but being hurt shows signs of remorse."

"Enough! Both of you stop!" Maynard rose to his feet by placing a hand on the desk for support. "Cameron, you act like everything we told you was a huge surprise, but you hid artefacts and continued to protect them. We've already shared our knowledge – does that not show trust? I think it's about time you shared *your* insights. What have you hidden? And why do you refuse to tell *us* the truth, knowing your own daughter is being threatened?"

"Cameron… I understand the reasoning behind your state of mind, but ask yourself how else could we have acquired the bottle of wine? Plus, who else would know the meaning behind its relevance? Think, Cameron, remember the past, the work we accomplished. If I didn't care about Emilie or your daughter, would I be concerned about their safety? What would it matter to keep them hidden?" Maynard asked Cameron and waited.

"I…" Cameron paused; he hung his head.

"Cameron..?" Maynard prompted while he glanced at the clock.

"The temple..." Cameron began after sighing deeply, "…within the building lay clues that tie to the bigger picture. The artists that came centuries later left clues in their paintings about the aspects that occurred in that temple. Or what secrets the temples hold from a time long past. We all know that churches commissioned art in the Renaissance period and some beautiful works were created at that time. But when I saw that those same frescos of art depicted the clues in the Mithras Temples, I knew there was more to it. How would a Renaissance artist know what was hidden in a buried temple so many years prior to them, creating that artwork? And why would they put such artwork in a Catholic cathedral? Especially since those two faiths were at war with each other." Heather and Maynard watched with wide eyes, and so he continued.

"Emilie educated me about the magical romance surrounding Michelangelo and his masterpiece, *Creazione di Adamo.* History has taught us that humanity is, in essence, a single family, where Adam and Eve were at the base. However, Adam and Eve weren't born of a man and woman; they were created by one God. Which got me thinking, what if the timelines were incorrect? What if Michelangelo was trying to show us the historical events unfolding? In the temple, there are references to life being created from one entity, a uniform beginning."

In seconds, the atmosphere in the room altered to a dynamic lesson of instant sharing. Any distrusting suspicion vanished for that moment due to the distraction of the lesson. Cameron flashed from present to past, to the long evenings locked away with Maynard in Vienna scanning documents for clues to history's timeline. The thirst they shared for knowledge drove their insatiable hunger back then and that energy was now contained within this room.

The present situation brought Cameron to an impasse; did he fall to temptation and share his prize secret? Or let the voice of reason stay in control? The predicament had him perplexed. Before him stood two people whom he'd once trusted and sought counsel from, yet now he asked himself if there was a need to maintain his defences around them. He couldn't deny within himself the thrill and excitement at the discovery that he felt he had made all those years ago and the chance to share it now, finally.

On one hand, Cameron stayed quiet, reflecting on the

situation. *On the other hand*, he thought, *they have deceived me, lied and conjured a world around me for their own sense of meaning and purpose.*

He knew what he had to do. He really had no choice but to remain calm and to allow the foreplay leverage to win this game. Until this moment, he had remained in the passenger seat, however, it seemed he had just gained control of the car.

Cameron could finally see the events with some clarity. Without him, secrets would remain hidden or be lost forever if the codes were unable to be unravelled in this mystery. For Cameron, his focus was the safety of Emilie and Siena, but others seemed not to have this as the main agenda.

The faint resonating aspects of a breathing house surrounded all three from various sounds of material that made up the structure of the house, giving it an air of life. The wooden floorboards expanding and contracting as the heated pipes came to life in the building. The hum of the boiler located in the hallway cupboard. There was a calming nature to the house that eased Cameron's mind to contemplate the next course of action, and he glanced at the clock once more, such elegance, in perfect precision with time. Time is time. No way to stop it or alter its effects.

"Cameron… what exactly did you take from the temple? What do they seek from you?" Heather's voice startled him as she broke the silence.

He replied while looking at Maynard, speaking directly to him. "I knew you were focusing on the Mithras in Vienna, Maynard. It was clear, with all that research directed at one aspect of history. My research just continued from where we stopped, I mean, where *you* stopped. The quest was to uncover as much as I could about them."

Maynard clapped him on the back and smiled. "I knew you wouldn't rest; nothing could have stopped you from carrying on what we started. My lifelong work took everything from me, including Sofia."

"Maynard, you missed a large piece of the puzzle, the one section you needed Emilie to uncover. How good are your biblical texts?" Cameron turned away from the pair of them and continued. "*'... Now no shrub had yet appeared on the earth and no plant had yet sprung up, for the Lord God had not sent rain on the earth and there was no-one to work the ground, but streams came up from the earth and watered the whole surface of the ground. Then the Lord God formed a man from the dust of the ground and breathed into his nostrils the breath of life, and the man became a living being'.*"

Maynard sighed. "From the book of Genesis. I didn't take you for a religious soul, Cameron."

"I'm not, far from it, actually. But it's becoming clear that religion is about keeping us blind to the truth. Isn't that what this is all about? The truth and how it has been hidden?"

"What did you learn in that temple, Cameron? Why are they hunting you? You know they won't stop." Heather spoke with urgency. "They will kill you, Emilie and the child. You do understand that, right?"

"Then I'd say it's time for confusion and espionage; some payback." Cameron walked over to the big sash windows to plan carefully what he needed to say to both Heather and Maynard – or rather, what they needed to hear from him.

"What did I learn? What did I take? I gained what may be part of the truth that the Mithras was, is and always has been… something that, perhaps, you both also know but have just been too blind and stupid to put together. It's only now that I see how it's all becoming clear with Emilie and her work. Look at what we have all sacrificed to get to this point. Maynard, would you have risked Sofia in this if you had known of the outcome? Heather, I ask myself, are you ever capable of being the real you and loving someone who isn't just work-related to reach a target or complete a project? I am sorry about Sofia, I truly am. But I cannot fully trust you both until I have Emilie and Siena in my sights. The choice is yours. Take me to her or I'll find my own way to her without your help. We have wasted enough time over this past year, don't you think?"

Cameron focused on Maynard who seemed to be looking past, out into the night sky, with the mention of his daughter's name: Sofia.

CHAPTER TWENTY-ONE

1992

Maynard

"Papa, I like holding your hand when we walk; it lets me go without needing to think about where we are going. Why, Papa, do more people not do that?"

Maynard smiled at his ever-inquisitive daughter, eager to respond, but quickly interrupted by Sofia as she continued, "Why do children get taught to read simple things if they are only going to end up reading more important things?"

Sofia was a Benjamin Button, born to take on the adult world. Though Maynard took pleasure in the fact that the ignorance of her youth kept her safe from it for a short while, even if she did feel so obviously restricted. Maynard could remember early mornings; she'd wake from a deep sleep, her hair matted from the pillow, although any talk of brushing the mop was infinitesimal compared to the important events of the day. Her long, flowing hair, often with a co-ordinated collection of knots, would bounce as through it had a life of its own. In an act that remained standard for years to come, Maynard finally gave up fighting it because it only drove more passion into her defiant behaviour.

When she was old enough to understand age, it became a direct point with her father. Maynard remembered the long conversations discussing the subject: "I am twelve years, four months, twenty-two days and twelve hours old at this hour, Papa." Sofia's desperate bid as a child to stand out from other children gave her father the validation that she was different; she was special. The exact details of her age and life could not be challenged.

As a parent, Maynard found himself biased in many ways; however, he knew his favouritism was mild compared to his daughter's talents. Sofia worked intensely with her father before she even began school and never saw the relevance of wasting her days sitting in a classroom. The idea of listening to a teacher drone on about things that did not matter seemed pointless. Especially when she could just read a book and learn the subjects on her own. Her days in her father's study, mimicking his habits and characteristics when it came to research and study, taught her more than any teacher ever would.

"Sponge, you should really try to have some of your friends around more. Surely they'd like to have afternoon play dates with you in the garden?" Maynard suggested.

Sofia had only shrugged, her mind too consumed by the book she held.

The drive to learn was the light to her very soul. It started the moment she woke to the fight before sleep invaded her mind. The energy, along with the endless searching questions, never stopped. However, the passion did not surprise Maynard; after all, he was a published academic professor well known for his work. Children are products of their environment; all that she knew of family was her father, so that was what she emulated.

In the beginning, Maynard was thrilled to always have his daughter by his side in the study, at the library or at his university where he lectured. It allowed Sofia to observe his work. They were family; he was her best friend and she was his. Maynard did not realise, until it was too late, that she had indeed become her father. Sofia had literally absorbed every nuance of his life.

Accomplishing anything she set her mind to, Maynard knew she would one day surpass his intellect and began to find it increasingly difficult to distract her. So, he gradually began to test her knowledge, hoping to judge her best career path.

He thought that one such field that could always keep Sofia occupied was the health industry. Since she had grown up with a scientist as a father, her knowledge of medicinal practices was impressively extensive. Medical faculties were too mechanical for Sofia, however, as she would constantly voice. "Papa, humans are working too hard on fixing people from an illness, but it is not an illness, but evolution. So, we are harming our future survival aspects."

The legal realms angered Sofia; she saw them as an elaborate cocktail of lies to gain purpose for the client being represented. Teaching, nevertheless, engaged Sofia's attendance, yet not in the conventional sense. She not only wanted to share her knowledge but push the boundaries, to raise the dynamics of learning. It was clear that there was only one way she was heading... to follow her father.

CHAPTER TWENTY-TWO

1998

Maynard

As dawn broke, the morning chorus of birds took flight with their voices. The day was blessed with a lazy sunrise, yet one full of hope. The flirty fowls sang in tandem with perfect harmony. Beams of white laser lighting etched the wall of Sofia's bedroom. She slept contentedly after ingesting the works of Michelangelo; only today was a special day, the morning of her sixteenth birthday.

Maynard crept into her room singing, "Happy birthday to you, happy birthday to you and happy birthday to the Sponge frizz head!" He held out a tray filled with breakfast; fresh orange juice, oats in coconut milk sprinkled with berries over the top and a slice of rye bread. Her favourite.

Sofia had a look of wonder. "Papa, I do love you so much!"

"Not as much as you love Michelangelo, I see. I hope the amazing facts you learned were worth sleeping in your day clothes and missing out on your beauty sleep!"

Sofia looked flushed and rubbed the sleep from her eyes, moving the hair off her forehead and to curl behind her ears.

Maynard swallowed the lump in his throat and blinked back tears. "You are beautiful, like your mother." Clearing his throat and not wanting to allow the emotional turmoil of missing his dear wife, he said, "Obviously the day is yours. I am hoping you have plans involving some friends that I completely disapprove of. Along with some behaviour considered socially inappropriate?"

Sofia rolled her eyes, "Well... Papa, I thought perhaps hanging out with an old-timer who pretends his taste in clothes and music are refined might be an exciting occasion. If that old-timer has time to spend with me?" Maynard smiled, "Are you sure..? Don't you have friends to frolic about town with, instead of hanging with the old-timer?"

"Papa, you are my best friend. The only place I want to be is with you; besides, who else could I find to be as mentally stimulating as you?"

"I admit, Sponge, you are your father's daughter. I just don't want you to waste your life away researching the past and not living in the future. I want you to create your own life."

"You have taught me everything. I am doing what I love; being in this place excites me, Papa. It stimulates my mind. Most people are ignorant, impossible to have an intelligent conversation with. You taught me to be who I am inside. Be confident and go after my dreams, right?"

Maynard nodded to her statements and felt proud inside of what his daughter had become.

He knew arguing was pointless once Sofia made up her mind. "My dear Sofia... please do not ever lose your passion for life, just don't forget to live."

"I won't... pinky promise."

"Now, how about you get dressed in a nice pretty sundress and this old-timer will change into one of his divine outfits and we will go enjoy this perfect spring day?"

"You got a date. I will be ready in a jiffy."

Maynard kissed Sofia on the forehead and left her to get ready.

It felt as though it were only yesterday when Maynard would hold baby Sofia, swaddled up in her pink blanket. *Where did the time go?* he wondered. The blanket hadn't lasted long, of course. Sofia hated being fettered, even as a newborn.

He'd never forget her first words. That's right, not word... words. She was a genius from the very beginning.

"Papa... out," she'd said from her cot, refusing to sleep in it yet again.

Too powerful a force to ignore, Maynard had bought her a regular bed, attaching rails to the side to keep her safe.

Sofia's birthday was a beautiful spring day: bright and fresh with a gentle breeze that made the leaves on the trees whisper songs of life. Nestled in the centre of the city was a park filled with elegant flowers and shrubbery covered in brilliant green growth from the warming spring sun. It was a perfect setting for a picnic.

"What do you say we stop at the bakery and pick up a slice of birthday cake? Along with all the fixings for a delightful lunch?"

"Papa, I'd say that sounds amazing. I love these warm spring days; after the chilly winters, I could use some bright sunshine. Plus, I have all our favourite music on my phone to keep the day in a party vibe!"

"Well then, Sponge, are you ready?" He held out his

arm for her to take hold of.

Sofia smiled and entwined her arm with his.

The two had set out on many adventures through the years, but Maynard found that one to be his favourite. He raised her alone for many years, but he'd never felt it a chore. While many of his colleagues would harmlessly complain about their children, he always saw the objections as ridiculous. His only protest was the passage of time; it stopped for no-one.

CHAPTER TWENTY-THREE

London, now

Cameron

As the silence disinfected the room, cleansing traces of lies and betrayal from the open, Cameron took a good, hard look at Maynard. Cameron couldn't put his finger on it, but it was more than being estranged from his daughter – Maynard was sheltering something else too. An unsettled, seething anxiety brewed within that seemed like yet another deception. He looked gaunt and pale. Maynard's eyes met Cameron's. "Maynard..." Cameron announced, but his speech went unanswered, as Maynard didn't seem to have registered anything and looked straight through Cameron. A few seconds later, Maynard started to falter and lean to the side, with a bead of sweat on his forehead travelling down the side of his face. His face turned to a pale shade of grey and Cameron leaped to his side to catch him just in time. "Maynard!" Heather shrieked.

Cameron placed him gently down, tapped him slightly across the cheek that was damp from the sweat and he started to regain consciousness. "When was the last time he ate, Heather?"

"I am not sure; we made arrangements for him to come

here just before you and I arrived. So before then, I do not know."

Cameron scowled.

"He doesn't look well. Has he gotten much rest?"

She shook her head. "I think he's been too nervous about meeting with you again."

"Have you at least tried to get him to rest?"

Heather scowled. "I am not his babysitter, Cameron. He is a grown man. We have *all* been running on fumes for a while now. Not just him!"

Cameron sighed and shook his head.

"Stay here with him; I will go out and get us all something to eat. I assume that is allowed?" He turned back to Maynard who was still pale, his eyes open, wiping his lips with the back of his hand.

"Please do not take too long, we have to get back on track to what we need to focus on," Heather stated.

"I will be back as soon as possible. There was a café we passed on the way here; I'll go there." Cameron placed a hand on Maynard's shoulder and left the room. As he stepped outside onto the pavement, he looked up and down the street. Nothing out of the ordinary, it seemed. He pulled the phone out of his pocket and checked the screen – still no contact from Sofia, which made him slightly anxious.

CHAPTER TWENTY-FOUR

Heather

Heather wandered in darkness to the back of the property where the kitchen was, to get a glass of water for Maynard. When she returned, Maynard was beginning to regain some composure. "What… happened?" He looked around, startled. "Where is Cameron?" In his tired, hoarse voice.

"Shhhhh, it's alright. He just went to get us some breakfast."

"You shouldn't have let him leave… What if–"

"He will be back; you need food and, frankly, so do I. We've been here all night and it was time for a break. Besides, what good are we if we cannot focus and keep our composure?"

Maynard blinked in a long, lazy manner and nodded in submission.

"Do you think he is on board now? We need him, Heather–"

"I think he is still sceptical but, yes, he will come around. Remember, we have the pull of Emilie. He wants to get Emilie and his daughter back. It gives us great leverage."

"You do realise that Cameron doesn't need us to get his family back, right? Especially with what he knows now." Maynard rubbed his damp forehead with the back of his hand and shuffled in the chair to sit in a more comfortable position.

"I know, but he won't betray us. I know him. I'm sure of it. Also, if anyone can get through to Sofia, it's Cameron. So, we need Cameron to keep her at bay and to still get your daughter back."

"Sofia…" Maynard's voice trailed off. "I messed up, Heather. I failed her; she didn't deserve the hell I've put her through. I wouldn't blame her if she never forgives me. As long as she is safe when this is all over, I can live with that."

Heather pushed the glass of water towards Maynard. "Have some water and don't think like that. She will forgive you. Everything we have done was to keep them safe. *All* of them safe."

"Heather, I let my daughter believe the lie that I was dead and that Cameron was the cause. What kind of a parent does that?" Heather lowered her head at his words and the silence was interrupted by a soft knock on the sash window that disturbed them both. They looked over to see Cameron's face peering through the glass back at them.

"Cameron's back; stay put. I will go let him in." Heather sighed and left the room.

CHAPTER TWENTY-FIVE

Cameron

Cameron walked through into the room without saying a word to Heather.

"I am sorry, dear friend; I must have been more exhausted that I thought." Maynard sat up straighter as he looked at Cameron walking through the doorway.

"Oh, I never thought coffee could taste so good," Heather smiled while she blew the steam away from the coffee cup handed to her in silence from Cameron. "You even remember my macchiato. Cameron, I am impressed."

Cameron glanced at Maynard, ignoring the act of friendship from Heather. "Are you feeling better? Your colour seems to be getting back to normal."

"Yes, Cameron. I guess my age is catching up with me after all these years."

"No-one can go without eating and expect to be at their best." Cameron laid out the bags of breakfast on the desk in front of Maynard. He paused just for a second before continuing. "Have some of this and when you are ready, let's get a plan laid out so we can get this mess over and done with. Maybe we can finally have somewhat of a normal life once this is over."

The walk had given Cameron some clarity of thought

and he had decided it was in his best interests to work with Maynard and Heather if he ever wanted a fighting chance of safely getting Emilie back with their daughter. Right now, he had to try and play along and trust these two.

Maynard sighed softly. "Cameron, I know after what happened you don't trust me and I don't blame you for that. We drew you into this. But now, the only way to get out of this, all together, is to help each other and work for the same outcome. It's the only way. You know the organisation; they're ruthless and will stop at nothing to put an end to us. Our deaths will just seal humanity's fate. We must succeed and we cannot do this without your total commitment. Do we have that, Cameron?" He was exhausted, but Maynard needed Cameron's attention.

"As I said last night, or should I say, this morning, I am here to protect Emilie and my daughter. I am aware of the organisation's tactics, but we are not friends. I hope I've made that clear. Please spare me the fake softness. Your lies and deception are now all too clear to see so, if you two are done, we can get on with the plan."

"Cameron..." Heather shot a glance over to Cameron, but saw his jaw clench at the sound of her voice and she paused.

Maynard cleared his throat and both turned to him as he spoke. "The truth must stay with us in silence. Do you understand that?" His eyes met Cameron's and did not look away.

"Yes, yours and mine." Maynard looked perplexed at Cameron's reply. "Go on, Maynard, what is your suggestion on how to play this?"

Taking a sip from his coffee, Maynard replied. "Sofia is the link to our success. But we have to get her out in the open, and vulnerable." He sighed before continuing. "Once she is exposed, we have the leverage to take them down. We lead them on a wild goose chase, a smoke and mirrors play and then you two can work on getting Emilie and Siena out and away from all of this." Taking a deep breath in, Maynard tried to keep his composure and concentration and the coffee was obviously helping with that. "If they truly believe the answers are in London, we have a chance. But you must sell it to them and make them believe it. Cameron... do you understand?"

Cameron's eyes feeling heavy like lead weights. "I know," he answered. "But we also know that the deception won't last long, so we have to get Emilie and Siena further to safety in a short time."

"Alright, but before we go any further... Cameron, this may be just another mission to you, but the target is my daughter, you must understand. I know you have lost trust in me, but she is all I have in the world. I must know that you will do everything in your power to protect her." Maynard's voice softer and more fragile than it had been all night.

Cameron raised his eyebrows and scoffed. "Let me be clear." The tone direct and cold, facing Maynard. "I know Sofia is your daughter; however, she has been on the dark side for many years it seems and we have no idea what they have done to her or taught her. I will do my best to get her out alive and she is our best option to succeed. She probably knows more about their inner workings than anyone. But I will not hesitate to take her out if I feel my life is in danger, or for that same reason, the safety of Emilie and Siena. Do I make myself clear?"

Heather turned to Cameron. "Cameron, listen–"

He held his palm up. "Heather… of everyone right now, I trust you the least. You lied to me right from the start. How do we know you aren't a mole, sent here to spy and run back to your precious organisation with our secrets?"

Heather paced across the room while she spoke. "After the last few hours, everything I have told you and you still don't trust me?"

"What have you told me that I don't already know? Please, yes, you brought Maynard and told me things about Emilie; nonetheless, all of that could have been part of the plan to draw me out and to use me for your own needs."

"Cameron, enough!" Maynard's voice startled Heather. "We need you more than you could ever imagine; the only thing we can do now is to try to rebuild your trust. That means getting your family back to you safely."

Cameron looked from one face to the other trying to evade his gut gnawing at him to not trust anyone. The stare from Cameron made Heather feel uncomfortable, as though he could see through her. She interrupted the atmosphere.

"Please, you started on the right path, with a building in London to draw them out. Where did you have in mind?"

"The cathedral… St Paul's," Maynard and Cameron announced at the same time. Heather looked puzzled at the unison of their voices.

"Are you going to explain?" Heather asked Cameron.

"No… go ahead, Maynard."

"Are you sure? I know you have studied every inch of that cathedral and done your homework."

"No, my secrets will stay with me; it's the only leverage I have to secure my safety. The stage is all yours, Maynard."

With that, Cameron moved over to the window and looked out onto the street.

Maynard took another sip of his hot drink and turned in his seat to face Heather.

"It's said that below the crypt of St Paul are many secrets about the truth of Christianity. The tomb is more than just a burial place. It serves as a structural support for the building. The massive piers were designed to balance the weight of the building. It is said that the cathedral has many secret rooms, which staff members are unaware existed. During the war, the cathedral was almost destroyed and in the devastation the Freemasons build an underground cavern to store some of humanity's most hidden secrets." Maynard was in full flow now and broke off a piece of his bagel and chewed on it. Crumbs dropped onto his lap. Cameron looked over his shoulder at Maynard and enjoyed seeing the old man rekindle his art of lecture.

"If you look closely at the architecture, the secrets will reveal themselves. Over the entrance of the south transept, Sir Christopher Wren, the Freemason architect responsible for the structure we see today, sent a workman to bring a stone marker to the centre of the new building and he grabbed a broken gravestone inscribed *Resurgam*, meaning, *'I shall rise again'*. After this, Wren inscribed a phoenix rising from the flames. Across that particular area, the blank second storey walls are cleverly concealing Gothic flying buttresses supporting the cathedral's clerestory, while eight hidden columns support the massive dome."

Maynard paused as Heather opened her mouth again, but she was instructed to wait with her thoughts. "Hold on, Heather, I am not done yet. In the choir beyond the dome are stalls carved in 1648, then the wrought iron screens by Jean Tijou. Then, there is the effigy of the poet and Dean of St Paul's, John Donne, which was the only monument to survive the Great Fire of London without significant damage." He drew breath. "Keenly aware of his own mortality, Donne wrapped himself in a burial shroud as a macabre model for the sculptor, Nicholas Stone. Not to mention Wren is buried in the cathedral's crypt with an inscription on his tomb – *Lector, si monumentum requiris, circumspice* – meaning, '*Reader, if you seek (his) monument, look around*'."

Maynard paused for breath and took another bite of his bagel. He took a sip of his drink and looked directly at Heather.

"My point, Heather, is that there are enough secrets to get Sofia's attention. We just must hope that she hasn't studied the history like Cameron and I have. However, not many people have actually seen the hidden rooms." Then turning to Cameron, "Cameron... what are you not telling us? You know the cathedral better than anyone."

Cameron shook his head and turned back to gaze outside. "As I said earlier, those secrets stay with me. They're my lifelines. Just know that there is a lot more than what meets the eye. All of which is in plain sight. If Sofia has done her homework, she will not fall for our bluff. But I have my ways once I am in there."

"Cameron, our secrets of the Mithras cannot be found in St Paul's, but it holds some very pertinent information about our enemies. We must protect that knowledge. Do you understand me?"

"What knowledge?" Heather chimed in.

"Heather, some information must stay between

Cameron and me. The less who know in relation to the truth, the better."

"You have got to be kidding? How am I supposed to be of help if I'm unaware of the truth here?" She glared at Maynard.

"No, Heather, you don't. Maynard is right. When the time is right, I will tell you, but for now, it's best to stay between us."

"It never stops… the lies, deceit. I am tired of risking my life for everyone, just to be left in the dark. How can I help if you lie to me?"

"We aren't lying, Heather, just not telling you everything – there is a big difference," Cameron announced. "Like *you* always told me everything? If I am not mistaken, you have been lying to me since we met. Besides, are you going to tell us that *you* don't have secrets?" As Cameron watched Heather, he could see her shoulders tense slightly at his accusation. She did not answer and broke her gaze from him.

Maynard's face was one of fear as he began to speak again. "Cameron… I know you've already stated your mind about my daughter, but please, you are the only person who can save her from this also. When you confront her, remind her of me. Remind her that her first word was 'Papa'. Most children say 'Mama' because the 'P' is difficult to say for young children. Remind her of the picnic we went on for her sixteenth birthday. Cameron, I wish I could tell you this is going to be easy, but it won't be. The best way to get my daughter is to give her a challenge. Make her see the truth, but make it difficult for her to reach the real truth. She will bite if it's difficult for her."

Cameron wasn't someone who would intentionally hurt

someone. It wasn't his style. But the priority was his family. Just the thought of having a family seemed totally foreign to him. It was the last thing Cameron had ever imagined could happen. He now had a path to perhaps follow to bring his family home by using people whom he'd thought he could trust many years ago as his friends.

CHAPTER TWENTY-SIX

Sitting there in silence, all three had a worn look to them, bodies exhausted and drained of all energy. Even Cameron felt as though he had aged an eternity, though he was more concerned about Maynard and his health. Cameron concluded that Maynard's decision to go into hiding without his daughter would have been a heartbreaking one to make. Cameron cared for his dear friend, and despite his disappointment at the deception, he did not want any harm to come to him. In reality, he was the closest thing to a true friend he had ever known. However, the details of his well-being could not divert Cameron from the task at hand, as even the history between Maynard and Cameron was not enough to keep Cameron from Emilie and his child.

Heather, meanwhile, was a different story – she tried to show loyalty and openness now, but Cameron had serious doubts. If push came to shove, he could not trust her. He needed to maintain his wits about her with every move and statement made.

It was quiet and the stillness of the room allowed thoughts to fill the dead space and create a peaceful atmosphere to rest in that was broken by Cameron's voice as he saw the strain of Maynard's fatigued body.

"Maynard," Cameron spoke in a low tone, "let's get an

hour of rest. We are all exhausted and will need to be on top form later."

There was no further invitation needed. Maynard settled on the sofa to rest with no word of protest. Just a sigh and nod as he slowly moved to the sofa. Cameron gestured for Heather to leave the room with him. Cameron gently closed the door to the room and walked with Heather closely behind him towards the back of the property.

"We should let Maynard rest for a bit. The last thing we need is to worry about his welfare while we are dealing with Sofia." Cameron looked around the small kitchen, took a glass from the sink and poured himself water to sip on.

Heather looked across at him while she leaned against the wall with her arms folded. "We should go together and meet Sofia when she contacts you…" She kept her tone neutral.

"No, absolutely not – we cannot risk her knowing that I have help. Besides, I don't want to leave Maynard alone. The last thing we need is for them to find out he's alive or for him to try and contact Sofia himself." Before Heather could reply, she was cut off by Cameron. "Heather, you know I am right. I cannot protect you and him at the same time."

Heather's voice rose. She took a step closer to Cameron with her hands on her hips in a defiant pose. "I don't need you to protect me, ever!"

Cameron let her comments slide and they turned their attention to what needed to be done. "Heather, do we agree on St Paul's? It is the best place to show Sofia we can be trusted. Obviously, she will know the location of the car I am using as they have that tracked. Thanks to you following me, I didn't park too close to the Temple of Mithras, so it's easy to get around that point if needed."

"How do you plan to make this work?"

Cameron took another sip of his water and shook his head.

"I have no idea yet, but it will come to me when the time is right."

Heather sighed in response.

Cameron had to keep his plan to himself; he needed to get the location of Emilie and Siena confirmed and safe. He needed to gain the upper hand in all this and Heather was one that could not be trusted at present. He took another sip of the water and eyed Heather standing there in front of him with eyes narrowed.

In the other room, they heard Maynard beginning to stir.

"Listen," Cameron said, "Maynard cannot know I have gone to meet Sofia. I have no idea which way this may turn or end at present."

"Fine, what now? How are you going to get in contact with her?" Heather scoffed.

"They have my number; this is one of their phones. The car hasn't moved for a few hours and I am nowhere to be seen and so I am sure she will be calling soon."

Cameron reached down to grab the phone from his pocket and Heather's eyes widened at that moment as the phone came to life with an incoming call from an unknown number.

"What? Is that her?"

He nodded.

Cameron turned his back to Heather as he answered the call, putting the phone to his ear. The conversation was short, with Cameron only saying a few words in response to the voice on the other end. Cameron mentioning the meeting point of St Paul's Cathedral.

"Well, here we go. Heather, stay here and help keep Maynard stay put at all costs."

CHAPTER TWENTY-SEVEN

Sofia

Sofia pulled into the hidden underground parking with an air of anxiety and focused determination within her. She'd been summoned in to speak with the organisation, which she understood was to give updates on her progress with Cameron. As usual, she approached the grand desk with the solitary chair that played host to an individual sitting in it. A low voice with strong character directed the attention of Sofia to approach the desk.

She quickly gathered her thoughts before approaching; it was unwise to show emotion when called in to speak with any of her superiors, as emotions were seen as a sign of weakness, which would mean that she was no longer needed within the organisation and to help with its purpose.

Quietly, he presented her with two questions. "I assume Cameron has been approached and briefed on the urgency of what is needed? And I would hope you have an update on his progress?"

"Sir… until the last twelve hours, he has done nothing out of the ordinary."

"What do you mean, '*until the last twelve hours*'?"

"He, uh… disappeared, Sir."

"He what?"

"I don't know, Sir, he just… well, I tracked the car, only it hasn't moved for a while and so I can only imagine he is on foot. Still in London. My fear is perhaps he is getting help. Maybe from Heather?" Sofia tried to hold her voice strong without it wavering, but it was a struggle. She needed to maintain composure.

"You *think*, Sofia? You know what happens to people who think? I don't pay you to think. I pay you to get the job done. Why did you lose him? Do I need to find someone else for this assignment? Maybe I misjudged your abilities. Do we need to worry that you have let your emotions cloud your objectives?"

Sofia shifted from one foot to the other. "No, Sir. I am the only one who can complete this assignment. I know everyone involved and I know the weakness that Cameron possesses and how to apply the appropriate pressure on him. I have done all the research and groundwork. You need me, Sir."

"*Need* you, Sofia?" his voice commanding and ice cold, cut her down.

"Yes, Sir. I am the best person for the job. I know Cameron inside and out."

"Well, up to this point, Sofia, you haven't shown me that you are capable at all."

"Sir," her voice peaked. She cleared her throat. "Sorry, I can do this – please, just give me the chance? I want him to pay for what he did."

"This isn't about payback. You have a job to complete, not a personal vendetta – let me remind you of this. You need to get control of your emotions now, Sofia. Or I will find someone who can. Do I make myself clear?"

She nodded firmly. "Yes, Sir. Perfectly."

"Good – now where do you think he is?"

Sofia looked at the floor, searching for an answer, but before she could answer…

"I don't want guesses or shrugs. I want answers. If not, you know what happens, right?"

Sofia looked worried. "I believe so, Sir."

"It will be the end of everything for you, plus any chance of getting your revenge for your father. Now, can I count on your commitment to getting this done?" She nodded anxiously.

"You have been watching him; where do you think he went?"

"Sir, my guess is he and Heather are planning to locate Emilie. That is the only reason I could think for him reaching out to her."

"Or Heather reaching out to him. We should have dealt with her when we had the chance. The thorn in our side is a complication that we didn't anticipate." A sigh escaped him and he continued, "I would say, on this note, that you are correct. Heather is smarter than you think. Perhaps she is leading Cameron along with the lure of Emilie also, and she may be more persuasive than us, it seems. That cannot happen, do you understand? We need Cameron to be focused on us and doing our bidding."

The dark outline of the figure at the desk leaned forward to rest on his elbows, with his hands crossed in front of his face.

"Sofia, did you hear me?" he demanded her attention.

"Oh, yes, Sir. I'm sure I have a way of routing Cameron out and making him comply with us. I haven't called him again yet, as I was waiting to see the relevance of the location he drove to."

"Fine, see that you do. Keep me updated immediately when you find out." Sofia nodded. "And Sofia?" She turned. "It would be disappointing to lose you like we lost your father."

"Yes, Sir. I understand." She swallowed hard into her throat that was dry like stone. She knew the meeting was over.

Sofia managed to maintain her composure until she got back to her car. Once inside, she felt like she wanted to collapse. The pain she'd endured since the alleged disappearance of her father and missing out on a normal relationship, had been hard to come to terms with. She missed just doing normal father-daughter things. No matter how much time had passed, her anger only grew, and moments like this were a reminder to her about how she could not fail at trying to fix this pain and trying to salvage normality in time.

A car alarm sounded in the parking garage, startling Sofia. She reached over to the glove box and grabbed a wet wipe from its container; the last thing she needed was to have someone see her in tears.

Sofia looked around the parking garage, and as she glanced back to the exit, a notion flooded throughout her body. She remembered what she was doing here and the need to contact Cameron. She reached over and grabbed her phone that was resting on the passenger seat.

She dialled. "Hello, Sofia." Cameron's voice came through on the other end, calm and composed. His demeanour threw her train of thought off for a moment.

"Cameron… It's time to come in; we need to meet. You've had more than enough time to gather your thoughts and get us the needed information to start with."

"Only when I have your assurance that Emilie and Siena are safe. Then, we can arrange to meet–"

"Do you honestly think we would harm them without having what we need from you? There would be no bargaining power left if that was the case…"

"Give me your word. I will not hesitate to hunt you down if anything happens to them."

"Be mindful of your tone, Cameron. Remember, you have more personal things at stake here."

"St Paul's Cathedral. Come now; I will meet you there to put an end to this all." The tone went dead and Sofia looked at the blank screen of the phone.

CHAPTER TWENTY-EIGHT

Vienna, before

Sofia

One thing she had learned from her father was how to hide her emotions from the world, and for the most part, she excelled at it. But in private, it would often torment her and she would buckle in pain. As she sat in the car, Sofia was drawn to memories of when the nightmare started to be exposed for her.

Back in Vienna, they had been busy with their jobs and hadn't spoken much for a few weeks. Maynard had called and wanted to take her out for lunch. The date was set and they were to meet at one pm, at their favourite restaurant. He had told her that there was something very important to discuss. It was the urgency in his voice that made her realise perhaps she had been missing something over the past few weeks of her father's life.

When she arrived, Maynard was seated in the back of the restaurant at a quiet table in the corner. "Papa, is everything alright? Are *you* alright?"

He nodded. "Sofia, I am fine. How are you?"

"I'm good; you worried me on the phone."

"I guess, with the anniversary of your mother's death, it

has left me feeling nostalgic and obviously that is affecting my emotions."

"Papa, it's not just you that is hurting over her."

"I know, I know. I am sorry if I sounded selfish. That's why it is important we spend time together; now, please sit down."

She smiled and her face softened as she took a seat opposite her father. There was already a bottle of still water on the table and she poured a glass for them both.

"Sofia, it was never my intention for you to take on this life. I wanted you to have a normal life – go to college, get married, have children and grow old with a man you love. I feel responsible for you living this life in the dark of night."

Sofia shook her head. "Papa… I am not upset. I love my life with you. I don't want to be anywhere else. Having a nine to five, Monday to Friday job just isn't stimulating for me in any aspect and you know that."

"Sofia! No… this is not a life for anyone. It's filled with mysterious, dangerous people and secrets that those organisations will do anything to protect. It has become more obvious to me of late. I want you to leave, go and be safe, and start a life for yourself away from me and this."

Sofia eagerly leaned forward, studying the worried look that her father wore. "What do you mean you have become more aware of this recently? What have you found out?"

"This is not a life, Sofia – you must get out while you can."

"You sound so serious, calling me Sofia." She reached across the table for his hands.

"Because I want you to listen. Do you understand? I mean it."

"Yes, I understand. But I am not a kid anymore. I have grown to make my own decisions – be they good or bad – and contrary to what you think, Papa, I can look out for myself. We're both working for the organisation here in Vienna and, so far, we have been happy and well rewarded."

"You have not got all the information at hand to make these decisions. These people are dangerous, Sofia. I was young and stupid and thought there were no other options. I was drawn into the promise of my research and teachings being safe and being allowed to continue without any barriers. But at what cost? I did not question that at that time. Please don't make the same mistakes!" Maynard looked nervously around the room and his attention only returned as Sofia gently squeezed his hands.

Sofia leaned back in her seat and crossed her legs beneath the table, but keeping her arms on the table holding her father's hands. "Papa, what is wrong? Tell me, please."

"I am missing your mother. She was strong and stubborn, just as you are. The strength of character she had was unbelievable."

"Tell me again what Mum was like. Remind me of her."

"Oh, Sponge… She was beautiful like you and smart, but in a different way. When we found out she was pregnant, it was the happiest day of our lives. Your mum had a way of making me fit in the world. I think you have that trait of mine. In here, I feel normal and out there, I feel like a freak. Nothing makes sense, it's all chaotic, although she could calm me and make me believe to never give up on my dreams and passion." Maynard smiled fondly, his eyes glazing over.

Sofia returned the smile and Maynard nodded towards her. "See, that's what I want to see – you happy with happy memories – not being made to look over your shoulder all the time."

"Papa, I am happy right now. Right here, doing this. This is my life now, just like it is for you. Maybe someday, I will find someone like Mum who can help me make sense of the world but, for now, I am comfortable. Now that all this is settled, can we eat some lunch and perhaps you can tell me after our stomachs are full what you wanted to tell me?"

CHAPTER TWENTY-NINE

London, now

Cameron

It was mid-morning by the time Cameron got back to the car and drove toward St Paul's. The angelic cathedral, one of the largest in Europe, watched over the patrons of London. How Cameron wished it didn't watch over him at that moment. Being here now reminded him of the lazy conversations Emilie would have with him when she tried to educate him on the comparison of this dome with the structure of St Peter's Basilica in Rome.

They had explored the five hundred and sixty steps to the top of the cathedral to view the large lantern, which weighed eight hundred and fifty tons. The Whispering Gallery was on the ascent to the lantern, and Cameron remembered the tender touch of Emilie's hand when they had visited.

Cameron knew it was prudent to meet Sofia in a very crowded public place, to minimize any risk of the meeting getting out of hand. He regarded Sofia as a volatile risk at present. The weekday services at the cathedral began early, with tourist guides and visitors hustling around. Various friends and family shared moments and pictures together in this mystical, alluring place. Cameron would hope that Sofia would be able to see some family bonds in action, which he could use to tease out her emotional side that he knew was still there, deep down somewhere.

Cameron spotted a car parking space just past the lay-by and steps leading up to the cathedral. There was a bus just pulling away past it and he slowly managed to slip inside the space. Checking the signage next to the space, he wanted to be sure it was a pay and display slot and not a permit only space. The last thing he needed was a clamp on his wheels if he needed to make a quick getaway. As he stepped out of the car to locate the machine for the parking ticket, he glanced up at the great entrance that stood before him. The sight took his breath away, not only due to the amazing structure of the building, but because of the memories with Emilie.

CHAPTER THIRTY

London, before

Cameron

Cameron followed Emilie up the steps of the cathedral towards the great towering doors that acted as a gateway to the great hall inside. The checked flooring of the nave that led toward the dome above was hidden in a deceptive way from outside the cathedral. Religion wasn't something either fully believed in, but they both respected traditions of all aspects of various religions at the appropriate time. The image of Emilie walking in front of him put Cameron in a trance that day; he couldn't believe a woman of such beauty would be in love with him and he constantly questioned the basis of that emotion she showed. Emilie looked back over her shoulder at him and gestured for him to follow; she pointed to the spiral staircase toward the corner of the hall and he followed close behind.

As they gradually made their way up the five hundred or so steps, Emilie would sporadically turn and look back at him. Each time Cameron caught a glimpse of her looking back at him, he would hide how unfit he felt walking up the steps, matching Emilie's pace. Every time he looked into her eyes, it took him back to that day in hospital when he first saw her. But now, knowing the personality, passion and intellect of Emilie, it made his attraction to her insatiable.

As the ascent came to an end, the staircase gave way to a circular room filled with mosaics and paintings and, at that moment, Emilie whispered, "I love you, Cameron Hope."

Cameron started to reply when she put her finger to her lips and stated, "Shh! Listen!" The sound rolled its way around the room in a graceful and elegant manner.

"This is the Whispering Gallery; the sounds echo off the walls. Amazing, isn't it?" She giggled, her eyes wide and bright like a child, and continued, "Come on, the Stone Gallery is next and we're almost to the top." Cameron nodded and smiled to himself at the boundless energy of this woman. He willed himself to keep up to her pace so as not to look incompetent.

After another one hundred and seventeen steps, they stepped out into the Stone Gallery; the sun was setting in the western sky by this time. Brilliant shards of purple and yellow rays lit up the horizon. Cameron was about to experience one of the most breath-taking sights of his life.

Emilie took his hand and said, "Over here." He followed her to the west end of the dome's platform.

Cameron was so content. He felt love like he'd never known and never wanted that feeling to stop. He felt safe. The couple stood at the Stone Gallery wall and watched the sunset while inching closer to each other, ending with a passionate kiss. It was tender and soft as their lips explored one another, trying to discover higher aspects of hidden emotion and feeling. That moment could have lasted forever and Cameron promised himself to protect this woman for the rest of his life, no matter what that entailed.

CHAPTER THIRTY-ONE

London, now

Sofia

The dial tone hit hard when Cameron hung up. Sofia felt a sense of ease within her now that she had something to go on and to get the next part of the plan into play. She immediately called the organisation to inform them that Cameron had been in touch, as they had demanded to be kept abreast of all and any developments. Sofia threw the phone across the car, slamming it against the passenger side door after she terminated the call. Anger, frustration and fear all merged into one emotion, which festered within her every time she was met with an unimpressed reaction from the organisation.

Sofia wasn't used to being told how to handle situations, especially with the man who had supposedly killed her father. Plus, this meeting was different – Cameron had the upper hand and she knew it. Sofia turned the key in the car and took another glance in the mirror at her tired and worn face before putting the car in reverse.

Time had not been good to Sofia since the days in Vienna with her father. The circumstances around his disappearance caused the rage to build within her, which became so strong it consumed every inch of her soul. She hated living under this emotional stress and being unable to control her feelings. What would her father have thought, seeing her so full of hate now? But that source of hate involved her father and all Sofia could see at that point in her life was that she had no foreseeable normal future. It was a black hole that was slowly pulling her inside. She couldn't even remember how long it had been since she'd smiled or found some joy to celebrate. Her life had become a cascade of suspense, lies, calculated risks, deception and pain.

The journey was short to St Paul's and Sofia parked the car in a street facing the great steps leading up to the imposing doors of the cathedral, the doors that were the trademark of precision design and build. Perfectly balanced doors were typical of Freemasons architecture. Turning the key and pulling it out, the car came to a deafening silence. Her eyes narrowed as she saw the figure she was after. As she watched Cameron in the distance, standing there, she knew she had to have her mind focused and clear as it was nearly time for all the preparation to pay off and there was no room for mistakes. This would take skill to navigate.

CHAPTER THIRTY-TWO

Cameron

Cameron glanced across the road. He spotted a woman walking tall, with her shoulders relaxed and arms moving confidently by her sides. The determined look in her eyes was focused directly on him. She looked hungry for her prey. Eyes wide open and no indication of any form of blinking to break the gaze. From everything he recalled from Maynard about his daughter, he was to not underestimate anything about her.

Cameron watched Sofia intently, his eyes trying to match her stare – never straying – and she repaid the gesture by not looking away. Then he waved and smiled, showing his teeth and tilting his head in a friendly manner. Cameron smirked to himself as Maynard's advice worked. Sofia seemed taken aback while she continued to the steps. Her gait changed for a short time at Cameron's motions. The steadfast, co-ordinated pace became a loose, carefree movement, if only for a couple of steps. She quickly regained her composure and continued directly to Cameron who had moved toward the large doors that lay open. Cameron knew that when an opponent is left in the dark, an attack is much easier, leaving room for the element of surprise. It was a little trick he'd learned from reading *The Art of War* by Sun Tzu, a brilliant strategist – that there is more to battle than the physical fighting. It is won and lost in the mind. The poker face was key for Cameron. He knew he had to maintain control and the upper hand at all times.

Sofia seemed a little perplexed on her approach, in contrast to the steely, firm and confident woman that approached Cameron on the Embankment at their first meeting all those hours ago. She looked more troubled and distant.

As she came closer, Cameron could see deeper into her eyes. Despite the outlook of composure that she tried to maintain, he could sense the pain hidden behind them. It became obvious they both had suffered over the loss of a loved one, only in Sofia's case, she thought her father was dead. Cameron knew he could use this information to gain control of the situation; nonetheless, he needed to get Emilie and his daughter to safety before exposing the truth about Maynard still being alive.

"Sofia, it's a pleasure," Cameron choked out as she reached the top steps to stand a few feet away from him.

"I'm sure it is, Cameron. Let's get this over with. Tell us what you know and have discovered, so we can put this to an end. You have had enough time given to you by the organisation over the last few hours to get what you need and give it to me."

"Always in such a hurry, Sofia. You waited all year. I am sure a few more minutes can be offered by you. I need something from you." He maintained the forced smile on his face but with his fists in a tight grip to keep his emotions steady.

"Right. The reassurance you want in relation to Emilie and Siena. At least they are alive to come home… Can you say the same about my father?" Her eyes narrowed.

"I cannot, Sofia, and for that I am truly sorry, but I did not kill Maynard." Cameron's voice wavered slightly at saying his name.

"Are you back to that again? Please, spare me the insult of your perpetuation with ignorance. You can spare the act too; it's just us here now. At least honour his death by admitting the part you played."

"I'm telling the truth... Can't you see the lies, Sofia? The people we both used to work for are using you for their own gain. They don't care who gets hurt or the damage they cause in the process. If you come with me, we can at least have a chance to take them down together." He wondered what would happen if he just told her now that Maynard was alive. But, at this moment, she was not on their side.

"I always think what life would have been like for my father if you were not part of his..." her voice trailed off.

Cameron could feel the bitterness and, deep inside, his heart ached at lying to her more now, but he also had duties of a father now and needed to get his own daughter to safety. He sighed and took a moment to look down the steps and along the road that led away from the cathedral. Looking to see if there were any sign of others out there watching and waiting to pounce.

"Sofia. You have my word. If you come with me and listen... I can show you the truth."

"Please, Cameron, spare me the lecture. Just... why do you want me here? Is the cathedral holding the secrets you have discovered?" Her voice now showing irritation at Cameron's words and attitude.

"Look, I know how you feel about me and what

happened, but we can work together and get what we want the most… peace and safety," Cameron pushed.

Sofia's voice rose. "Are you stupid or something?" she shouted. "You killed the only person I have ever truly loved. How am I supposed to find peace?"

Cameron watched Sofia's actions and mannerisms as she spoke. Something did not add up in the statements she was making and in her actions. *Very much staged*, he thought. To the extent that it was a show for someone other than him. "Sofia… I–"

She cut him off.

"Cameron, tell me why we are here or I am leaving and that would further piss off everyone involved, which will only end up with an inevitably fatal end for you and others!"

He scoffed in response. "Fine, then come with me." He motioned for her to follow through the doors to enter the cathedral. Sofia followed without a word.

Cameron turned around slightly and tried to take her hand. "What are you doing?" she demanded.

"Shh, Sofia, just play along, please. We need to try and blend in." She sighed and reluctantly took his hand.

The two quickly moved through the breath-taking vista of the nave with the long central aisle that led to the dome towering above. Both took care to weave through the other visitors present, but tried to maintain an air of blending in and taking in the monuments on display.

Moving down the nave, they both turned to look at the largest memorial in the cathedral: Wellington's monument. Sofia and Cameron couldn't help but be taken aback at the immense structure. The towering white beacon with columns and arches allowed the statue of Wellington, who was sitting upon his horse, Copenhagen, a vantage point over the cathedral floor.

Cameron picked up the pace slightly and continued to walk towards the grand organ. They passed in silence under the magnificent dome. Cameron glanced back to make sure Sofia was still close. He noticed her head tilt upwards to take in the paucity of colours on the interior of the cathedral dome. The paintings created a sombre atmosphere, which was reflective of the mood in the pair – a stark contrast to the emotion of power that had radiated from the previous monument a few moments ago.

"A very romantic tour, Cameron. Perhaps Emilie would value this atmosphere better than me right now. This had better be leading to what I need to know."

"Be careful with how you use Emilie's name... Tell me one thing – what are you doing for them, Sofia? Is this really what your father would have wanted? Did he raise you to be a hired thug?"

"Wha–? Is that what you think I am? Really? You have no idea what this is all about, do you?" Sofia let out a controlled chuckle.

"You didn't answer the question, Sofia…"

"How dare you mention my father's name! Was it not enough that you led him to his grave? And now you use his memory like some sort of ransom note?"

"I am glad he doesn't know what you're doing; he would be embarrassed and disappointed. Do the right thing here, Sofia. Tell me where Emilie and my daughter are; help me get them to safety. Then, we can take the organisations down together."

Sofia paused. "You know I can't do that, dear Cameron."

"What happened to the Sofia your father spoke about? That Sofia would never have followed blindly like a servant. Do you have any idea how much your father loved you?"

"Yes, Cameron, I do! But how would you know anything about love? You are the one who killed him. And if I did not care about rules, you would have been dead a long time ago. So, in that case, you should be happy the old Sofia is gone. Now, answer my question: why am I here?"

Cameron shook his head sadly. "You're right… this is a pointless gesture. You're too far gone to even listen to the facts or voice of reason; everything they have told you is a lie. If you come with me, Sofia, I can show you the truth, I promise." A last desperate attempt by Cameron to make this easier for Sofia, but he could tell it was becoming a futile process.

"You promise? And I am just supposed to trust you, just like that?"

"Yes, you are. Why would I be lying?"

She threw her head back and laughed. "Simple… You want your precious Emilie and daughter back, so you think by snuggling up to me I will help you, and you're trying to do that by taking me back to memories of my father. Can you bring back the time lost with my father?"

"Sofia! Yes, I want my life back, but you can have a life away from them. A safer life. Maynard would never have wanted you to go down this path. You know that deep down inside, don't you?"

"Do not mention my father's name!" she cried. "Keep walking and take me to where you need to before I totally lose my patience with your company." Her voice attracted the attention of a group of tourists standing nearby.

Cameron sighed and turned to continue, with Sofia

following him.

The two continued to head for the crypts. There was a rope dividing the section where the arch contained the stone steps down into the rooms below. Cameron took another quick glance around and gestured with his hand to Sofia to follow him quickly. Cameron led with the torch on his phone illuminating the way when he was sure no-one was watching.

They entered a chamber at the bottom of the steps and walked over to the south aisle at the east end of the crypt. There rested Sir Christopher Wren in his tomb. The architect of St Paul's. A simple stone marked his tomb, with memorials surrounding it to other fellow Masons and Wren's family. Cameron stopped at the foot of tomb and took a deep breath in and, as he slowly breathed out, he said to Sofia, "Okay, we are here."

"At a dead guy's tomb, so..?" Cameron heard the annoyance in her tone.

"Christopher Wren, the Freemason architect of this church. Born –"

She interrupted this time. "I know who he was; you knew my father so you should know I am well taught about such facts of history."

He nodded. "Yes, I found what you want. Don't you see?"

"No, Cameron..."

Cameron pointed to an area above the tomb. "On the wall above his tomb in the crypt is written in Latin: *Lector, si monumentum requiris, circumspice.*"

"Yes, so–"

"The significance of this statement always puzzled me, as did why it was put here to begin with. Then it came to me that it was actually indicating a code, an instruction."

"I know my Latin, Cameron. It translates to: *'Reader, if you seek his monument, look around'*. So, are you telling me that this is a code and that it holds the secret you now hide?"

"Give me something to go on, Sofia. My family; where are they?"

CHAPTER THIRTY-THREE

Heather

The priceless clock on the mantle seemed to chime incessantly. Heather listened to each tone resonate throughout the room, each creating uneasy echoes in her head. She wasn't used to being made to wait and to be patient with unknown aspects out of her direct control. The intensity of the situation was growing by the minute. Heather tried to maintain a calm appearance, but inside she was having emotions of anxiety, frustration and anger at not being able to push Cameron to get on with what was at hand here under her own direct supervision. She wanted the control.

As she sat in the Chesterfield chair, she concentrated on the steam coming from her coffee, the only thing soothing her apprehensions. The thought of comfort with a warm drink to ease and calm the start of the day and to give that needed boost was reassuring, but that was in a normal lifetime, which seemed so distant at present. She looked over to the sofa where Maynard was beginning to wrestle with waking after a much needed rest. She remembered back to the time she'd taken Maynard under her wing to protect him in London. She wondered if she could have done anything differently with him and how the situation had unfolded to date. Had she missed something, as it had felt all so easy with Maynard? This unsettled her.

Heather cleared her throat loudly, feigning surprise when she looked up to find Maynard swinging his legs over the sofa.

"Oh, you are awake. How are you feeling?" she said, glancing over to him.

"Much better, almost human again. How long was I out?" Maynard looked around the room, patting down his hair. "There is only a limited time that one can run on pure adrenaline for." Heather saw the fight of stiffness in his joints as he wrestled with his posture on the sofa.

"Of course; you are no good to anyone if you're exhausted or ill and you did look pretty pale earlier. Coffee?" Heather gestured to Maynard. He nodded.

Heather stood and hurried out of the room to get a fresh pot of coffee for him.

She returned a few moments later holding a mug in her hands. "Here you go; I made it just as you like." As she focused on Maynard's face, she noticed the concerned look he held with his jaw slightly clenched.

"Heather, where is Cameron? We have work to do; he should be here. Where has he gone?"

"He just stepped out for a short time; I am sure he will be back soon enough."

"Cameron doesn't just step out without a reason. Where has he gone and for what? Did he go to find my daughter?"

"I am sure all is good; you need not worry." Heather looked down at the floor, feeling flustered.

"Your body language gives away more than you realise, Heather!" he snapped. "I may be old but that does not mean I do not have my sense of intuition."

"I… really, that is ridiculous. He did just step out. But we need to talk before he comes back anyway."

"Talk, about what? The plan has been set in motion… we can't go back now."

"Go back? I don't want to go back. But we need to be sure Cameron is doing what we want him to and, if not, what is our risk and how can we protect our position?"

Maynard put down his coffee. "Where has he gone, Heather?"

"He—"

"Sofia called, didn't she? Why didn't you wake me up?"

"We actually thought you needed to rest. Maynard, you almost collapsed. I need you alive – Cameron may be a lot of things, but I am sure he can handle Sofia."

"I am not concerned about Cameron; it's my daughter I'm concerned about. If she finds out this is a deception, then what? He will put her life in danger too. Heather, we agreed on this. My daughter was to be protected. We do not know Cameron's state of mind right now! The man has just found out he has a daughter!"

"Maynard, I couldn't stop him from leaving. He was determined and he was even more determined that you remained sleeping while he left! What was I to do?" Heather whined, near to stomping her feet. The redness spread from her neck up into her face.

"If you seem to think Cameron will not find out the truth, you don't know him very well. He is just as ruthless as my daughter when necessary." Maynard looked directly into Heather's eyes at this point. The assertiveness of his statement felt like a warning to Heather. She could not help but wonder if Maynard had found out what she was hiding.

"Please, sit… It will be alright. We just need to go over everything to make sure all tracks are covered. We have worked too long and too hard for this not to work. We need to remain as strong as a unit." Heather pleaded with her voice.

Maynard paused at Heather's words. "I… don't know. It's just…" Maynard leaned on the desk with his right hand. Heather watched with her arms folded and she glanced again to her watch and waited for him to respond.

"Maynard..?" Heather questioned.

Maynard replied, "What if she finds out he is lying and that this is all a deception?" He repeated his concerns. "How do you think she will react?"

"What if she doesn't? That's what we must believe. Cameron seems to be smart and has his wits about him. Besides, we both know Cameron isn't telling us everything."

Heather took a seat on the sofa where Maynard had been sleeping a few moments ago. She crossed her legs and sat up. "Cameron thinks we have Emilie and Siena in a safe space."

Maynard turned to look at Heather and found her studying her fingernails, sitting there on the sofa.

"Yes, and what are you going to do with them? You can't just–"

Heather interrupted Maynard without looking away from her fingernails. "I can, and you know I can… if Cameron does not give us any other option. We cannot let him get the upper hand again." Her voice had a cold calmness to it. "If he thinks there is a chance to get his family back safely, we are safe and in control."

Maynard frowned now, his eyes narrowing at her.

"Heather, what do you mean by 'if he *thinks*' they are safe?"

"If he continues to think they are safe, we are in the clear and he will do what we want."

"Is there something you are not telling me, Heather?"

"No… not really. I mean, what does it matter, as long as Cameron believes what we tell him?"

"Heather, I believed and trusted you when you said you have Emilie and Siena safe. You gave me your word!"

Heather stood up. "I am not the one you need to be worried about playing games here."

"Cameron will not stop until he knows the truth and gets Emilie and his daughter out safely. You *do* understand that, Heather, don't you? God forbid something has happened to them."

"How dangerous can Cameron be? You forget, I have survived the wrath of the organisations already."

"Oh, Heather, I hope we never have to find out. You'd better pray this works. I spent a long time by his side, working out who he is and what character he hides beneath that mask he wears. Don't be fooled by his charm. And, oh, if he gets through to Sofia and they pair up, that will not be good for us."

"What do you mean if 'they pair up'? Is that not what Cameron went to do? Turn your daughter to our side?" Heather's voice quivered slightly.

"Yes, *our side*. Not his side. We need to get Sofia to come back home, but with the confidence to be able to tell her the truth. How do you propose we do that if she sides with Cameron? Because at the moment, we still don't fully understand Cameron's intentions."

"Do you really think she will side with him? After all, she thinks he killed you, remember? From what Cameron told us, she hates him and that is driving her thirst for revenge."

Maynard let out a sigh. He ran both hands through his silver hair and sighed again. Then he slowly remarked, "Maybe it is time we showed her the truth?"

"What truth, Maynard..?" Heather's demeanour changed to the stance of someone worried.

"She sees me alive in person."

"No… No way... Get that thought out of your head. The reason you fled was to be safe and if she finds out, you will not be safe anymore and neither will she for that matter!"

"Heather, it is the only way she will see the truth. I don't see any other way for Cameron to succeed. We need her help and that will be the only way to keep her safe. It's only a matter of time before the organisation finds out I am still alive and then Sofia will be an enemy to them too – and they will use her as bait and then destroy her also."

Heather shook her head frantically, grasping for control. "What about Cameron? How do we control him and his reaction if we just show up unexpected?"

"I think maybe it's a risk we have to take."

Heather frowned at this.

"Why don't we just wait? I am sure he will be back very soon." Her voice now in a rushed pace as though she wanted all her words out at once.

"Yes, and maybe he won't. I don't trust Cameron with my daughter. If she does or says something to upset him, it could put her in harm's way. No, we have to try and catch him. Don't forget, Sofia is using Emilie and Siena to get Cameron's attention and he will be aware of that fact. It will be forming some of his actions and thought processes right now, as we have also said we have Emilie safe."

Heather wondered what had changed Maynard's mind; he had been totally against letting Sofia see him before and, now, suddenly, he wanted to rush out. She couldn't help but think maybe Maynard and Cameron had a plan that she wasn't involved in. But how was that possible? There has not been any time for the two of them to be alone to discuss anything between them. Or had there been and she has missed something? Or was this just Heather's paranoia getting the best of her?

Maynard walked over to the edge of the sofa where his coat was draped. Pulling it over his shoulders and putting his arms through, he declared, "Yes, we have to go now, before it's too late—"

"What do you mean 'too late'; too late for what, Maynard? You are starting to worry me that I am missing something here?" Heather's voice rose slightly.

"Nothing, I don't mean anything. We have to go. Now, are you going to drive, or am I?"

"I will take you, but please tell me what you are thinking!"

"The only thing I am thinking about right now is how I can protect my daughter. This has to work – Sofia is my whole life and I don't know what I would do if something happened to her because of my mistakes."

"I understand, but we don't want to make matters worse. Cameron can be overzealous at times, but he is a good agent, you must know that. Just maybe we have to trust him, despite the situation."

"Heather…" Maynard's voice rose to match hers, "I will not repeat myself one more time – stop trying to stall me. Or… do *you* have some agenda that you are not telling me or Cameron about? Maybe he is right not to trust you. You lied to him for many years; how can I know for sure you are not lying to me as well? We know the organisation has moles. Maybe *you're* the one they sent to spy on us. My daughter might be a lot of things, but she isn't a traitor."

Heather rubbed her fingers together and felt the raw skin around her nail bed. It was a nervous habit that she had. She stared directly at Maynard; words just did not come to her at that moment.

"Heather... say something or I am leaving without you. Can you prove that you are not here working on behalf of the organisation? Can you tell me that Emilie and Siena are safe and hidden by you?" The room stayed completely quiet for the next few minutes and Heather seemed to feel that what she thought was so sure, having someone on her side, was slipping away from her. Heather replied, "Maynard... you know I have no way to prove my loyalty. Other than to say that I am not here as a spy. They have done horrible things to all of us; I want this over as much as you do."

"Yes. That I can agree with, but you have the least to lose out of all of us. But for now, I have no other choice but to trust you. Get the car keys."

Heather felt as though she'd lost the momentum and control of the situation. All those years planning and waiting and, in a matter of hours, she had let Cameron slip away with his own agenda and now she had Maynard wanting to face his daughter, the one thing she had tried to stop from happening. *This is not going to end well*, she thought, as she got her coat from the hallway along with the car keys.

Maynard followed her into the hallway and saw her standing using the baluster as support like it was needed to keep her upright.

"Heather, I apologise for being short with you," Maynard had a softer tone now, "it's just that this whole situation is getting to me and I don't know Cameron's intentions. I don't think we convinced him enough to trust us."

"I know, but if we turn on each other, nothing will get accomplished and all this planning will have been for nothing." She turned in the gloomy hallway as she replied. Maynard's face seemed even more blanched in the hall than it had in the room. Maynard sighed and walked past her to the door and pulled it open, daylight pouring in. "Shall we?" Maynard offered. Heather noticed a different look in his eyes. A look of control and confidence compared to a few moments ago. "Maynard, I'm not sure this is the right thing to do." She shook her head and walked outside, letting her eyes get adjusted to the daylight, reminding her how tired she was.

Heather had her car parked close by and they set off to St Paul's Cathedral. There was no further conversation in the car. Heather wasn't sure what needed to be said as it was now worrying her that they would have to face Sofia. This was not how she'd wanted to tackle her. The thoughts and potential ways to navigate this were racing through her mind while she concentrated on getting to the cathedral.

"Do you think it is wise, Maynard? What if Sofia doesn't react the way we need her to?" Heather stopped at the traffic lights approaching the Strand from Aldwych. She was heading east straight to Fleet Street and then onto Ludgate Hill.

"Maynard?" she said when he didn't reply.

"I heard you, Heather," he replied in a sombre tone. "My daughter needs protection now, also. Not just others and our own selfish importance. Just drive."

Her foot hovered anxiously on the accelerator as she waited for the red light to turn green. She was certainly not in control now and was concerned over what to do and how to salvage something from this. *What have I missed?* she asked herself in her head. Right then, she wished the road were unending, so she was able to drive for miles and work out a strategy in her own mind. But then, what could she change that could not have been planned through all these years? "What have I missed?" She bit her lip while pressing down on the accelerator on the amber light change.

"Heather, you haven't missed anything. I think we all have missed everything!"

Heather was startled at Maynard's comment, as she was not sure if her last words were out loud or in her head.

"Look, I just feel as though we have Cameron on our side, seeing things from our point of view. We were sure he could protect Sofia and get her to understand and see what is really going on only a few moments ago. What has changed for you, Maynard?" A bus cut in front of Heather as she pulled onto Fleet Street. She was reluctant to overtake. It got her a few more precious seconds in the car with Maynard.

"Heather…" After a long pause, thinking and calculating the words to come, Maynard questioned, "Do you think Cameron believes us?"

CHAPTER THIRTY-FOUR

Cameron

Cameron could feel the air of tension continuing to build between him and Sofia. He waited patiently for her response, keeping a steady eye on her face, trying to drown her in subconscious thoughts. Cameron was desperate to get an idea of who knew the truth of Emilie and Siena's location. Was it Sofia or Maynard and Heather? Or the more concerning answer to this question he worried about was, did they all not know where his family was? What he *did* know was that he had Sofia intrigued by being here in the crypts of St Paul's Cathedral.

"No – you're not going to fool me into thinking that this inscription is some kind of secret message. If you want me to tell you anything, it had better be more powerful than some old text on a tomb. We don't have time for these games!" Sofia's eyes showing determination when she spoke.

Cameron shrugged and gestured around her words. "Yet, Sofia, you know the mystery of this place. You know the hidden truths and lies that surround this very structure we stand in." He slowly raised his hands and pointed with his fingers to the left of Sofia and hinted, with a tilt of his head, to look over in that direction.

Sofia followed his hands, allowing herself to be entertained by Cameron's words for a while. Her eyes moving over the tomb.

Cameron continued, "I wanted to remind you by bringing you down here that the writings were a message by Wren back then. He knew the secrets and he also kept them hidden. But, at the same time, he wanted them to be known to others within reason for those who wanted to do something with the truth."

This seemed to get Sofia's attention. "Carry on, I am listening." Her tone softened as she walked closer to the tomb with her arms folded in front of her.

And so Cameron did. "We see masonry trifora in the upper spaces, above the cathedral floor. And you know the Latin word *'triforium'* means the opening of a tall central space. What if the masonry trifora were built to create vaulted and separated areas to hide secrets? To give clues for the truth."

"Cameron. Are you asking me or telling me?"

"I am showing you what I discovered after all the years in London – the work that your father and I started in Vienna. Above us, above the Whispering Gallery, there are dark corridors with ancient stones that create concealed areas. A hidden door to the south side of the triforium that leads to an office. This office was used by Wren himself. To this day, the office has only been accessed by a miniscule number of individuals and enclosed within the confines of these walls are some of the most sacred artefacts of humankind."

Sofia walked the length of the tomb, reading the inscription silently to herself. "Cathedrals were commonplace to store educational books, religious texts and business documents such as leases and property deeds." Her comments more of an assessment for her own benefit rather than for Cameron. "Documents with sensitive scripts that needed to be hidden, would be great to have stored in such an office." She turned, looking over her right shoulder to see if Cameron was following her train of thought.

"My discovery involved the ledgers of Humfrey Wanley, the library keeper in the 1600s. In his catalogue, he logged every book retained by the church. You know of the saying 'lost in translation', right?" Cameron let that hang in the air for a while.

Sofia didn't answer, so he continued. "Don't you understand? The more a script is translated into different languages and through time, the further it gets from its original meaning. The original meaning is far from what is shown on this tomb."

"Give me the answers to all these riddles, Cameron. You know the organisations want the answers, not the clues!"

"And I want my family safe and in my arms, Sofia!"

Cameron started walking, brushing past Sofia's shoulder on his way toward the narrow staircase.

"Where are we going?" she demanded.

"To the triforium," Cameron stated without stopping or looking back at her.

Sofia stayed close to Cameron; they needed to navigate out of the lower levels and back to the nave. As they steadily moved to the steps to climb towards the triforium, Cameron was conscious that Maynard and Heather, by now, would be discussing a plan amongst themselves. He hoped Maynard had reacted how he had hoped he would at this point.

Cameron paused as they reached the top. "Shh…" he whispered, while putting his finger to his lips. "We must be silent right here – as we move along this balcony, stay close to the wall and move slowly. It would be easy for people below to see us moving up here to areas we should not be in." Sofia nodded and followed his lead.

Cameron cautiously walked towards an unassuming archway that was only a metre high. He stopped and got down on his knees. Sofia peered over the arch at the darkness beyond. "Are we supposed to be going in there?" she whispered. Cameron didn't reply; he was busy concentrating on the inner aspect of the arch. He leaned his body forward to place his right hand onto the inner stones and felt the cold, dusty surface. He let his fingers explore the contour and smiled to himself when he felt the groove that he was looking for.

"This is it; get down and follow me." And with those words, he crawled through the archway into the darkness beyond.

"Cameron!" Sofia bent down and called again. "Cameron?" There was no answer. She reached in with her right arm, tentatively, feeling blindly in the darkness. There was no resistance. She waited for what seemed like minutes, but which was only a matter of seconds, and when there was no further sign from Cameron, she sighed, "Dammit," and looked around before bending down onto her hands and knees, tucking herself into the archway and making her way into the darkness.

Cameron made his way through the darkness, eyes fixated on a glow in the distance. He could hear Sofia scrambling behind him. As the end approached, there was a small hatch-like doorway, which led to a room. Slowly uncoiling his body as he got up from his knees, dusting off the dirt from his trousers, he went and stood by the far wall, looking at what seemed to be ledgers and books on shelves.

"Where are we, Cameron? What is this room and all these writings?" Sofia asked, slightly breathless from crawling and finally emerging through the door behind him. Hands full of dust and dirt and her hair had fallen over her face with strands in her mouth.

Cameron did not turn around, but kept running his fingers over the edges of the books with his head at an angle. "You still haven't given me any confidence that Emilie and Siena are safe." His voice was low, but strong and forceful and full of determination.

"You have the envelope with—"

"Why give me that envelope in the first place, Sofia? Something doesn't add up with you and maybe there are other things you want to tell me but cannot!" He turned to look at her over his left shoulder, his hands still on the books in front of him as though he did not want to lose his place of concentration with them. Sofia just looked directly at him as she stood up, moving the hair from her face and rubbing the palms of her hands on her trousers, not replying, and eventually she broke eye contact with him. Cameron could tell she was hiding more and he felt justified now that he had convinced her to meet him here, in St Paul's Cathedral, rather than at the Temple of the Mithras.

"The organisations you work for depend on lies and pain to do their bidding. Remember that, Sofia."

"Show me what you brought me here for, Cameron."

Sofia stepped closer to him. "What is that book?" she asked, glancing at the one his hand rested on.

Cameron pulled it out. Delicately, he brought it into the light. It had a toughened, bound look to the covers. Worn away, but still sturdy. There was a faded golden leaf pattern around the edges and spine. The dust fairies ran and bounced around the book from the beam of light peering into the room and made the object seem like it was commanding attention.

Cameron kept the book closed in his hands with a firm but delicate grip. "Sofia. This was written in 1637 by Brian Walton. He was a prebendary member of the Roman Catholic clergy and spent twelve years translating and working on this version of the Bible. This is a Polyglot Bible."

Sofia raised her eyebrows and put out her hands in a gesture for Cameron to explain more.

"A Polyglot is someone who speaks, writes and translates languages; in this case, ancient, forgotten languages."

Cameron carefully opened the book to its inner pages. What unfolded in front of Sofia's eyes were pages made up of parallel columns of scripture. Her eyes widened. "What languages are these?"

"The left-hand side of the page is Hebrew translated text. The middle column is Vulgate, which is a late 4th century Latin translation, and the far text is Septuagint from the Greek Old Testament. And towards the bottom of each page is the Targum Onkelos, which is the translation of the Five Books of Moses." Cameron looked at Sofia as he finished speaking and could see her eyes fixated on the page of the book. He waited until she looked back up at him and he gestured with a nod to look along the rows of books on the shelf. "All these books are the complete translations and comparisons of every one of those scriptures. Upon completion of his work, he was ridiculed, ordered into custody and branded a delinquent by powerful establishments, in order to undermine his translations and publication. His writings disappeared and were forgotten about over the years."

"But what did all his translations uncover?" Sofia asked.

"Sofia, the powers and influences of the organisations were working, even back then. Who do you think manufactured his reputation to be branded, as it was then? Who do you think made all his work disappear and be hidden, here, like this, away from all?" When Sofia didn't answer, Cameron prompted her. "The organisations that you now work for."

"So, you mean to say that even as far back as then, they were hunting for answers and clues?"

"No, Sofia, what I'm saying is that, back then, the same organisations were killing and destroying the truth, just like they're trying to do now. Using me and Emilie, they are using you to do the work for them."

Cameron closed the book slowly and returned it to the shelf. This secret room held so many answers, but also so many dangers. With his back to Sofia, he paused, wondering if he should, and then voiced the challenge.

"What makes you think they didn't try the same with your father?"

Cameron could hear Sofia's steps behind him as she walked towards him. She got close to his shoulder; he could feel her breath on his neck.

She whispered, "*Acta Sanctorum*. I am aware of the lists of names. So is my father. *Acta Sanctorum*, a collection of names and knowledge spanning over four hundred years. Disguised as a principal source for research into the societies and cultures of early Christian and medieval Europe." Her voice crept around Cameron's neck, bringing the small hairs to attention on it.

Cameron could feel purpose in her voice. She brought her right hand up to his neck, placing her thumb behind his ear with her fingers reaching down to the front of his neck. And then, finished her statement. "A list that continues today and which has three new names on it. My father's, yours and Emilie's."

"How can our names be on that list?" The calm, controlled manner of Cameron changed when faced with this new statement from Sofia. He continued when she did not answer. "*Acta Sanctorum.* It is a document composed in the 1600s. It is impossible for our names to be on it!" He turned to face her. Standing close to feel the steady air coming from her mouth as she breathed.

Sofia's face softened. A warm tone radiated from her voice. "The list didn't stop back then. It continued over time and is maintained with names through these times."

"I don't understand!" This was a statement from Cameron, perhaps aimed at himself. Was it his thoughts telling him out loud that this was not something that he had imagined? Was he realizing he now did not know what the 'why' was of all this? The why and the who made no sense to him.

Sofia stepped back, reached into her pocket and took her phone out. She swiped the screen and opened the messages. No change of facial expression from her. She gave a sigh and turned to look at Cameron.

"Is there anything else in this room you want to show

me, Cameron?"

Cameron walked closer to her to stand a few inches from her again. "What is the meaning of our names being on that list? What *is* all this?"

"Cameron, you've done enough. It was a clever move of you to bring me here and show me these artefacts. It seems my father taught you well after all."

Cameron looked to the books lined up like soldiers, awaiting orders to strike. He was hoping answers would leap out from them to help him untangle and decipher all of this, but all he could see was haze. He hadn't known how he was going to get the truth of where Emilie and Siena were when he went to the cathedral, but now it seemed perhaps he was on the wrong path and in need of guidance.

"There was no other way to deal with this, Cameron. I needed you to call the shots and make the first move. It was important for the optics of the situation that it all came from you."

Cameron walked over to the far wall and turned to lean against it. He sat on the floor with his knees flexed in front of him and looked up at Sofia. "There is more to this, isn't there, Sofia?"

"I'm afraid so," she replied in an endearing manner. The softness to her eyes made Cameron feel that perhaps she was not all she seemed. She walked over to where he was sitting and kicked him on his shoes. "Move over, make some room for me." And she sat down next to him.

"You know your father is alive, don't you?"

Sofia let out a long sigh at this.

CHAPTER THIRTY-FIVE

Sofia

Sofia closed her eyes while she moved her neck to the side. Her shoulders were tight and she felt as if her neck would fall off at the slightest movement, fragile as it was from all the tension. She knew there wasn't much time now after checking her phone and seeing the message just a few moments ago.

"Cameron, there was no other way to make sure we all could come out of this in the least damaging way. Yes, I know my father is alive. I know you were with him just before you came to meet me." She waited for Cameron's reaction, but he just sat there next to her on the floor looking straight ahead at the brick wall.

"He and I have been working closely together ever since Vienna. In fact, since he knew he was in danger. Well, when he knew we *all* were in danger, he told me that something needed to be done at a rapid pace."

"So, his death? That was engineered by you. To protect him and hide him?"

"Not directly, Cameron. My father knew the organisation were worried that he'd managed to uncover the real reasons behind his work. He understood that the organisations wanted the research and work for something sinister. For something that may, one day, cause concern for all of mankind. When you both focused on the site here in London, the Temple of Mithras, my father mistakenly voiced his findings and concerns to the board of the organisations in writing. It was at that moment that he knew his life was in true danger."

Both Sofia and Cameron had become accustomed to the dim light present in the room. The faint echoes of voices and footsteps from the visitors and staff that roamed outside could be heard, most of them on the lower floors. The need to be conscious of their own sounds diminished as the time went on and the whispers progressed to a normal volume of speech.

"So, what happened in Vienna when your father disappeared?" Cameron looked at her, nodding for her to go on. She sighed.

"I was working in another department for the organisations at that time. My father reached out to me and explained everything. At first, I thought he was exhausted and perhaps going through a depressive and paranoid state. But his behaviour was always rational and he convinced me to get closer but in a covert way, to the top tier of the organisation. It was to gain their trust. My father and I needed to find a way to double bluff them to get my father out to safety and this was the only way to make them believe they had my loyalty and that I was willing to do anything they asked of me."

Cameron stood, dusting the small stones and debris from his trousers like they were crumbs from food he had just eaten. "And Emilie. You truly *do* know where she is, don't you?"

CHAPTER THIRTY-SIX

Heather

There was no time left for Heather. They had arrived at the foot of St Paul's Cathedral. Heather turned down a street opposite the towering steps for the cathedral, Godliman Street. A narrow street, only wide enough for one car at a time. It led into Queen Victoria Street, and she spied a parking space and swung the car into it.

She turned the ignition off. Maynard unbuckled his belt and reached out to open the car door. "Wait!" Heather voiced, in a manner that came out a bit more urgently than she had hoped. "I mean, what is the plan here? How do we know exactly where they are, what we say or do when we see them? We need to be sure Sofia has been turned by Cameron so that she is either on our side or is totally blinded by the truth, but will not put all of us at risk."

Maynard opened the car door and swung his legs round to get out, holding onto the inner handle of the car door for support. "Heather, come on, follow me. This will be OK. Trust me. I know Sofia will know the truth from the hidden agendas here. We will be OK. Now, come on."

Heather wanted to say something more but was unsure of what or how. Maynard was out of the car; he pushed the door closed and headed north onto Godliman Street towards the cathedral.

Heather took the key out of the ignition and watched Maynard walk away, sighed, and closed her eyes. She placed the key in her jacket pocket and rubbed her thumb and second finger nervously together, feeling the rawness of the skin again around the nail bed. Then, opening her eyes, she gently rubbed her right-hand jacket pocket and sighed again.

Letting out a puff of air from her mouth making her cheeks blow out, she got out of the car to follow Maynard.

Heather sprinted to catch up to Maynard. He was just going up the main street to cross to enter the front courtyard of the cathedral.

"Where do we go?" she asked Maynard, slightly breathless as she caught up beside him.

"I know where Cameron would have taken Sofia. The artefacts he would have enticed her with. That's where we go. I'm hoping by now Cameron has done enough to get Sofia to be thinking more rationally."

Heather tied her hair back in a ponytail as she looked both ways to cross the road. The wind was blowing and she wanted to remove any distraction from her sight. "I doubt it. Sofia has been under for too long. Whatever Cameron says will fall on deaf ears. That's why I still think this is wrong. We need to get Cameron to tell us what he knows, get him and Emilie to safety and out of the equation while we deal with the rest."

Heather knew she sounded desperate and uncertain. No matter how much she told herself to stay calm and to stay in control, it was no use.

Maynard stepped into the road off the pavement and crossed, with Heather following. "We will go up the steps and into the cathedral from the main entrance." Maynard pointed to a kiosk on the pavement by the foot of the steps. "Grab a tourist guide leaflet from there. We will need to blend in."

Heather shook her head and put her hand in her jacket pocket for comfort and reassurance, hoping for her new plan to gain control.

CHAPTER THIRTY-SEVEN

Sofia

"Yes, Cameron." Sofia watched Cameron pace around the room. She stayed sitting on the floor with her back against the wall. "Only I know where she is. Again, it took planning and skill over all this time to get her hidden safely."

"But, the organisations... the ones that are hunting her and the ones that you say you're working for, even if you're undercover – what do they think has happened to Emilie?"

Sofia glanced at her watch again. "Cameron, we don't have much time at all. Please. You need to put your trust in me. All will become clear; just *please*, I need to be frank and straight with you."

"Look. Whatever you need to do, go ahead and do it." Cameron folded his arms across his chest and leaned on the bookshelf. "As you said, I've given you enough to go on here at St Paul's for you to be able to work on. What troubles me is the fact that you used Emilie and Siena as a plot to get me here in the first place, which means the organisations would have known you did that."

"Yes, Cameron, they knew I used them as a ploy to get to you and to get you to play the game. But there is one big difference. The organisations think Emilie is..." Sofia paused and sighed.

"…Is what, Sofia? Finish what you were about to say!"

"Well… dead. The organisations think she's dead." She took a deep breath and continued. "Please, remember they're not. I have them safe and hidden. Both Emilie and Siena." Her voice more rapid now to reassure Cameron. "But again, I had to convince the organisation that they *were* dead so that they would stop looking for them. That was where Heather came into play."

CHAPTER THIRTY-EIGHT

Cameron

"Heather?" Cameron asked. "What do you mean by that is where she came into play? How, in relation to Emilie and Siena?"

There was no answer from Sofia. Cameron waited and then allowed conversations of earlier which were left unanswered to come back for Sofia.

"The list that is encompassed within are the documents of *Acta Sanctorum*. If my name is on it, along with your father's and Emilie's, as you said, that means it's a list of names that have all been connected throughout history." Cameron did not let Sofia respond and continued.

"It is a list of names who all have known something or discovered something of great importance, but knowledge which has been deemed to be dangerous if communicated out into the open."

Sofia stood up. Another look at her watch. "Cameron." She paused and looked to the dark exit out of this hidden room that they'd both crawled through. Cameron caught the direction of her eyes.

"Who is coming? Who are you waiting for?" he demanded. "Why are our names on that list?"

"The list is maintained by the organisations. It was

started and has been handed down in a fashion to have a record of people who are of interest to them. You are correct in thinking that every name on that list has been close to unlocking a piece of what has been hidden over the centuries." Her voice hurried.

"And now they are all dead?"

"Yes," she replied. "But not my father, not you and not Emilie. We have a way of protecting you all."

Cameron glared at Sofia with his eyes fixed on her pupils, making no movement other than the rise and fall of his chest with deep breaths of intensity. "Who is coming for me, Sofia?"

PART TWO

CHAPTER ZERO

Now

Emilie

The sun reflected high in the horizon – it was the type of day that people felt a warm inner glow, a sense of fulfilment. Emilie walked up the steps, sun reflected in her almond set eyes, hair gracefully moving across her face and coming to rest on her shoulders. The sun's rays gave her a glow with a vivid brilliance of veracity, the type that would magnetize one's soul. Her smile could penetrate every aspect of your body and would pull you into her. A safe invitation.

She hugged and kissed Cameron passionately as they met on the top step. Her left hand on his face while holding a bag in her right hand. She gripped the bag much more tightly than was needed, her knuckles turning white with the pressure. She handed him the jacket and smiled again. This smile seemed slightly different. An intimate yet shy smile, speaking a thousand hidden messages.

Emilie had battled this day for weeks, yet she was no closer to resolving the agonizing decision that she'd been forced to make. The thought of hiding anything from Cameron, let alone of lying and deceiving him, went against every fibre of her being. Inside, Emilie ached from the pain of leaving Cameron; how she'd tried to come to terms with the numbness that enveloped her soul. Nonetheless, the truth that had become apparent in the last few weeks left her no choice but to succumb and surrender to this path. There wasn't even a question of choosing an option; she would have to be strong. It was time for her to focus on the current task. But behind the façade, an outward charade, her world had become a bitter reality of unbearable sadness, filled with deceptive risks.

The last thing Emilie wanted to do was meet with Cameron that morning; it took every ounce of strength within her to make her remain focused on the task ahead. It would have been easier not to face him that one last time for fear that he may see through her false surface and into the inner depths of her deception. Normally, she would have inner butterflies when knowing she would be meeting Cameron, but that day it was far from that – more of an inner sickness of betrayal in her. But it was the only way to save humanity. Well, that was what she'd been led to believe, of course. The trade-off was not being able to spend the rest of her life with the man she loved. Their meeting had to be fleeting if she was going to pull off the deception, as she knew he could read her like a book.

"Thank you for bringing the jacket. Do you have time for a coffee?" he asked.

A slightly chortled response flowed. "Super busy day, let's get coffee another time?" They rubbed noses, confirming the affection shared, then she turned and walked away.

The tears welled up as Emilie walked down the steps. Shooting pains surged through her ribs, knowing the turmoil of her decision. She felt unwell from the lack of sleep and the constant adrenaline running through her over the past few days. It was a sickness that she wanted to get rid of, but she knew it was just the beginning. It would be unbearable for both of them; she ached to turn around and explain everything to Cameron. *'He would understand, maybe even be able to help...'* Emilie fought with her thoughts the further she got from the steps. "Stop this weakness. This must be done; there is no turning back..." she repeated to herself as she walked towards Sofia, who was waiting for her.

CHAPTER ONE

London, before

A few weeks prior to the fateful day of walking away from Cameron, Emilie had been approached by Sofia, a stranger in her world, but someone who rocked all understanding of what Emilie thought she knew of Cameron until that moment. She learnt from Sofia about Maynard and the work that he and Cameron did together in Vienna, before Cameron came into Emilie's life, and the hidden worlds they were uncovering with their research. Sofia informed Emilie that Cameron had spent much of his adult life as a very lucrative treasure hunter of sorts, locating and acquiring priceless artefacts from around the world and passing them on for handsome rewards of profit. His skills and work were soon noted by two powerful organisations when they were alerted to the fact that he was searching for a particular artefact of interest to them. It was then that the organisations realised the potential damage he may cause if this knowledge breached the walls of the few, to diffuse into the public domain, in relation to impressions of humanity's evolution. This prompted the organisations to act. They convinced Cameron to work for them under the guidance of Maynard, to complement and complete each other's work. At that time, both Cameron and Maynard were kept from the dark truth that was unfolding in the shadows.

The confessions from Sofia caught Emilie off-guard and she found her claims far-fetched at first, yet concerning and logical at the same time. As the conversation expanded and the trust slowly developed between them, the wonder turned to questions. "Wait… you are saying that Cameron… *my* Cameron, is a hired thief, involved in some sort of global conspiracy?"

Sofia replied, "That is an interpreted choice of description and an expression; he is much more than that, of course. Cameron has many hidden talents but, yes, he is very good at finding things of value and using his acts of persuasion to get what he needs."

"And he found something of priceless value? That now these secret organisations want, whatever or whoever they are, because it has the potential to destroy humanity?"

"Yes, Emilie – in a nutshell. However, it's much more than that. Your work, the research you've been doing all these years, is fundamental in all this and it's critical we protect it and protect you."

"My work… I am a doctor, not a treasure hunter…" She looked puzzled and replied in a very defensive manner.

"I know the truth – there is no reason to lie to me, Emilie. We know of the research you've been doing for the last few years and know you're on the verge of an extremely important breakthrough. You've worked long and hard for this and even harder to try to keep your research secure."

"…But how does my research help Cameron? He doesn't even know the full details of my work. How does this all connect to each other?"

"It all ties in together with how we have all come to

be, how humanity has been and is present at the moment. Have you heard of the Mithra? The religion…" Sofia began explaining to Emilie as they sat opposite each other, like two friends catching up over coffee.

Emilie paused in thought. "I think so, but it's something that I recall only from brief paragraphs that I may have read at some point."

The table they sat at was opposite the busy counter where people queued up for their latte orders. There were the chinks of cups and saucers as the baristas worked to keep the orders flowing smoothly. Every now and then, the sounds of the steamer and froth machine would disturb the atmosphere and grab the attention of people sitting nearby. But not those two. Both Sofia and Emilie were far too engrossed in the intense conversation unfolding between them.

"Okay… Sofia, please tell me. I am sure you can imagine that my mind is thinking and racing through a million thoughts right now. It is a lot to deal with. What has all this got to do with the other stuff? What are all the links between Cameron, you, your father, the work they did or *are* doing and me and these organisations?" All these questions and more were circling in Emilie's mind, but these were the only ones that she could focus on and vocalize at present. Her tongue moving in her mouth as heavy as a concrete slab, struggling to keep up with the words that she wanted to get out.

Sofia took a deep sigh in, ready to explain. "Let me start with some history. It is the only way you will understand the meaning behind the importance of all this. The Mithra faith dates to the Roman Empire; well, way before the Roman Empire, but that was the time when it came to the forefront, and it was also known as the 'mystery religion'. This may get a bit much, but please stick with it and be patient."

Sofia continued in her business-like, formal tone. "In the second century, Justin Martyr, a Christian apologist, was regarded as one of the foremost experts of the divine world – later he was venerated as a Saint by the Roman Catholic Church. He adamantly disagreed with the Mithra faith and denoted it as demonic and not a true faith. Until the fourth century, Christianity stood in competition with the Mithra. Most of the mysterious religions were cast out as being devil-worshipping and denounced by mainstream Christian thinking models." Sofia held her warm cup between her hands, taking a sip before she continued.

"The last known practice of Mithraism is dated about 408 CE. The followers at that point were driven underground to practice their faith."

Emilie almost growled in frustration. "This history lesson is very interesting I'm sure, but obviously with such a religion that was older than Christianity, and us in this day and age, I still am unable to see any obvious connection here."

"I'm getting to that point, Emilie; please, that was just an overview."

"I'm sorry, Sofia, but I'm still rocking and reeling a bit from all this... Sorry, the Mithra – that is key to all this then?"

"Yes, the Mithra religion dates back to 1400 BC onward until the fourth century. Literally thousands of years before Christianity even existed. Mithraism is the worship of the so-called god, Mithras; it was best known as an ancient Roman mystery religion due to the Roman

Empire at the time driving it underground, with a view to create the thought that it was just folk stories. It is said that the Mithra faith was associated with the Light of the Sun, Truthfulness and Meditation.

"Text written over the years mention Mithras. From being mentioned both in the Vedas, the ancient holy books of Hinduism, which were written between 224–640 CE, to areas across the far east and also the middle east and Africa. It was global. However, almost all written text pertaining to the specifics of the faith have been destroyed by the powers that were at the time. Only some of the scriptures survived. But it is the similarities in Cameron's and your work that are the most important aspects of the reason for our interest in you both."

Emilie, at this point, seemed to have the colour drained from her face. It was the first time she'd understood and retained the fact that perhaps she and Cameron had been under surveillance for a long time. *If this is true, what else has been hidden or manipulated?* she thought.

Sofia continued. "The symbols, over time, contrasted but also had shocking similarities. Christ and Mithra were described in various ways; however, Jesus could only be represented as the son of God – the messenger. Mithra is often presented as carrying a lamb on his shoulders, just as Jesus was at times. Both religions have midnight services. Then there are the similar images of the two. Mithra is depicted as a sun disc in a chariot drawn by white horses, another solar motif that made it into the Jesus myth, in which Christ is to return on a white horse. What is really interesting is that, in the fifth century, the Roman emperor, Julian, having rejected his birth religion of Christianity, adopted Mithraism." Emilie was sitting upright and alert in her chair, taking all this in.

Sofia turned her wrist to glance at her watch, let out a breath of air and continued. "Over the centuries – in fact, from the earliest Christian times – Mithraism has been compared to Christianity, revealing numerous similarities between the two faiths' doctrines and traditions. In developing this analysis, it should be kept in mind that elements from Roman, Armenian and Persian Mithraism are utilised, not as a whole ideology, but as separate items that may have affected the creation of Christianity, whether directly through the mechanism of Mithraism or through another pagan source within the Roman Empire and beyond. The evidence points to these motifs and elements being adopted into Christianity, not as a whole from one source, but singularly, from many different sources."

"Sofia, my head's starting to spin. This is a lot to take in within such a short time, but I still don't see the connection here." Emilie's face was pale and drawn as she spoke.

Sofia shook her head at Emilie. "I promise, just listen – it will all fall into place." She continued in the same breath, without awaiting Emilie's acknowledgment. "Christianity was formed from the tails of Mithra, and just as the ancient powers tried to suppress the faith back then, they are still fighting it today. If it were true that the Church tried to suppress it all, it would destroy all aspects of what power it holds today. The common references between the two religions are astonishing, but none more so than one key fact. Mithra was born on December 25th and the babe was wrapped in swaddling clothing and placed in a barn to be attended by shepherds. Next, he was considered to be a travelling teacher or a master. Mithra performed miracles and was accompanied by twelve disciples. As the great bull of the sun, he sought world peace. After his death, it was said he ascended into heaven and the Mithra considered Sunday a sacred day. He set marks on the foreheads of his soldiers and Mithraism is founded on baptism."

Emilie's eyes darted around the room and then back to Sofia's face. She could feel her pulse quickening and the slight tightness sitting in her chest like a rugby player was holding her down. She was trying to register Sofia's words and gestured with a nod of the head for her to continue.

"The comparison of texts over time suggests that Jesus wasn't born on December 25th, but instead, the sun god, Mithra, was. The *Catholic Encyclopedia* says the birth of Jesus was chosen for that day, and called a rebirth of the winter sun, unconquered by the rigours of the season. Christmas was therefore founded by the Calendar of Filocalus or Philocalian Calendar circa 354 AD, which represents the 'Birthday of the Unconquered' – the winter solstice birth of the sun – as that of *natus Christus in Betleem Iudeae:* 'Birth of Christ in Bethlehem of Judea'. So, in essence, the effect is the same: 'Christmas' is the birth, not of the 'son of God', but of the sun with a 'u'."

Sofia took another sip of her drink while Emilie remained silent, allowing everything to sink in.

Swallowing deeply, Sofia continued, "Okay, so, the birth of Mithra. The analogous; Jesus was said to have been born from a virgin, Mary. But Mithra was born out of a rock... the cave shown at Bethlehem, as the birthplace of Jesus, was actually a rock shrine in which the god Tammuz or Adonis was worshipped. In history, the worship of a god in a cave was commonplace in paganism: Apollo, Cybele, Demeter, Herakles, Hermes, Mithra and Poseidon were all adored in caves, and Mithra was *rock-born*." She paused just for a few seconds, taking a breath. Then, she leaned slightly forward over the table. "Emilie, I know you know your history of Rome. You know where this is going."

Emilie avoided Sofia's eyes while replying and looked over her shoulder to where the counter was. "It is difficult to truly want to believe what I think you're getting at. But the reason why Vatican Hill was located across the Tiber river and the location of St Peter's Basilica–"

Sofia cut Emilie off, "Indeed, it may be the reason for Vatican Hill in Rome being regarded as sacred to Peter – the *Christian 'rock'*, – it was already sacred to Mithra at that time. Mithra was 'The Rock'. When Jesus mentioned in history that the keys of the kingdom of heaven are given to 'Peter' and that the Church is to be built upon 'Peter', as a representative of Rome, he is usurping the authority of Mithraism, which was precisely headquartered on what became Vatican Hill. In fact, while Mithraic ruins are abundant throughout the Roman Empire, the Illuminati, the Freemasons and even the Templars have scrambled for centuries to keep this evidence secret. Ancient Rome tried to destroy any references to this."

Sofia's voice began to soften. "My father's work uncovered one of the largest Mithra temples that was ever built under the City of London, which isn't surprising as it's the site of a Roman settlement on the banks of the Walbrook – a long-lost tributary of the Thames. In 1954, during construction of an office development, the temple was uncovered. During some very heated debates, the London authorities struggled with whether to make the discovery public. But thanks to some very influential people, the archaeological site was preserved and renovations got underway to secure the precious artefacts for public viewing. A museum was erected around the temple and opened to the public for many years, then in 2009 a shift in the government took place and suddenly the temple was moved, with the intention of relocating the site – however, legal issues prevented the reassembling. Or, what really was the organisations commanding their influence to hide the temple."

Emilie sensed a shift in Sofia's tone at the side mention of her father's company and something close to pain flashed across her face. Nonetheless, she nodded for her to continue.

"My father was researching the relevance of that site in London, the artefacts present there and the potential way the hidden truths could be unlocked. On that ground was one of the richest archaeological sites in London. As a matter of fact, there were some of the oldest handwritten documents ever found in Britain of the Roman invasion there. Over fourteen thousand objects were reported to have been found on the site, but most, if not all of the important artefacts, have been hidden…"

Now it was Emilie's turn to speak. "But not hidden well enough for someone like Cameron to find and acquire, I gather. Yes, I understand now his relevance to this. I also see how my work ties into it too. It's about creation. How life came to be, the meaning of how it all started. In other words, the key link between science and religion. My work joins the dots that history has kept hidden."

"Emilie, these people are very powerful and will do anything to keep this from the public. Which is why we must take you into hiding. They know what your work entails and will come after you to get what they want. No-one, not even Cameron, can safeguard you. They will destroy you and hide your work and never let it realise its true potential. Please, you must believe me and know that we can protect you. My father and I have infiltrated the organisation, so we know what they know and that means how to keep you safe."

Emilie was succumbing to the truths that Sofia had revealed, including the dangers of what this all meant for her and Cameron. Her breathing quickened, she tapped her fingers on the table haphazardly and managed to stumble some words out.

"I... I can't just leave Cameron. Surely he's also in danger?" Her eyes started to fill with tears, but she held them back.

Sofia leaned across the table to place her hand over Emilie's and said, "He is capable of taking care of himself, and as long as you are in hiding, the organisations will need Cameron to get to you and to understand what he also knows. They need him alive. We have been planning this for a long time, down to every single detail. I know this will be hard and I wish there was another way, but my fear is that there is work underway to have you and Cameron compromised."

Emilie just stared into space past Sofia and voiced, in a monotonous tone, "I need to see him, one last time. Give me that right, at least."

CHAPTER TWO

London, now

As Emilie sat in the back of the car, she knew she had to play her part. She had no choice but to put her trust in Sofia and hope that she would be true to her words and keep her safe.

The driver was working for the organisation and both Emilie and Sofia had to be mindful of their actions and words around him. This made it that much more difficult for Emilie than it already was. At least when she was alone with Sofia, she could question her and get reassurance of the plan and of what would happen to Cameron. But now in the vehicle, she had lost that right.

"Do I have the right to ask where you're taking me? Where does my fate go from here according to you?" Emilie's voice was barely a whisper; she knew where the car was heading. They were travelling west out of London along the A4, which would soon become the M4 motorway, which leads to Heathrow Airport.

"You will know when we get there," Sofia replied sternly.

CHAPTER THREE

Before

Sofia

Although it was September, the day outside was cloudy and overcast. Perhaps it was a reflection of the mood within Emilie's two-bedroomed apartment. The sky had the dull matt look of a grey blanket being pulled to cover the vast open space outside Emilie's bedroom window. Emilie walked over to the far side of her bed and sat by the bedside cabinet. She stared at the picture on the cabinet; she saw the laughing moment that was captured with her and Cameron on their trip to Santorini. How she remembered that day; hot, sunny and humid. The thought of that day now seemed like make-believe and she sighed.

"What happens with my life now, Sofia? What happens with Cameron's life?" Emilie continued to look at the picture on the cabinet, with its air of happiness and a moment full of hope and safety at that time. How she had clung on to those feelings for months on end since that trip. Every morning she would wake and have that feeling that there was a purpose to Cameron and her being together. "The life we had and the life we were going to have together. It's all been ripped away from me." Emilie's voice had a tremble to it, just barely coming out. She felt breathless like the air was lacking in the room for her lungs to be fulfilled.

Sofia took a deep breath, swallowed hard and gathered the strength to hit Emilie with more revelations. "Emilie. Cameron and you. Well…"

Emilie interjected, "What, Sofia?" She spun around on the bed to look at Sofia.

"How you both met, it was… well, it wasn't by chance." Sofia's voice had nervousness to it. She knew that telling her this would risk Emilie being able to stick to the plan. Emilie had built some sort of trust now in Sofia, but this was going to test that thin thread of a bridge between the two.

"What… what do you mean? We met in the hospital where I was working at the time. He spotted me while accompanying a patient there!"

"Yes, you did, but the lady with the sprained ankle, the patient that accompanied him – do you remember her? Well, it was suggested that she should attend with a sprained ankle to the hospital that day, all in order to get Cameron there while you were working and to allow the both of you to meet."

Emilie's face tightened. Her eyes narrowed and she glared at Sofia in disgust. "Excuse me?"

"Obviously, there had to be some sparks and for you both to have some sort of degree of chance to notice each other and some initial attraction, but it wasn't all how it seemed."

Emilie stood and stepped closer to Sofia. She could see the sheepish look on Sofia's face. Emilie's voice now agitated, making Sofia feel slightly uncomfortable.

"What exactly do you mean by 'it wasn't all how it seemed'?"

Emilie was breathing quickly now, her hands making fists by her side with her nails digging into her palms. There was no answer from Sofia.

"How was it done?" Emilie's voice was monotonous in nature.

"A woman called Heather," Sofia replied, with a reluctant apologetic sounding tone to her words.

"Heather. Who is that?" Emilie snapped.

"Look, there is no easy way to–"

"Just bloody tell me!"

Sofia sighed heavily. "She's the one who arranged for the two of you to meet. She works, well, worked for the organisations as a field operative. At first, her remit was to work on the field to gather information and to keep tabs on all interested parties."

"Let me hazard a guess. Me and Cameron were part of the 'interested parties' that she was keeping tabs on?"

Sofia paused for just a moment at Emilie's comments, just the right amount of time to look directly into Emilie's eyes, to give the message without any words, for Emilie to stop and remember who was really in charge here. Emilie tried all she could to stare Sofia down, but it was not in her nature to be that person, and she took a deep breath and looked away over Sofia's shoulder to the window.

Sofia continued, "Heather was brought into the project before me. She was already tracking your work, here in London. This was before she was also assigned Cameron." At that moment, Sofia knew she'd used the wrong word. She hesitated before continuing, being mindful not to lose Emilie's focus.

"As your research gathered pace, she reported your advances to the organisations. Obviously, she was handsomely rewarded for her work. Then, Cameron started working with my father in Vienna. I still recall the time my father used to tell me about Cameron and how much he impressed him." A gentle smile spread over Sofia and her tone softened for a slight moment.

"I don't know when Heather actually started her surveillance on Cameron and my father, but it was a few weeks before my father started getting upset and mentioning things to me. You see, the organisation would have various people working for them on various tasks and others would never know what the real purpose was. But my father was rattled. He had never met Heather, but was aware that someone was keeping a close eye on them."

Sofia took a moment to sit on the edge of the bed opposite Emilie, giving her feet a rest.

"I was working for the organisation also, but in a different department. It was when my father told me of his suspicions that I knew I had to find a way to work to get closer to the top tier of the board and to excel with my abilities and get noticed. I needed their trust. This took time and effort, but eventually, I was given more and more pivotal roles. It also worked to the organisation's advantage that I was the daughter of their lead professor – a professor who had discovered more than he should have done, and so they had me as leverage."

Emilie moved to sit next to Sofia on the bed. Both seemed exhausted now, mentally and physically. Both were looking to the window. The dull light coming through the windows was still bright enough to have them both squint, but this was more due to the lack of sleep and burden of tiredness.

"You see," Sofia continued, "I never met either Cameron or Heather face to face. At first, I didn't have any time to meet Cameron, but then as my father became aware of the deceptions, he knew to keep me away from him while we planned how to keep my father safe."

Emilie hung her head and looked into her hands as she clasped them together as if in prayer. "Seems like all of you are very good at deception from where I am sitting. How could I have been so blind to Cameron all this time?"

Sofia patted her hand. "He wasn't all that bad. I truly believe that he thought he was doing something good and meaningful with my father. When my father and I discovered that the organisation was planning to kill my father, we managed to plan his death and disappearance. We had to keep Cameron away from this truth otherwise he would also have been in danger. What we didn't anticipate was Cameron coming to London to continue their work."

"Do I even *want* to know how you went about planning your father's death?"

"I think we can leave that for another time, Emilie. But, what you *do* need to know is that Heather was sent to London to follow Cameron and to find out what he knew and what he was planning to do with the discoveries. She was already tracking your work in London and so she was the obvious choice for the organisations to send over here."

"And you?" Emilie asked. "What were *you* doing during this time?"

"I continued to work within the organisations. To get deeper into their cell and penetrate and extract as much as I could about who and what they are. They began to trust me more and primed me to have Cameron blamed for my father's death." Sofia put her elbows on her knees and placed her head in her hands. "It was a dark time for me. To act with anger towards Cameron, yet at the same time mourn my father's death and also help keep him hidden and protected." She paused and then sighed before continuing, "It was a dark time for me."

"Was Heather following me and my work for a long time?" Emilie asked, ignoring Sofia's guard dropping.

"Your research work into auto-insemination in humans got the attention of the organisations and it was obvious when they then looked at my father's work on the same aspects of the Mithra – they saw that the two were connected and would have a very powerful meaning if they had both pieces of work in their hands completed. That was why Heather was sent to London to follow Cameron as she had been following your work too. So they used her to report on all aspects."

"How long did she follow me for?" Emilie pressed.

"I do not know, but it started before Cameron arrived in London."

Emilie tightened her grip further between her hands. She made an interlocking pattern with her fingers and slid the second finger of each hand over one another. "So, this Heather is an assassin? But are you both not on the same side right now? For the organisations?"

"Emilie, this is where it gets a bit uncomfortable."

"Ha!" Emilie chuckled sarcastically. "What do you mean 'this is where it gets a bit uncomfortable'? Do you think it has been *comfortable* until now?"

"Heather started to have an unhealthy fixation with Cameron and you and the power of both of your research and discoveries. She was getting more and more rogue and the organisations even became cautious. She wanted more. She felt entitled to keep your work and Cameron's discoveries for herself."

The words from Sofia made Emilie feel so inadequate, so redundant at forming a rational response to all these allegations, which were being thrown around the room. She felt that they were immeasurable to any form of normality she'd encountered. She was a doctor and scientist and had everything under control in life. But this? This felt like it was uncharted knowledge – it just seemed ridiculous to even fathom it was reality!

Sofia cleared her throat and continued, "I was sent to keep an eye on Heather and also to take over the surveillance of Cameron in London. It became clear that Heather was planning to get all she could from Cameron and you by using the organisation's resources to do it. Hence why I am here. I am under orders from the organisation to find you, to get your work and to relocate you into hiding so that Heather cannot get to you and so that you can finish your work for the organisations."

"Thank you for the valiant effort, Sofia. But what do *you* get out of this?"

"I get to protect my father, protect you and Cameron and a way for you to complete your work. I get to keep my cover within the organisation and burrow deeper within them to destroy them."

Emilie stood up and paced around the room. "And what makes you any different?" she blurted out. "Don't you also want me to complete my research and learn about it? After all, Cameron was also set up to come across me. You mention this woman Heather, but was it really *her* or *you* that made that happen? Or maybe Cameron is in on all of this too!"

"Emilie, please calm down and breathe. Cameron is not part of any deception. Yes, it might have been arranged for you two to meet, but he fell in love with you. That part was all true."

Emilie collapsed on the floor, leaning against the wardrobe, knees drawn up. The silent cry and the dry tears were taking so much more energy than if she could vocalize her suffering. "How do we get out of this, Sofia?" She succumbed to the helpless state she found herself in.

"We use the organisation's means and reach to get you safe from Heather and we use Heather as a puppet to keep us all safe as time goes on. We deceive them all and get you and Cameron out for good."

Emilie looked up from the floor at Sofia who was still on the edge of the bed. Without saying a word, she got up and walked out of the room. She returned a few moments later holding a bottle in her hand. A bottle of red wine. She placed it on the bed beside Sofia. "We will need this token for trust when it comes to Cameron." Emilie closed her eyes and took a long, deep sigh. "On one of our holidays, we brought back two bottles of wine. Cameron usually drank red, either Merlot or Malbec. We always called the bottles sisters and promised to only open them later in our lives; however, it had to be in London. Then we would see if they still tasted the same."

CHAPTER FOUR

Now

Emilie

Everything had a grey, dull, flat look to it. All her surroundings seemed benign and lacking any substance or character. Emilie walked aimlessly along the aisle of the plane. As she suspected, she was being flown to Italy. Unlike her previous visit, she was not excited. Instead, filled with dread and anxiety toward the unknown.

Occasionally, a passenger would glance her way and she'd wonder whether they could feel her fear, perhaps mistaking her for a nervous flyer. Emilie could feel Sofia trailing behind her, acting as a babysitter she absolutely did not need, guiding her towards the seats 26B and 26C.

Emilie felt a light tap on her shoulder and turned to Sofia, who said, "Over there, to the right," while pointing to the seats in front of them. Emilie strode toward the seats without so much as a nod.

Emilie slumped into the seat and placed her bag on her lap. As she struggled to find the seat belt and buckle, a wet tear dropped onto the back of her hand. She furiously wiped her cheeks, ashamed and distraught at the tears she'd unknowingly allowed to fall. No sooner had she cleared them did fresh ones fall, followed by an increasing ache in her temple, a constant pressure, tightening whenever she found it unbearable.

Now that she was aware of the tears and the pain, she did everything she could to keep them hidden. *Don't show the tears*, she thought as the cabin crew began to make their announcements. She closed her eyes and willed her emotions to stay buried.

The next thing Emilie knew, she was in the clouds. Whether minutes or hours had passed, she was unsure. She didn't have the pleasure of such routine facts anymore.

Emilie found herself torn between her worlds; the life she lived as a scientist, a passionate doctor, and the life she lived as Cameron's lover. Now she was faced with the agendas potentially hidden behind each of them. Her mind shifted to Cameron. How would he feel upon realising she had disappeared? Would he bemoan the void left or was he part of this conspiracy? Would he ever know their child?

With this thought came a new inconceivable realization… that Emilie would be a mother, alone, unable to tell Cameron of his child's existence. She placed her hand gently on her lower abdomen, so gentle in her touch that she was afraid to disturb the fragile growing foetus. She looked down at her abdomen, still wrapped in her coat and the memory of when Cameron and she had jested together about having children.

CHAPTER FIVE

Before

Emilie

The first Valentine's Day that Emilie and Cameron spent together was a strange experience for Emilie. She struggled with the feeling of perhaps being in love with this man and the idea of sharing her life with another person just felt so foreign to her. Since their meeting they had spent every spare minute together, night and day. She was very busy and engrossed with her work, from being a doctor to the research she was undertaking. There were only a few days that she had off and those days she made sure she made time for Cameron. Cameron, also, was as busy with various aspects of work and meetings. They mutually accepted, somewhat reluctantly, that around their various responsibilities they would spend time with each other. This reluctance at the time was, on Emilie's part anyway, due to her trying to get to grips with having a meaningful relationship with someone, as she was new to such trust. Science and medicine were so much more logical for her.

She could feel the changes in her emotions gradually. They made her feel unfamiliar in her skin. From what she was used to as her normality, which was a combination of facts and proven evidence of statements and to be able to justify decisions based on those statements, she was now faced with what was a departure from her world of ordinary and how she had viewed the world through her lens.

It was far from just physical attraction for Emilie when it came to Cameron. That was too easy for her. It was all the other hidden attributes. The longing for him to know and challenge her work and her thinking. The thirst to want to prove him wrong all the time and, in a playful manner, to have him get irritated at that quality. The seamless ability to go from serious to clown in a matter of seconds, with him.

They had just spent the day at a Body Worlds exhibition at the London Pavilion in Piccadilly. A strange destination for Valentine's Day, unless you were a dedicated scientist, such as Emilie. They took a gentle stroll for dinner, along the streets of London toward Charlotte Street for a cosy Japanese restaurant that was themed with the upcoming blossom season of Japan. They stumbled across a small toy shop in a side street just off Regent Street. Cameron's eyes lit up when he looked at the window display. In the corner stood a toy van from the American TV series called *The A-Team* – a show that Cameron said he'd watched religiously as a child.

He commented, "Oh, look at that... that takes me back to my childhood; I wonder if our children will remember such icons."

Emilie shrieked, "Children..." After the words blurted out, louder than she had expected, she noticed a disheartened look on Cameron's face.

"Yes, haven't you thought about having children one

day?"

"To be honest… Cameron, I haven't. My focus has always been about work. I have just never thought of myself as a parent. It always seemed as though the maternal instinct skipped past me. I mean, it's not something that has really taken my thoughts or desires so far. Does that bother you?" Her voice slightly anxious.

"Maybe…" his voice trailed off. Emilie looked slightly on edge. "It's not a dealbreaker. But anything is possible, right? And feelings, desires, wants and needs change, right?"

"Yes, anything is possible. I suppose it wouldn't be the end of the world. And if I *were* to have a child, you are the most likely candidate." Emilie changed her demeanour and put on a cheeky smile. Cameron smiled in return.

"'Candidate…' What does that mean; am I being chosen from my genetics? I had no idea you had screened my saliva already!"

"Well, yes, as a matter of fact. Remember that day we shared that milkshake with the straw? Well, I used that to cultivate your DNA."

"I will say one thing… you are honest, cold and calculating! You always say what you mean. It is nice knowing where I always stand. And on a serious note, I am not sure if you are joking or not!" Emilie punched him in the abdomen and ran off with him chasing her with laughter.

It was the last time they had spoken of having children, but somehow the idea never strayed from her mind after that night. Cameron's presence had changed Emilie in more ways than she could ever imagine.

CHAPTER SIX

Now

Emilie

The captain announced the plane's descent into Firenze airport and Emilie found herself catapulted back to the last time she'd heard its name, on her trip to the Tuscan hills with Cameron. She let her gaze get lost outside the window of the plane, past the clouds below and deep into the rolling Tuscan hills.

CHAPTER SEVEN

Before

Emilie

On the first morning of their arrival, Cameron and Emilie visited Chiusi, on the southwest side of Siena – an ancient Gothic abbey that dated back to the thirteenth century, adorned with charm. Emilie had always loved history, especially the Gothic period, and was excited to see one of the most pivotal landscapes of that era.

The drive was long across the Tuscan countryside, via winding narrow roads that Cameron navigated in their Fiat 500 rental car. They approached the village and saw an incredible image imposing the skyline. The Abbey of Saint Galgano stood proud, even in the twenty-first century. Its most famous attribute is using the sky as its roof. Laid open on Emilie's lap was a local tourist information guidebook. She read to Cameron as they drove.

"It says here that the abbey was built during the thirteenth century by the Order of Cistercians and soon became a monastic centre in Tuscany." Her voice excited. She continued to follow the page as Cameron concentrated on the winding roads.

"The monks that resided there were dedicated to manual activities, mainly land cultivation, but also to study and prayer. Saint Galgano became quickly a small, flourishing area of Tuscany. However, by the end of the century, the monks abandoned the place and the building decayed. But ironically, it was this process of isolation in aging that gave the building its romantic, mystical appeal."

"Ha! Remember those words of aging and romantic when you make fun of my age again!" Cameron jested with Emilie.

"Shut up and listen. I will be testing you on this later!" Emilie continued. "So, it says that Galgano Guidotti was a noble knight who belonged to the Knights Templar. But he turned to religion and turned to a monk when he had a vision of St Michael." Emilie glanced over at Cameron. "Honey, do you need your sunglasses?" She noticed the sun directly in his eyes while he drove.

"No, its fine, we are nearly there anyway. Go on, anything else in that guide?"

"Well," Emilie turned the page of the guidebook, "as legend goes, Galgano visited his family and put the sword in the rock for safekeeping, but when he went to retrieve it, the hardened rock had absorbed it and refused to budge. So, the story of having undeniable faith was the only way anyone could pull the sword from its eternal home. After Galgano's death in 1811, a structure was built and transformed into a beautiful circular Chappella of Monte Siepi."

At that moment, the car turned around the corner to have the magnificent abbey in both of their sights. The area surrounding the building had remnants of frescos scattered in the fields of grass. The church itself was an incredible sight to behold.

Emilie let out a gasp. "So, so beautiful."

As Cameron pulled up to park, Emilie placed her hand over his and turned in her seat to face him. He looked back at her, both sitting there in front of this magical setting of history, not saying a word. Emilie was deep into him. Her phone to this day carries a picture of them posing next to the glass-covered dome of the sword.

CHAPTER EIGHT

Now

Emilie

The jostle of the turbulence brought Emilie back to her depressing reality. She rubbed her temple with the palm of her hand, the ache now an agonizing pain, and turned to look at Sofia, who was standing in the aisle by their seats.

"Would you like something to eat?" Sofia asked, upon meeting her eye.

Emilie moved her dry, cracked lips to say, "Yes, please. Do you have any painkillers at all?"

Sofia nodded. "Of course. Is everything alright?"

"I have a splitting migraine, that's all."

"Okay. Give me a minute and I'll get some food and paracetamol for you."

Emilie watched her walk away and then turned to the window, her hand gently resting once more on her growing stomach.

CHAPTER NINE

Before

Emilie

The morning of her first scan appointment, Emilie felt like a kid at Christmas, excited and anxious. She wanted to be sure all was OK with the pregnancy and to finally share the news with Cameron. She took leave early that afternoon and snuck upstairs to the pregnancy unit. She wanted to avoid being seen by any of her colleagues on the way there. No matter how she tried to keep busy and in control all day at work, nothing could have prepared her for the scan. Emilie had looked over to the monitor, a black and grey pixelated image on the screen. The Doppler handheld monitor was placed and slowly glided across her bare skin. Emilie had listened to thousands of heartbeats from her patients over the years, but nothing could compare to hearing the sound of her own child's. It took a minute or two to wrap her head around the situation. *I'm pregnant, oh my…* It was the most beautiful sound she had ever heard and, in that split second, Emilie's life took on a whole new meaning for the future. Life would never be the same again. At times, she'd heard women speak of never feeling alone once they got pregnant, but the concept seemed crazy to think a foetus could make someone feel accompanied. Now she could relate to that saying, emotion and feeling. The feeling of meaning, of being worth something and creating something of meaning. The feeling of the moment of creation.

Emilie had every intention of telling Cameron right away, but as the news settled with her, she wanted to keep the feeling just to herself for a little while longer. She had planned on going back to work, but once the appointment was over, trying to concentrate was impossible. At that point, Emilie thought she had all the time in the world to tell Cameron. As long as it happened before she started showing, everything would turn out just perfect.

CHAPTER TEN

Now

Emilie

Minutes turned into hours and the hours turned to days. Weeks and months passed by as though they had no meaning or purpose. Emilie refused to acknowledge that her days were travelling past her without a feeling of ownership or permission. It felt as though she had no right to the life she was inhabiting, at present. As much as she was told that she was not a hostage, she demanded to be told what the new definition of hostage was – her life of liberty had been stripped away. Being forced to complete her research in such conditions of duress had made her lose the passion she'd once had. Time in this place seemed to be never-ending. Yet, her work created a strange addiction for her. A toxic relationship to complete and to hate every aspect of her work as it had caused so much pain to date. So much anger, misery, distrust, bitterness, deceit, envy and mostly, fear, were the effects of her research, her discovery, her legacy, which she would leave behind.

Emilie had been approximately nine weeks pregnant when she'd turned her back and walked away from Cameron on those steps. She recalled that futile day. She now looked out of the window in her new surroundings and placed the palm of her hand on her growing belly – now with a visible swelling at thirty-four weeks. She gazed out of the window, watching the white netting and drapes falling to the floor and blowing in the breeze, creating a picture frame for the lush green lawn outside the window and the hills canvassing into each other throughout the narrative of the scene playing outside. A perfect picture postcard of Tuscany. How this place was so full of fond memories. Sofia had convinced the organisations to have her hidden here, as it would be familiar to Emilie and allow her to have an environment calm enough to allow her to continue with her research.

Emilie wondered what Cameron would think if he could see her now. Would it be delight and excitement that he would display in relation to the unborn child or would he show uncertainty and anxiousness? It was these same thoughts she'd had in her mind that day she'd walked away from him. She was now kept awake every night with the nightmare of not telling him when she'd had the chance. He had a right to know and that moment had now been taken away from him forever.

Sofia had spent some time with Emilie over the weeks. Although the organisations knew that Sofia was leading on the project of Emilie, they still wanted some further safeguards in place and so always had other agents present on the complex that Emilie was living in. Sofia had to get pockets of time with Emilie alone, every now and again, to keep her focused on the long-term plan.

Emilie looked over to Sofia. They were alone in the apartment and so could speak freely. "Sofia, you know my research will take years yet to complete. There are so many missing aspects to it, which I know I will not be able to solve in my lifetime. How are you planning to have Cameron and I safe if I cannot do this in time?"

"I know that, Emilie. Your work also will not be completed until we know what Cameron has discovered and how that fits in to help complete your work. But this is the key aspect of what I want to speak to you about."

Sofia shuffled her chair closer to Emilie. "I need you to start making duplicate, carbon copies of your work. Every calculation, every sequencing of the cells, every messenger protein. The lot."

"Do you know how—"

Emilie was about to finish when she was interrupted by Sofia.

"I know; it will take years. But that's OK. We must allow you to safely deliver your child now and to allow the child to grow for a couple of years. In that time, you will be kept under my watch according to the organisations. They have my trust, as long as they keep seeing you progress with your work."

"But what is the aim of creating duplicates of all my work? Surely that creates more risk?"

Sofia placed her elbows on her knees and made a bridge with her hands interlocking and placed her chin on her hands. Her eyes full of concentration, her reply was in a hushed voice. "One accurate version. The other should have delicate changes done, just enough to create a non-functioning version, yet on the face of it, still seem like it is groundbreaking work. But only *you* know the changes, of course. And make sure you make many of them."

"The false version of my work will be used to blindside the organisations, right?" Emilie's realization at Sofia's intent.

"No. The false version of your work will be destroyed, along with you."

Emilie gasped and leant back in her chair. There were the faint sounds of a bird singing in the trees in the distance. It sounded like the birds were also conspiring with Sofia. Emilie stood up and walked a few steps toward the banister of the balcony. She looked out into the evening unfolding around them. It reminded her of when she and Cameron had visited Tuscany and fallen in love with the area. They were enchanted by the medieval city of Siena on their visit, with its buildings adorned with frescos on the ceilings, which were restored from the sixteenth and seventeenth centuries.

"Emilie, are you OK?" Sofia asked with a slight look of concern on her face. Emilie paused for a moment before her careful reply.

"I don't want to forget Cameron's face. I mean, not just how he looks, but his mannerisms. The way his facial features change when he is curious or upset. How his eyes slant upwards when he is smiling and happy."

"There is no easy way to remember someone so close. Over time, the worry is that you forget the beauty of them. The beauty of the things only you came to know and love. Try to picture and develop a context."

Emilie raised her eyebrows at Sofia's comments. "What do you mean?" she asked.

"Well, you have to think about something specific, like something the two of you shared. Only the two of you. The scene. Where you were, what day it was, the colour of the top he was wearing or how you wore your hair that day. Only when you develop these specifics and create the narrative will you be able to remember every crease, every touch, every smell, every wrinkle and every mannerism of Cameron." Sofia's voice trailed off. She turned away and sighed.

"Cameron and I visited this area. We dined in this quaint restaurant within the Palazzo Ravizza Hotel." She closed her eyes and took a moment before continuing, keeping her eyes closed to recreate the atmosphere of that evening with Cameron. "We had a long, lazy dinner full of laughter and conversation. We drank a couple of bottles of wine that evening, so you can imagine how jolly we were. That wine, that evening, was one of the bottles we took back to London. To join the other one we had taken back from Santorini."

Sofia smiled sadly.

Emilie continued, "Those bottles of wine had a deeper significance than just a souvenir from a holiday once in the sun. It was a deeper bond between the two of us, a bond that at that time would keep us both safe together forever."

Emilie felt her abdomen again with the palms of both of her hands while looking out towards the distant hills, again focusing on the mystical lights of the Piazza del Campo in Siena, flickering away. She whispered to herself, "We will find one another again, my love. We'll share that bottle of wine as we planned. That is my dearest hope. Siena… what a beautiful name."

CHAPTER ELEVEN

Now

Emilie

The delightful small shops are nestled in-between small cottage houses and apartments on narrow, quaint cobbled streets, like bright coloured jellybeans in a jar – tightly packed and enticing to anyone that walks by. The hilly contours of the city of Siena exposed tangled webs of tall buildings, with smoke rising from the terracotta-tiled rooftops with their chimneys erupting from within. The narrow streets and alleyways would wind off into corners, all whispering to be explored.

This was now home for Emilie. Home for Emilie and her family – Siena, her newborn daughter. How the last couple of months had forged the character and will of Emilie to become one of stability, courage, protectiveness and single-minded survival for her child. How the temperate of Emilie had become one of resolve. The journey into motherhood was a choice that was made for her prior to arrival here, but she owned the path it had taken since then.

Emilie remained in the same apartment and complex that had been provided for her by the organisations, under the ever watchful eyes and supervision of several rotating personnel that lived onsite too. Their remit was to facilitate Emilie to continue her research with any resources needed and allow her to fall into motherhood. 'Allow' being the term that Emilie chose to put onto this. It was a notion that she would not normally seek permission for – to be able to fulfil her right as a woman to be a mother.

"She is beautiful, Emilie. Look at her thick, flowing hair." Sofia walked with Emilie through one of the charming narrow streets, which were packed with local bars and pasticcerias, pushing Siena in a pram ahead of them. They were on their way to Orti dei Tolomei, a park full of lush green colours where local families went to enjoy time away from the stone buildings. They walked along the Via Giovanni Dupré towards the Fontanelle di Contrada de la Onda.

Sofia had witnessed Emilie become stronger within herself. She'd become a more determined individual.

"Do you dream?" Emilie suddenly asked.

Sofia raised a perplexed eyebrow. "I don't understand. What do you mean?"

"It's a simple question."

"Yes. Ummm, I guess I do dream, Emilie. Why?"

Emilie bent over and smiled at Siena, who was peacefully sleeping. She placed a hand gently over her forehead and stroked slowly towards her ear. "Don't you ever wonder how you get into a dream in the first place? You never remember how it starts. You always start in the middle of the dream. That's how I feel every day. I am in the middle of the dream. Never remembering how I got here and never knowing how or when it will end." She stood and turned to face Sofia. "It's getting late. I need to get back to my work." She turned the buggy around and moved past Sofia, back the way they had come.

"Emilie?" Sofia tried to grab Emilie's arm as she brushed past, but with no success. Emilie shrugged her off.

Sofia hurried to catch up with her. "How close are you to being able to give some of the duplicate work to me?"

"I am close and I have enough for now. A couple more months and I will have done enough to keep them baffled for a while. It will give them enough to go on, and before they notice the key missing aspects, I trust you will have a plan to get us all away from them!"

It was moments like this when both Sofia and Emilie felt pressured to tell and ask all they could of each other. It was the only time they had without the eyes and ears of the minders from the organisations. "Siena must be safe from all this, Sofia. You have to promise me that is the priority here."

Emilie's voice was shaky at the thought of Siena coming into any harm without even having the chance to witness all the splendour and marvel of the world. She slowed as they walked past a stone bench. She sat on the cool, smooth surface of the bench and pulled the buggy close to her so that Siena's face was always in view.

Sofia sat to the far edge of the bench and blew her cheeks out as she spoke. "Heather is becoming a problem. I feel she may make her move soon with Cameron and I fear the organisations will take her out before…" her voice trailed off and she hesitated.

"Before what?" Emilie prompted Sofia to finish.

"I want to use Heather to help make you disappear. She will need to find out where you are and knowing that she is hungry to get your research, she will come looking for you. With that, we will create an opportunity for your disappearance."

"What do you mean, make me disappear?" Emilie looked over to Sofia, eyeing her stiff and anxious posture. She was sitting there cross-legged and rubbing her palms and fingers together, agitated.

"The only way you and Siena can be safe is if the organisations and Heather, and anyone else that may learn of your work, thinks you are…" a hesitation from Sofia before finishing her sentence, "…dead." She let that hang in the air for a while before continuing. "We will use Heather to create that narrative and the organisations will then think that Heather killed you because you refused to divulge your work." Sofia let her words out in a breathy rush.

Emilie sighed. "You had better start planning what you need to do then and figure out the bits you don't know."

Sofia choked out the response, "Yes, I am." She swallowed hard, looked at her wrist to check the time. "Tell me, where is the research stage at? I mean, the version you have been working on for the organisation to see."

Emilie yawned. She replied slowly and with an air of deliberation. "I will be brief. As you know, the whole underpinning of my work is to prove my hypothesis that humans can indeed procreate in an asexual manner. We know that there are cases where people are born with a mix of male and female sex organs, but that alone hasn't been enough to prove the hypothesis, as those individuals still need the male sperm and female ovum to create life." Emilie looked over to Sofia to check she was listening. Sofia responded with a nod.

Emilie continued, "My work has documented the parallels with such individuals and also the aspects of how the ecosystem around certain species makes them adapt to find a solution to create a new norm of species to survive. The aim of this adaptation was to allow the species to flourish and reproduce without barriers."

"A form of hermaphroditism?" Sofia asked, with a sense of achievement.

"Precisely. My work will show and prove the complex similarities with the genome of such species and how this progression of changes in the genomes have adapted over time." Emilie paused, took a breath and looked into the buggy to the peacefully sleeping Siena, smiling before continuing. "What was fascinating is the fact that stages of the changes in the genome mirrored some of the changes in the chromosomes of certain human karyotypes, which I have been able to map and sequence. The X and Y chromosome makeup of the genetic profile of a human was the blueprint of us as species. What my work and results show is that the cross-sectional comparison study, which took years to build and engineer in the lab, has enabled me to test my hypothesis."

Sofia was keeping up with Emilie's explanation and did not seem too confused with what she was being told. "Is it this study that we will let the organisations see and have?" she asked.

"Well, yes, and also that I have proved that what we feel are certain 'defects' in the human chromosome are actually the windows into the human's true hermaphroditic processing. The work proves that we can build, well, in the lab, anyway, a way of real and successful self-fertilization. I will show them how the human organism could, in fact, be an organism that can create a fusion of early embryos, with grafting and mutation to create the duplication of genetic code – from a single cell to a multicellular structure." Emilie closed her eyes and took a deep sigh.

"But if you give them all that, will that not give them the answers for all your work, your secrets and your discoveries?" Sofia asked.

"They will see it is possible to be done. They will see that I have proved my hypothesis, but not actually done it. Certain engineering techniques will be left out and it will be for them to try to experiment with the knowledge, but I know they will have no idea how to create the final answer. In any case, Cameron's knowledge and secrets are needed to finish the puzzle. Certain aspects need history of our species to unlock and allow us to discover."

"I pray this works, Emilie." Sofia put her head in her hands and leant forward, her elbows on her knees. Emilie looked across at her bent over posture and reassured Sofia. "It will. The rest is in your hands, to pull through as you promised."

Sofia stood. She took a couple of steps forward and placed her hands on her hips, then moved them to cross her arms out in front of her. "My father and I have been aware of Heather's plans since Cameron was in Vienna with my father. My father befriended Heather back then, knowing that her greed would be useful further down the line. We will use her to help my father hide in London and together they will monitor and work on Cameron until the organisation wants me to approach Cameron. My father will leak to Heather where you are hiding and that will be your way out when she comes hunting for you."

"When?" Emilie asked flatly.

"Once she comes and feels she has inadvertently caused your death, the organisations will be made aware by me, and that's when the heat will be on, as Heather will need to get to Cameron to find out the remaining secrets and the organisations will do the same. She wouldn't want Cameron to know that you are dead and that she was the cause of it."

Emilie looked up directly into Sofia's eyes. "Give me eight months and you can have the research to give to the organisations and make me disappear."

CHAPTER TWELVE

Now

Heather

Heather sat nervously at the table, rubbing the raw skin around the nail bed of her thumb with her fingers. She looked at her watch again and realized that it had only been twenty seconds since she'd last checked it. Her water was untouched on the table in front of her. The atmosphere around her was busy and noisy. It was drowning out her concentration, which further unnerved her. St Pancras station always trapped in the coldness from outside and if Heather concentrated on her breath, she could just make out the steam coming from her mouth, making a mist that drifted away into the ether. The location for the meeting was to be at the south end of the upper level of the station, sitting outside the Italian chain restaurant of Carluccio's. The tables and chairs were huddled under a makeshift veranda on the concourse, with overhead heaters beaming down on the patrons having their lunch.

"Would you like a blanket? We have them inside if you would like one for your legs." Heather was startled by the waiter who had suddenly appeared beside her. "No, no, I am fine, thank you," she replied in a hurried voice.

To Heather's left stood the 20-tonne bronze sculpture called *The Meeting Place*. The 9-metre-high structure that cost one million pounds was intended to unravel the romance that was attached to the travelling experience. Heather watched with her eyes darting to everyone who walked past the sculpture, looking for the person who she was supposed to be meeting. She rubbed her face, the tight skin around her eyes pulled, straining with the effort of keeping them open. She felt how cold the tip of her nose was from sitting out here and wrapped her scarf tighter around her neck. "Is this seat taken?" The voice came from behind her, one she knew very well. She composed herself and took a breath before getting up to turn around.

"Maynard. You are safe." And she hugged him.

As Maynard sat opposite her, she gestured to the waiter for another glass. "I was so worried when I received your note at my workplace. I thought they had found me." Heather held Maynard's hands across the table as she spoke.

Maynard gave a slight smile and with a hushed voice replied, "I am sorry to have been very cloak-and-dagger with getting you here to meet. But as you can imagine, a certain level of discretion is needed." Heather squeezed Maynard's hands tighter, then let go and sat back in her chair.

"I was so worried when I didn't hear from you when I was sent to London, after the news that you had died. I refused to believe it. I knew it was not true. How did you—"

Maynard cut her off. "It was a difficult thing to plan, but I managed to stay safe and, more importantly, keep the organisations off my back." He watched Heather intently. She could feel his eyes burning into her, looking into her thoughts and assessing her convictions about what she had done and what she would do next. "I need your help, Heather. I need to be able to trust you. My life depends on it." Maynard put his elbows on the table and brought his hands to his face, making a bridge with his fingers across his nose, and sighed.

"But…" she paused, as the waiter approached.

"Are you both ready to order?"

"Just an English breakfast tea for me, please," Maynard said, looking up at the waiter and smiling. The waiter nodded in response.

"And for you, Madam?"

Heather shook her head without looking away from Maynard, and as the waiter walked away, she continued, "But why didn't you reach out sooner? Where have you been all this time? How did you manage to leave Vienna?"

"I couldn't risk putting you in danger, Heather, and I wasn't sure at that time if you would help me. But it is obvious that you are here in London because of Cameron."

Heather sat upright at the reminder of Cameron. The reminder why she had been in London for all that time. "Yes, it was to monitor Cameron, but I have no longer been willing to carry out the dark work of the organisations. I am afraid; I may be in as much danger as you are."

The tea arrived. Maynard poured it into his cup and put his hand around the heat. "Sofia does not know I am alive."

Silence followed. The screech of the Eurostar trains sounded just behind them. The announcements on the tannoy system indicating platforms for departures and arrivals. The distant, indistinct chatter of people as they navigated around the station. "I am so sorry, Maynard. I cannot imagine what this is doing to you or Sofia."

Maynard gave no response. He looked over Heather's shoulder into the distance with a vacant look on his face. "Maynard?"

He blinked and nodded his head. "Sorry. No matter how much time passes, the trauma of all this will never fully allow me to be at peace." He sighed. "Heather, in Vienna, I knew you were also doubting the work you were being made to do with the organisations. You understand that they will kill Cameron once they get what they need from him, right? That is the reason they sent you after all, isn't it?"

"They wanted me to track him down. They think he knows too much and that's what they want to find out. But also, there is something else." She looked down at the table.

"What is it, Heather?" When she didn't reply, Maynard took her hand. "Heather… they have taken everything away from me. My daughter – you know she works with them now and is too far deep in. You managed to see the true evil in the organisations and now you have a chance to help put some of this right."

Heather took a deep breath and nodded. "There is another woman. Here in London. She has been researching and developing a way to prove certain scientific facts in relation to humanity. Facts that augment the work both you and Cameron were doing. I was originally tracking her and her work here in London." She stopped and realized that her lips were dry and cracked and she took a sip from her glass of water before continuing. "But she has fallen off the radar. She just disappeared a year ago. I fear the organisations have her."

"Why have you stayed in London, Heather?"

Heather rubbed her thumb with her finger. She could feel the rough, loose skin around the cuticle of the nail bed. "I wanted to stay close to Cameron. I can't do what the organisations want me to anymore. It's not right. I..." her voice trailed off, "...I care for Cameron."

CHAPTER THIRTEEN

Now

Maynard

"Are you sure Sofia cannot leave the organisation and be safe with you?" Heather had seemed more and more trusting of Maynard over the past few months as they had both been working together to figure out a uniform plan to try and protect what Cameron and Emilie had been hiding. Heather brought Maynard up to speed on Emilie and her research.

Maynard, in return, over this time needed to understand Heather's agenda and to be mindful that she, too, once was very loyal to the organisations. "You know how powerful they are and how long their reach is," he replied.

Over the last few months, Maynard had been living in London, working deep undercover and staying away from the public eye. He needed to maintain a very low profile to ensure that there was no risk of word getting back to the organisations that he was indeed alive and well. He had Heather helping him to do that and, in turn, they both worked together to keep a distant eye on Cameron.

"Do you not fear for Sofia's safety?" As soon as the words

left Heather's lips, she recoiled at her own stupidity. Of course he would.

Heather had been working in a legal firm as a paralegal around the Blackfriars area of London. This gave her the perfect cover to remain in London and keep close contact with Cameron. She maintained distance from him when needed, but never let her covert surveillance fall below her high, self-set standards. When Maynard showed up in London, she felt further assured that Cameron must have had great secrets to uncover.

Maynard sighed and closed his eyes. He slowly tapped his fingers on the table. They were at his flat – a small studio flat above a shoe retail outlet on Camden High Street. The small, unassuming doorway to the side of the shop was squeezed between the two shopfronts: a shoe shop to the left and a souvenir shop to the right.

Maynard chose this area to hide. There was enough distraction that meant he was able to fade into the surroundings.

His room was small and sparse, without anything of note. A single bed to the far wall had its headboard under the sash window looking out over the street and, at its foot, a single wardrobe with uneven handles on the faces of the doors stood. To the opposite side of the bed was a door to a tight kitchen, with nothing but a small sink with a drainer, a thin fridge and small double burner cooker. Another door leading off the bedroom led to a toilet with a corner shower unit. It was cramped, but with a small basin and mirror to allow Maynard to shave. There was a small desk in the bedroom with a lamp and some of Maynard's reading material.

"We need to locate Emilie. We need to get to her before her completed research gets to the organisations." Maynard kept his voice low and steady.

"How? I would not even know where to start, thinking about where she could be. She could be anywhere, protected and kept in hiding by them."

Maynard stared out of the window, through the netting that had black pollution stuck to it from the street. The light grey outside typified London, even in the springtime. "I may have an idea where she would be."

"Where would you think she is? And even if we know where she is, how do we get to her and her research if she is being kept by the organisations?" Heather asked.

Maynard got up gradually by placing his hands on his knees for support, unfolding his recoiled body like a crane. His hands showing signs of osteoarthritis, with the typical swelling around his knuckles and finger joints. The skin on the backs of his hands was thin and wrinkled and so delicate that it would tear at the slightest abrasion across it. "She will be in Tuscany." Maynard's voice was breathy and raspy. "There is a complex the organisation has there."

Heather raised her eyebrow and asked, "How do you know this? What if you are wrong? I mean, will they be able to just take and hide Emilie there, away from the world?"

"You know better than anyone not to underestimate the resources of the organisations when it comes to being able to hide what and who they want to, when they need to. I need to do some investigative work, but I am sure I have an idea about where exactly she may be."

"In that case, we need to move now to get Cameron to open up. We need to know what he knows!" Maynard raised his eyebrows at her urgent tone, but before he could say anything, she quickly added, "I mean, surely we should get to Cameron before the organisations do, so we can protect him too?"

"Heather, please don't approach him yet. I am sure he will come to you if indeed he does see you as a close friend and confidant. We cannot risk alerting the organisations or, indeed, making Cameron suspicious until we have Emilie safe." He stood at the door and opened it a jot, motioning for Heather to leave.

CHAPTER FOURTEEN

Now

Sofia

Sofia sat on the fiftieth floor of one of the DC Towers along the eastern bank of the Danube. The building was the tallest skyscraper in Vienna, housing offices, exclusive apartments and a hotel on the upper floors. This building dominated the Donaucity district. The exterior of this building gave the tower a liquid, almost malleable texture to it that folded and unwound itself with the light. The interior used the raw building as its decoration, with exposed metalwork and beams with stone plinths to create both mood and functionality. Sofia had been summoned here once she'd delivered the recent update of all Emilie's research to the organisation. This had been obtained from Emilie eight weeks ago and the organisation had several technicians and engineers working on it in Vienna.

Sofia sat on the single chair in the room at the table, which was devoid of any objects apart from a telephone. As she looked over to the telephone, she jolted in her chair as the phone rang. She let it ring three times to compose herself and then picked up the receiver and held it to her ear, not saying anything, just listening. "The research is incomplete. But we have enough to work with and to help us decipher different complex systems of theories. We will have our teams in South America, China and South Africa work on what we have. Go and push Emilie to continue at speed to complete the rest." The phone disconnected. Sofia placed the receiver back and sat back in the chair, finally breathing out a sigh, with every muscle in her easing slightly from the wound up tension. She pulled her mobile phone from her jacket pocket, typed, 'Send her!' and pushed the send button.

CHAPTER FIFTEEN

Now

Maynard

The moment Maynard revealed to Heather that he'd confirmed the location facility where Emilie was being kept, she could feel her heartbeat quicken. The palpitations caused a surge of adrenaline throughout her body. This was the sign that she had been waiting for. Finally, her sacrifice and risk were starting to pay off. Maynard had worked with her all these months and they now had both Cameron and Emilie in their sights.

"You are absolutely sure that's the location of the research facility where Emilie is?" Heather's wide eyes were eager in their stare towards Maynard as they walked along the path around Hampstead Heath. It was early morning and Heather had bought them both coffees to sip as they spoke. There were a few scattered people around the park walking dogs and others undertaking their morning jogs. It was a clear morning so far, with the sky a beautiful shade of blue with the odd wisp of white clouds floating by. They approached the vantage point called Parliament Hill viewpoint, which was a summit at which one could view the skyscrapers and metal buildings of the city. Such buildings stood tall and distinctive, such as the Gherkin, the Shard and 'The Walkie-Talkie'. To the floor of the park was the Parliament Hill Athletics Track, with a local running club having a morning session.

Maynard blew into his coffee cup and took a small sip. "I'm certain. She will be monitored constantly and it will be extremely difficult to get at her. But I think my contact will be able to create an opening for you."

Heather was a couple of steps ahead of Maynard on the path, her nervous energy giving her that extra bounce that she struggled to contain. "Her research. I need to be able to get to her research."

Maynard stopped walking and only after a few paces did Heather realize he was standing still on the spot, looking at her. She turned and saw his gaze. "Are you OK? What's wrong?"

"Heather. This isn't just about the research. We must ensure Emilie is safe. She has a child. Cameron's child."

Heather let her mouth drop open, then closed it slowly and swallowed hard. Her throat was dry. "What? How? I don't understand."

Maynard moved a step closer to her. "She was pregnant when she was taken away from him." He reached inside his inner blazer pocket and pulled out a folded piece of paper and handed it to Heather. She took it without saying a word. "This is where Emilie is. It is a small area, just on the outskirts of Siena in Tuscany. When you arrive there, the contact I have will meet you and get you close to her. The rest is up to you. Remember – she will be watched at all times and..." He stopped talking and held his breath. He slowly exhaled and finished his sentence. "...Sofia may be there with the organisations keeping watch."

CHAPTER SIXTEEN

Now

Heather

The shaking just would not stop. Sitting on the floor, rocking with her knees folded into her chest and her hands shaking in front of her. Looking straight ahead at the wine bottle that sat on the table in the hotel room she was staying in while in Siena, Heather shook her head to get rid of the events that had just taken place. She had come here, under Maynard's trust, to speak with Emilie, to gain her trust, to find a way for her to be safe, to obtain her research and to protect the baby. That was far from what had occurred. She had managed to get into the complex and to gain entry to Emilie's private quarters. Heather thought she must have had the luck of the stars on her side that evening. But that was as far as the luck had shone on her. As she sat there, staring at the wine bottle with Emilie's handwriting on the side of the label, she remembered flashes of the last few hours. She could smell the smoke on her clothes, her hair; the black charcoal soot remnants on her fingertips like a scar, reminding her of what she had caused. She still struggled to think clearly of how the fire had started. It had seemed to come from nowhere, then the desperate cry of Emilie as she turned her back on Heather, running into the bedroom in the far end of the apartment. Screaming her child's name. There was a flash and the bright yellow heat glowed and raced towards Heather's face, like a swarm of locusts. She couldn't remember anything more until she woke up amongst burning debris in the room near the door leading out to the courtyard. Her head was sore from the fall to the ground and her bag was wrapped around her shoulder. She managed to pull herself up to her feet, but everything around her was in flames, burning to nothing but fragments of what was once Emilie's room, where they were confronting each other. It took her a moment to understand the reality that where Emilie had run to, she couldn't have survived.

She hurried back in panic to her hotel room to breathe and to think. It was only when she'd closed the door and collapsed on the floor next to the bed that she'd seen what was in her bag. She must have put it in there for some reason, but couldn't recall the exact moment she did it. She pulled out the red wine bottle that had a sentence written on the label, which she could only assume was in Emilie's handwriting. Perhaps this message was supposed to have reached Cameron by some other means? But now, it was in her possession.

How would she explain everything to Maynard on her return to London? Then it hit her like a bolt of lightning – the only chance at getting the research was lost. Only Cameron remained now, with his knowledge and secrets. That had to be the focus now. She had to be as cold and focused as she could possibly be.

PART THREE

CHAPTER ONE

Now

Heather

The little light present in the room was creating a ghoulish ambiance for Cameron and Sofia as they were hidden away here, high up within the Cathedral of Saint Paul. The patterns of decaying cement and crumbling bricks created shadows of faces, judging the contents and individuals that were present in the room. The whispers of confession and redemption over the years, passed over within these very walls. There, now, both Cameron and Sofia bore witnesses to them all and faced the consequences of the parts they must play.

Cameron repeated his question, this time more forcefully. "I said, who is coming for me, Sofia?"

"You have to trust me, Cameron. This will only work if you can totally put your faith and trust in me." She took a moment to find the words within herself to relay gently to Cameron what she had been planning all this time.

"The envelope I gave you; it does contain the true location of where Emilie and Siena are now. They are safe there, hidden, but…" she hesitated.

Cameron stared at her, his stance unwavering. When

she did not continue, he prompted her. "But what, exactly?"

"We don't have much time," Sofia sighed. "My father and Heather will be here at any moment." Sofia pulled her phone out from her pocket and glanced at the screen as she swiped to unlock it. "Look; I am sure Heather has told you she has Emilie and Siena safe and showed you the wine bottle as proof of this." Cameron nodded. Sofia continued, "Well, you know that isn't true, don't you?"

There was a sound, a faint sound, as faint as a feather falling against a window, but it was loud enough to startle them both in that confined space. The sound came from the dark mouth of the entrance to the room. It stood like the mouth of a beast, ready to devour anything that entered it. Just then, they both heard the delicate and aged voice of Maynard coming from beyond the opening.

Sofia turned to Cameron and said with urgency, in a hushed voice, "We don't have time; trust me, please."

From the dark mist, there was the glow from a torch, getting closer and closer into the room until they could see Maynard's shoe creeping through, slowly, so as not to disturb the ground beneath it.

Both Cameron and Sofia looked on as Maynard slowly appeared from the low, arched doorway and gradually uncurled his torso and straightened his back. Behind him was Heather, just appearing. As she took in her surroundings and her eyes became accustomed to the lighting in the room, she went to open her mouth to say something, but nothing came out. No words; just a faint gasp of a sound.

Sofia's face softened as she looked over at her father. Maynard smiled back at her. Cameron saw how his face had now started to regain some colour and life to it in the presence of his daughter. Sofia repaid the smile with a nod of her head and her eyes had an encapsulating warmth to them.

"Sofia!" Heather cried. But then, glancing between father and daughter, she frowned. Silence glowed and engulfed the room. She looked from Cameron's face back over to Sofia and then back to Cameron. "How?" she managed to say.

"All those years, Heather," Cameron broke the silence, "you always were good at keeping a poker face. But I never thought you would be the one to hurt me. To hurt Emilie."

Heather swallowed hard. Her mouth was as dry as sandpaper and it made the roof of it feel like the inside of the cave-like room they were in at present. "Cameron, don't believe them. Sofia isn't who you think she is. She would have twisted everything and told you only what you wanted to hear." Heather moved her gaze from Cameron to Maynard. "How did you…" but she was unable to finish her sentence.

Maynard, looking away from Heather and towards Sofia again, answered, "Heather, did you think you were the only one capable of deception and being able to plan things for your own gain? Did you really think I needed you to help protect me in London?"

Heather spoke to Cameron once again. Her voice with a slight tremble. "Don't believe them, Cameron. I know where Emilie is; she wanted me to get you to safety, to her. I have the bottle; you saw the wine bottle with her handwriting on. She told you to trust me." Her voice had a bleeding sorrow to it as she spoke.

"Heather," Cameron said in a low voice, "yes, the bottle was from Emilie. Indeed, it was her handwriting also.

However, when you showed me that bottle, it confirmed to me not to trust you at all."

Heather looked perplexed. "I don't understand," she stammered.

"Emilie and I joked about the wine bottles and how we could give secret meanings to them, that only she and I would know the true meaning of. At first, we would create images of keeping the wine bottles to hand down. To our children. Then we joked that we would open the bottles with friends or family, depending on our mood, and how we wanted each to be able to give good or bad meaning to the bottles, depending on the company." Cameron smiled slightly and chuckled to himself, followed by a pause for a moment to remain in that distant memory a while longer. "Then, Emilie had an idea that we could handwrite messages on the label of the bottles to confuse the meaning to others." He looked directly at Heather and asked, "Do you know what one of the hidden messages we joked about writing on the bottle was?" Heather just stared at him, waiting for him to reply to his own question. "You see, Heather, we *did* run in the hills and we *did* watch the sunrise. But," he stopped and took a deep breath to gain strength from this delicate memory, "it was in the West suites, not the East as the message read on the bottle you showed me. The hidden message we joked about was that the word 'west' would mean good or the truth, and the word 'east' would mean bad or a lie."

Heather stumbled back into the wall. "No, this cannot be. This is all wrong."

She looked past Cameron and over to them both. "You both worked against me! For how long? How long have you played me for a fool?"

Sofia stepped forward from the shadows and into a glimmer of light that was still pushing to get through into the room, to give some solace to them all. "Heather, you played a very dangerous game. How did you think you were going to get away with it? So many loose ends you have had to contend with. Surely you knew it would be impossible to cover all the angles?"

Heather looked dumbfounded. "No – Sofia, you're not going to twist the situation for your own benefit. I am in charge here, not you." She turned to Cameron. "You think you are so smart, don't you? You think you can keep your secrets from us all? It's a shame you will never get to tell your precious Emilie about your secrets either!"

Cameron felt for the envelope in his pocket. The one handed to him by Sofia. He needed to feel the attachment to Emilie as he moved to speak to Heather, but then he stopped and looked over to Sofia and Maynard. He needed to know for certain he could trust them. To gain some sort of reassurance from their facial expressions. "It's over, Heather. You are not in control anymore."

"Wrong… Cameron, I have been controlling your every move ever since you stepped foot in London. Without me, you would never have met Emilie."

Sofia sighed. "You were acting under the orders of the organisation, Heather. You were told of the task to make them meet. What made you turn rogue over time? What pushed you to put your*self* in danger?"

"How dare you question me, Sofia!" She looked over all three faces staring back at her. Their eyes were settled on her pale, ashen face. Her lips were pressed tight together with her teeth clenched. She spoke through the tension of her jaw. "You think you are the only ones who have suffered? You have no idea what real suffering is. All of you have had the opportunity and the means to follow your passion, your craft. To have an attachment to something, *to* someone. To your acts of self-indulgence!"

Cameron could see the slight tremor in Heather's tightly clenched fists. Her knuckles were white with pressure. He could tell the situation could escalate out of control at any moment. She noticed him studying her from the corner of her eye and remembered why she was there in the first place. She spat out the words to him. "Tell me the secrets you hold about the Mithras. Tell me!"

Sofia interrupted, "Why don't you tell Cameron how you *really* got the bottle of wine? Tell him what became of Emilie and his daughter."

"What did you do to them?" Cameron's voice was strong as he took a step closer to Heather, penning her in. She shuffled from one foot to the other, back against the wall.

"I was ordered to watch you, Cameron. To study you. To know you better than you even knew yourself. At first it was just surveillance, but the more I got to see who you were as a person, the more I craved interactions with you. Then, I had to plan the interaction with you and Emilie and watch how you both blossomed together."

"Tell me! What did you do to Emilie?" Cameron snarled.

Heather shook her head. "I worked for the same organisation as you all! So, I am not anything different from each one of you. You all enjoyed the money, the autonomy to follow your passions for your work. Why should I miss out on that? Why should I not have the opportunity to share in the secrets, in the power?"

She paused. Stood there, wide-eyed with hands trembling, sweat around her forehead and her damp shirt stuck to her back. Heather reached into her pocket to slowly pull out a small pistol; her painted fingernails curled around and caressed the trigger.

Heather pointed the pistol at no-one in particular, but in the general direction of all three of them. None of them moved or seemed fazed. There was stillness to the room.

"This is a mistake, Heather; you don't want to do this. There is no way out for you if you continue down this path." Cameron was the first to speak, while trying to edge slowly towards Heather and place himself between the cold metal of the pistol and the others.

"That's far enough, Cameron. Stay there. You have no idea how long I have waited for this day. To have all three of you in my sights and not needing to live a lie any longer." Heather rubbed her eyes with her left hand and flicked away a drop of sweat that was gathering on her temple while she continued to hold the pistol, firmly, in her right. She focused on Cameron.

"You have to understand, Cameron. It was an accident. I just went to speak with her and to convince her to share her work with me."

Cameron tilted his head. "What did you do to Emilie?"

Heather's eyes flickered under his direct gaze. His face was full of heat, rising from within him. His eyes were as wide as black holes, raking over her.

Heather's hand started to shake, moving the pistol in a haphazard manner. "I just went to speak with her; you have to understand that, Cameron. They were both there."

Cameron felt unbalanced standing there and the room started caving in on him. He went to open his mouth, but before he could, he felt Sofia move to his side and speak. "Heather. Put the gun down now. You don't want to do something you'll regret now, do you?"

Cameron went to step forward; Sofia grabbed him by his right arm, but he shrugged her off. Heather pointed the gun directly at Cameron. "Stop walking towards me, Cameron. Please stop. Please, I beg you." Tears flooded Heather's eyes, her vision became blurry, her mouth dry and heart pounding so forcefully and rapid.

Maynard cried out from the back of the room, "No!" There was a flash of light, a deafening sound. It echoed around the walls, bouncing like a ball on the playing field, lively and confident. Cameron fell to the floor, onto his knees. It took him a few seconds to become familiar with the floor so close to his face. His ears ringing with high-pitched tinnitus. As he blinked, over and over, the dust and debris slowly cleared from his eyes, clearing his vision. He breathed in deeply, then blew out and felt his breath on the back of his hands. He looked up toward the arched doorway where Heather was. The ringing in his ears made his concentration difficult. His vision was hazy and it was difficult to focus. He looked perplexed to find her slumped against the wall with a warm, dignified, rich red spreading from underneath her shirt, covering her chest. Her arms were resting beside her and no longer holding the gun. Her hands not clenched, but open and welcoming like a friend offering a sign of comfort and safety. Her lips were no longer trembling. Her breath was no longer momentarily halted, but permanently.

CHAPTER TWO

Cameron

Cameron looked on with shock. Frozen to the spot, for a moment not registering Sofia or Maynard's presence. Sitting on the floor in front of him was the still body of Heather. The woman whom he'd thought he had known for years. The woman whom, only some hours ago, he'd phoned to ask for guidance and support at a time in need. Cameron's mind refused to understand what he was seeing. What he had just witnessed. He was expecting any minute now to have Heather stand and explain that she had just been resting.

How have things got so bad? he thought to himself. Then, the slight whimpering of Sofia grabbed his attention and he looked over to see her huddled into her father. Cameron rose from the floor and walked slowly over to Heather. His legs powerless and to be dragged with effort. He knelt beside her limp body, rubbed his face with his hands and then reached over to touch her face, but hesitated. He recoiled his fingers and then rubbed them over her open eyelids to close them. He knew they must leave now. He was aware that each one of them now would be a suspect for murder. He was also aware that Sofia would now have to live with her act of sacrifice for the rest of her life.

"We have to get out of here," Cameron said, while still focused on Heather. There was nothing from either Sofia or Maynard. Only the soft sobbing sounds coming from behind Cameron could be heard. Cameron stood and turned. "Sofia!" His voice was strong and direct. It startled her. She turned slowly toward Cameron, staying in her father's embrace. Her breath was catching, her eyes now red and raw and tight, fighting to stay open. She focused on Cameron, consciously avoiding looking down to Heather.

"I will take care of this. You both need to go. Now." Sofia directed Maynard and Cameron, her voice quivering.

Maynard placed a hand on her shoulder. "Sofia, we need to get you to safety right now."

Sofia closed her eyes. "No, Papa. I have to settle this. There was never going to be any other way. Please, both of you; go now."

Cameron and Maynard both knew that she would have the organisations come and attend to it and no doubt this would take her deeper within them – and their trust in her would be further enhanced by this.

Cameron looked over to Maynard. "We need to leave."

Maynard followed Cameron to the exit of the room. He turned and looked at Sofia. "Be strong, my dear."

"Papa," Sofia responded, "I will make contact once I am sure the organisations are satisfied with what I tell them about Cameron's knowledge." She rubbed her eyes and pulled her hair back from her face and spoke to Cameron. "Take the car and drive to London City Airport. They will be tracking it. I will message you what flight to get on once I know."

Cameron was about to say something in return and

Sofia interrupted, "Keep the envelope with you. Now both of you go!"

CHAPTER THREE

Sofia

Sofia was left alone in the room. The eerie, spectral feeling surrounding her. "I'm so sorry," she whispered to Heather's lifeless body. Deep down, this sorry was meant for more than just Heather; also for herself, for Maynard, for Cameron, for Emilie and for Siena. She pulled her phone out and dialled. There was no voice, just silence, but she knew there was someone on the other end, and she spoke. "There has been a complication. Heather. I had to take her out. She was a risk and was going to destabilize Cameron." She swallowed hard. The faint noise of a breath on the other end of the phone could be heard. She continued. "Cameron will go to Santorini now. He will go there under the impression that he is meeting Emilie. He did not reveal anything here and after witnessing Heather's demise, I had no choice but to tempt him with the hope of meeting Emilie so he would tell us his knowledge on his arrival." There was a sigh on the other end. Then the voice sounded low, calm in demeanour.

"The body will be taken care of." A short silence again. Sofia could hear the faint ticking of a clock in the background. Then the voice again. "He must tell us before he realizes Emilie is no longer alive and I assume the child has not been found yet? We must hope she is also dead." The voice was cold and devoid of emotion. "If he refuses upon his arrival in Santorini to explain what he knows, we have no further use for him. His fate needs to follow Heather's. Go and do what needs to be done. Be sure of this." The phone cut off.

Sofia felt a wave of nausea through the pit of her stomach. Her legs buckled beneath her. The phone falling to the floor and coming to rest at Heather's foot. Sofia let her hands fall to the dirt floor in front of her. Her eyes flooded with tears. Pain coursed through every cell within her. She looked up and ahead at the pale face of Heather. Sofia's scream reverberated around the room.

CHAPTER FOUR

One Week Later

Cameron

The sun had a lazy feel to it as it tried to retire for the evening, though it gave the feel of an endearing, welcoming atmosphere. The type of feeling that no-one can, at that moment, upset any aspect of your life. This was no ordinary sunset. The world's greatest sunsets occur on the island of Santorini, the Greek island of volcanic remnants that have carved out romance to this part of the world. The town of Oia is placed delicately on a sloping cliff face on the northern tip of Santorini, with a vantage view of the volcanoes of Palea and Nea Kameni, looking over the vast, deep and unforgiving chasm of the Aegean Sea, which joins its big sister, the Mediterranean.

A solitary boat was present in the distance, on a journey to find meaning, perhaps. Cameron sat on the cliff face, watching the boat. How this visual focus brought back memories from what seemed like a lifetime ago. Once he'd sat alongside her, watching the same sunset, whispering to the same clouds that enveloped them both. Now it seemed they were just feelings of foolishness and both their lives were left to chance. That chance had ended on the road here. What awaited this new discovery? The question was both confusing and clear in Cameron's mind. How deeply he wished to meet with Emilie's eyes again in such a sunset. How he wanted to embrace her once again and feel her skin on his. Time has passed, many sunsets have gone to bed and many solitary boats have gone on to search for their meanings. *What has become of Emilie?* he wonders.

Cameron held an envelope in his hand – the very same envelope given to him back in London, at the start of his quest. Moments later, he was told by Sofia that the contents of that envelope contained information relating to Emilie. A handcrafted, delicate card lay inside. The edge had a hand painted navy border and, within the centre of the card with black ink in italic writing, with a slight slant to the text, were the words: *'Oia 1800'*.

He recalled that the trip here all those years ago with Emilie was special, but he did not realize she'd held it in her heart so dearly as to return. Yet now, it was with their child, Siena, a new soul who was as much Cameron's as she was Emilie's. Cameron wondered of the marvel of Siena. What would her eyes reflect when she looked into the sunset? Did she have Cameron's dark hair, with the same softness of velvet as Emilie's? Did Siena even know of Cameron? All these questions and more burned inside his mind, but one above all had haunted his thinking since that moment he'd met Sofia in South Bank back in London – why did Emilie leave and disappear without a trace? Why did she not trust him enough to tell him back then, so he could have helped all three of them at that moment?

He became conscious of the day moving on. He got up to head deeper into the nestling cliff face houses and apartments that made the picture-postcard village the envy of the world. The white faces of the buildings with domed tops had the occasional distinctive, deep blue colour to them and the cobbled streets with uneven surfaces were beneath Cameron's smart shoes. Although not the best choice of footwear for this terrain, it was Cameron all over, always elegant and well groomed – how she would remember him. Prestige twin monk strap shoes in oxblood. The dust of the streets and hillsides gathered on the surfaces and sides of the shoes to create a worn look. The micro 'fleck' detailed cloth of his navy trousers created an understated yet creative look, with mother-of-pearl buttons for the pocket on the rear adding a luxurious finish. To complement the trousers, he wore a sky blue cutaway collared shirt, crafted in printed cotton. The bold print pattern was a single colour print in an abstract floral design, which fitted in perfectly with the setting of a sunset evening in Santorini.

In his hand, he held the jacket that still had her grip interwoven into it from when she'd handed it to him on that fateful day of their goodbye. He did not realize until now that he had been holding the jacket so tightly that his knuckles ached from the hold, his palm sweaty.

As he navigated the winding, cobbled streets of Oia, the evening population descended onto the streets for the sunset romance and a night full of laughter, food, wine and contentment. It had a mixture of tourists and locals, both from the island of Santorini and the neighbouring Greek islands. Cameron walked along a busy street market covered with vibrant colours of fabrics and glassware for sale celebrating the island, which was very familiar to him. He traced his very steps, which now seemed to have occurred a distant lifetime ago with Emilie. This very street where they'd held hands together and negotiated the local sellers, all of whom were commenting on her beauty and how the colour of the fabrics they had would add to the elegance of her aura. Cameron could not help but smile at these memories and he almost reached for the cloth hanging from the stalls on either side of this street, which was so full of whispers of the past.

As the evening set in and the sun made its way for its finale before it disappeared for yet another day, Cameron arrived at his reservation at one of the historical mansions of Oia. Built in 1845, the mansion now hosted the restaurant called Oia 1800. This mansion was the home of influential sea captains in times long past. The building, now restored, housed one of the best restaurants in the town. This was where Emilie and Cameron had once sat to have dinner and watch the sunset while hiding from all the eyes watching them. Cameron walked through the gates; the mansion had a grand living room, with original furniture that had been restored over time. He was all too familiar with the works of art and history that lay before his eyes. Antique Santorinian sofas made from walnut wood and a Venetian bed with a hand painted baldachin that had been transported by ship from Russia by the captain to live in this grand mansion.

"Good evening, Sir; beautiful artefacts, are they not?" A young, smartly dressed gentleman greeted him with a European twist to his accent. "Will you be dining with us this evening or are you here just for drinks?"

"Dinner, please, and on the roof terrace. I have a reservation and will be meeting someone. You will have the reservation under the name of Cameron Hope."

The young man lowered his eyes and shuffled through the papers on his clipboard. "Ah, yes, Sir, you have the best table to view the sunset. Please follow me up the stairs. You are from UK, yes? I can tell from your speaking."

Cameron remembered how everyone was so polite in Santorini; always so glad to help in some way and to show appreciation of the time the visiting tourists gave them. Many of the staff came over from mainland Greece to work in Santorini for the tourist season.

The roof terrace was busy with diners in the evening, as always. A quick scan of the tables and Cameron could tell the majority were tourists with their phone cameras at the ready, for the views of the caldera and the volcano bathed in the evening fiery sun. Everyone was dressed in evening spring attire, pastel colours and flowery flowing dresses. Glasses of wine floated everywhere on the tables, amongst couples having romantic pictures taken with the horizon as a backdrop.

As Cameron took his seat, he couldn't help but acknowledge the sense of apprehension that rested within. He could feel the hairs on the back of his neck standing to attention. All the years of training and work he had undertaken and yet this feeling had arisen due to Emilie. The fog still clouded his mind, with his memories of the last day he saw her and the hours, days, weeks, months and year that had followed. Sitting there, listening to the laughter of people around him and feeling the happiness of strangers, Cameron felt he needed to suppress the resentment of the time lost that would never be recovered.

"Excuse me; may I get some still water, please? No ice." Cameron got the attention of a waiter nearby.

At that very moment, he spotted a woman's gaze fixed

on him. A strikingly attractive woman with hair flowing just below her shoulders, dark brown in colour with slight curls. Her pale, flawless skin looked so smooth. Wearing thin linen trousers, white in colour with an irregular striped pattern. High heels that were covered by the large flare of the trousers. She was a woman with a seductive presence, carrying a shoulder bag in her hand. A sky-blue, off-the-shoulder shirt detailed how defined her body was. Her green eyes reflected every aspect of her surroundings. They were like the sea that surrounded the island, vast and deep in nature, with passion and danger, yet with an invitation of calmness.

"The infamous Cameron Hope." She spoke with an eloquent British accent. At that moment, a waiter rushed over to pull her seat out. Cameron couldn't help but notice her alluring manner – not just her physical beauty, but how she moved, her presence, her pose and her demeanour.

"I take it you are my guest this evening; or should I say, I am *your* guest? May I have the pleasure of your name? Sofia did not mention any details when she told me to be here."

She smiled at this, took Cameron's hand across the table and felt his palm. "I have always wanted to feel the hands of someone who has touched so much history of mankind. Friday is my name."

Cameron pulled his hand away, recognizing that she may not be there on friendly terms, which further heightened his awareness of anxiety.

"You obviously know what this place means to me; I do hope you have some meaningful information to give me."

"Cameron, we have the whole evening ahead of us with one of the best backdrops for sunsets around the world –

let's not be too enthusiastic about wishing the time away now. Dinner and wine seem like a needed requirement, do you not agree?" With that, she nodded to the waiter to attend the table. "A bottle of your Vinsanto, please."

"I am in no mood for pleasantries. It's been a long road to get to this point. I suspect you are aware of who I seek." The longer this exchange took place, the more Cameron's thoughts sank deeper into concern that this was still the beginning of something that may or may not have an end.

"Look, Cameron, I am on your side here. Who do you think has looked out for and kept your girls safe while you have been primed for all this? Do you think this was all an accident, all a strange collection of random events? You may need some wine for what I am about to reveal to you." The waiter returned and showed Cameron the wine bottle. Cameron took hold of the bottle, poured two glasses and waved the waiter away, never once breaking the gaze of the woman before him.

"We have wine – now speak. Explain what needs explaining."

She smiled coyly and replied, "For centuries, as you know, the human species has relied on one aspect to get them to survive and to continue to excel in whatever they are trying to ascertain, before each of us reaches the end. One cardinal rule and belief is central to all this – faith. Be it blind faith, misguided faith or faith in the unknown. With this comes a human emotion to create the terror that is within us all – fear. Fear of failure, fear of success, fear of disappointment or fear of happiness. We find it easier to put all our fears onto others, to project them into other's eyes and actions, rather than hold them within us and to navigate them with our own strength."

She held his gaze and reached for her glass, the wine rich and deep in colour, smooth and inviting. She studied Cameron's reaction. He moved forward in his seat, reached for her hand on the table and took her by the wrist.

"You speak of fear and you speak of faith in the same breath. People like you pray on others' weaknesses. You infest and contaminate this world. The notion of your so-called bullshit, noble cause to promote and keep this so-called faith and belief in people is nothing but another futile attempt to have power and control. But you underestimate the true power of the human faith. You underestimate the true resolve and endurance of willpower. You will never comprehend the starving mother who will do anything for her child who only has his bare bones and torn skin to keep him warm at night. This is something you cannot steal, this is something you cannot take and this is something you cannot hide, even with all your conspiracy stories and layers of deluded theories. You can make all the threats you want, but you will never win this."

Cameron's knuckles were turning white, with his grip tightening around her wrist. She sipped the wine, seeming totally unmoved by his words. She put the glass down slowly on the table, placed her fingers over his and gradually picked his grip loose, with a touch that was both soft and endearing.

"Cameron, you and I, along with every living being on this planet, would not have any faith left if we were not to protect the burden unleashed on us. The burden that you carried all these years and the sacrifice you and your family are now making."

Those words – 'your family' – startled Cameron. At that moment, he felt he was transfixed in a dream, in a make-believe play on stage and he had forgotten his words, his lines. She smiled and moved back in her seat.

"I see these words have got your attention now. 'Family' – the cornerstone and foundation of humanity, some may say. After all, we both are sitting here because at some stage, two people decided to have a family."

"Tell me – your name, Friday – named after the day you were born? Or was it the day you decided to turn into what you are today – a deluded woman?" Cameron spoke through gritted teeth.

"We all have a past, dear Cameron, and sometimes that carries us to where the journey was supposed to take us and, at other times, it is a path that makes us blind. In my case, my name, Friday, is a clear meaning of what my path has been in life. My story is not your concern. My name; some hold it to its Latin origins, of *Dies Veneris* or *Day of Venus*. Others use my name in the literal sense – from the Greek meaning, *to prepare*. That is all I do Cameron; I prepare others for what they are about to uncover."

"Prepare me for what?"

"All is never what it seems it is, Cameron."

Cameron picked his wine glass up and took a long sip before replying, "Tell me something I don't know."

"You will meet her, soon – you just need to know in what capacity and why you are here to meet her. The danger is far from over; the story has just begun. This is what you need to come to terms with, Cameron. They will not stop; they are relentless in their quest for what we have so desperately been trying to protect."

"May I ask a question, Miss?" Cameron's tone was sarcastic, like a schoolboy wondering if he could leave the classroom to visit the bathroom. "Can you give me one good reason not to cut your throat right now and walk away from this table? After all, the card telling me of this restaurant was handed to me by Sofia who is, how can we put it, a murderer. Which, by the powers of intelligence, tells me you both are in contact and on the same team. So, what makes you both any different from the very organisation hunting us?"

"Has it ever occurred to you that perhaps, just maybe, we are the good guys? Moles are everywhere – the good use them just like the bad do. Take, for example, Heather… but on that note, my dearest Cameron, the organisation is taking one last chance at asking you now – tell them what you know, what you have discovered as the key to the Mithras and they will let Emilie and Siena go free."

Cameron sat back. "I came here without fear or needing to know if I have anything to lose. All this time that Emilie has been missing. All this time the organisations have tried to get me to falter and reveal my discovery. They tried to kill Maynard and I was the only one left able to solve the puzzle – to help, while pressure was put on Emilie to complete her research. I came here for Emilie and Siena, guided by Sofia. I can now see this was all designed to find out what I know. There is no end to this."

"End it then, Cameron. Tell me what you know. Give me the answers and we can end it right here and now." Cameron rose to his feet. "Friday, you all can go to hell. You were never going to let me see Emilie. She could be dead by now, for all I know. Heather certainly thought she was. You wanted me here to create the illusion of a chance. You will get nothing from me!"

"Well, in that case, there is no reason for this to continue – is there, Cameron?" She looked over past Cameron's shoulder and gave a nod. A shadow descended over the white cloth of the table; Cameron made an effort to turn around to see the cause of this, but at that moment he felt a mighty blow to his head and everything went dark, just as he started making out the eyes of Sofia looking back at him.

CHAPTER FIVE

Now

"Wake up, my dear. Wake up, my love. You are missing the amazing sky that hovers above us." The sweet whisper. That soft, delicate breath on the skin. The words lingered in the air as they floated like a dream to infiltrate the mind. "Wake up, my love. Let me see those eyes. Those caring, deep eyes that hold a million troubles. Those eyes that keep me warm in the wildest storm. Wake up, my love."

Cameron lays there on the cold floor. He heard the distant voice, unsure whether it was reality or within his own mind. It was difficult to decipher from all the surroundings that he was exposed to. Was it a voice he remembered? The voice once again – "Wake up." Yes, he recognized it. The voice he'd heard from a time long since passed. A voice so familiar to him. The voice that kept him on a good path that had taught him humility. The voice that had guided him to a better him. It was a voice that he had not heard in so long and a voice that he hadn't been sure he would hear again. Now, he struggled to be sure that this was in fact reality or if it was a mix of previous emotions caught within a desperate plea for him to survive whatever this was.

The cold surface he lay on was wet. He could feel liquid

trickling into his mouth and around his lips. It had a warm temperature to it. A taste on his cracked, dry lips of a warm, iron-based metallic liquid – blood. Did that instill panic and a desperate effort in him to move, to acknowledge if this was real by opening his eyes? No. He felt calm. He felt at peace. What drove him was the voice. The breath he felt just above his ear. The touch he could now feel. A hand. Soft skin, fingernails smooth on the surface. He could feel the stroke of the hand on his forehead. How he wanted to open his eyes, yet in the same thought he didn't want this perceived fantasy to come to an end. Would he wake from a dream if he tried to open his eyes? How did he get to this place? Was it his blood he felt on his lips? An effort to move his legs; yes, they worked. He dared to initiate a word, to speak. A futile effort – the same hand on his head moved to his lips. "Shhh, save your strength, my dear. You do not need to worry yourself with questions at this moment." Again, that voice. The voice he wanted to have wrapped around him for eternity. A voice that had no place on this cold, stone floor. A voice that begged for a different setting and stage. The words were comforting to his ears. Cameron searched for the memory of this voice. It came to him in a haze of mist around his thoughts. He then came to realize the intense pain that was buried deep within his head. The more his senses became aware of this, the more intense the pain became. Was the source of the blood from his head? Certainly, that would explain the pain he was now being subjected to. A sharp, intense pain radiated through his skull, penetrating in nature like a sharp metal rod had been placed deep within his scalp, turning slowly and winding deeper into his skull. *Back to the voice,* he tells himself, *do not lose this train of thought; block out the pain, Cameron. Block it out like your life depends on it.*

The ringing in his ears came and went and was surrounded by the deafness of what he could only recognize as a halo echoing in a large room. His memory started returning in broken fragments. A fall: no, definitely a push – he recalls a push, a struggle and a flash. Was it the sunlight, perhaps? A bolt of lightning? He's unsure. He struggled to open his eyes. The brush of hair tickled his outstretched arm as he lay on the floor. The smell of lavender in the air; it was coming in waves and he could feel the breeze it travelled on. Reminiscent of the lavender hills he'd once got lost and immersed in at Sénanque Abbey in Provence, France. He recalled the spectacular abbey where the monks grew lavender and where, as the sun came down over the vast fields of purple, it had the illusion of a spectacular light laser show on the floor. He remembered the walks through the fields, the staining on his cotton trousers from the buds. The laughter and the voice of happiness. That voice! The same voice that came to his attention now. The very one that caused him to try to stir and move there on the floor once more.

"Cameron, please don't move. You are bleeding, but you will be fine. I promise. This may hurt; I am going to apply some pressure on the wound. Please don't try and move and don't speak – save your energy, my dear."

That same voice: he struggled with his own mind and consciousness, aware that he was unable to place where he was or who that person was. This softly spoken, gentle woman. "I need to stem the bleeding, Cameron." There was a calm, controlled manner to her speech. Cameron felt pathetic, lying there, unable to respond to her and to say what he wanted, to reach out and feel this real person. In the distance, almost too faint to make out, being drowned by the persistent ringing in his ears, was the sound of bells tolling away. Birds were chirping, indicating a warning signal to others around them. Could he also hear water? The sea? A lake? No, definitely more powerful than a lake. The ocean, Cameron decided. That would explain the breeze he felt on his face, fresh and with purpose. A slap in the face of – get up and get going now! Back to the here and now, Cameron recalled the word 'bleeding'. The taste – it *was* blood; his own, he was certain now. Still confused as to what had occurred, but this voice obviously belonged to someone who could be trusted, someone to help carry him through this.

Why did that pale blue colour come to Cameron's mind at this moment? Was it the sky he could picture, as that was the last thing he saw? No, he remembered and started to try to move his arm on the cold floor's surface. A church. A blue domed structure, with bells. The faint sound of the bells he could hear now. He was lying on the floor of a church. Whitewashed walls, cold and calming to the eye, but blinding in the sunlight. It was all coming back to him now as he lay in a pool of his own blood swimming around his head. But whom did this voice belong to?

Piercing pain shot through his head; he groaned and the energy of the disturbance caused Cameron to open his eyes slightly. His lashes fluttered as he tried to adjust to the surroundings. Was this the white tunnel experience that had been used time and time again by countless people when describing a near-death experience? He found it difficult to navigate the spectrums of light, blurring what he thought was the ground, halos all around him, uncertain if he was seeing light or reflections from within his own mind. As his sense of vision slowly returned, he saw movement in the corner of his eye. Unaware at this moment as to who or what this movement was, he tried to manoeuvre his head slightly to get a better glance. There was that voice once more.

"It will be over soon. They are coming for you. You will be safe now. No more running. Just hold on a few more minutes; I know it hurts."

He could feel his pulse in his neck rising to a beat that was strong. Suddenly, the voice was no longer that of a stranger. The breeze no longer created the sensation of mystery as to the location of where he was. A breeze that he was now familiar with as he had been here before. The blue colour was now bright in his memory of the domes he'd once admired, standing against the backdrop of the most stunning, arching, vast fields of clear blue sky. The bells he could hear trying to sing in the whispers of the wind, the birds that mocked the people sitting by the wide waters that rested just beyond the courtyard below the hill. The voice that put all this setting into place. The touch that he remembered from all those years ago, which gave him a sense of belonging. Emilie.

"How..." He struggled to get the words out, to put his thoughts into coherent sentences. Then a sudden reminder of the intense pain on the side of his head. Was it a hot poker or was his head in a vice of some sort? All he knew was that he couldn't stand the pain, but felt powerless to act upon it. His eyesight was still blurry and trying to fully adjust to the environment and kaleidoscope of colours. Even the stony floor seemed as bright as the sun to him at present. He could hear the voice, but again, it was difficult to clearly differentiate the words. That touch again, across his lips and eyes. The soft fingers. "Shhh, rest and save your energy." A white cloth obscured what little he could see for a few moments. He was aware his head was being lifted slightly and then could see the cloth under his face. A buffer between the floor and him. Yes, he felt a sense of power was regained as he could make out this simple fact. *Must open eyes and speak.*

"If you can hear me, my dear, and I am sure you can, please listen carefully. I hope you remember what I say as we don't have much time." Cameron was sure those were the words he'd just heard. Determined to believe they were real words, rather than his imagination playing tricks on him.

"Remember when we came here; remember those warm evening sunsets. We would talk about nothing and yet discuss everything. You told me that was the very moment you fell in love with me – the moment we looked over the Aegean Sea. How I wished at that moment I could have run from you. I let my false sense of security trick me into believing I could have a normal life with you, Cameron. It was going to be just us in our bubble, against the world."

Cameron felt a drop of wetness fall on his forehead, light and delicate. A tear, Emilie's tear. He felt powerless being unable to comfort her, to tell her to stop and that everything would be OK. But he knew that was just a set of false hopes.

"The clouds that evening, Cameron, how they drifted over our heads. The thin whisper of clouds high in the mountains. That evening we went on a quest to find that restaurant. Do you remember the name? Of course you don't! You never remembered details. Metaximas. We ate nearly everything on the menu while a cat waited for us to feed it scraps of food from our table. The most tender roasted lamb shank, ever. The aubergines were lightly grilled and had feta cheese laid on the top. We were lost in the dinner, in our world. The temperature dropped dramatically as we sat outside, the night drawing near. You had red wine, as always, and were conscious only to have one glass as you were driving us back to the hotel." Cameron heard the sounds of a chuckle. "Ha! Remember the drive back? The parked car's wing mirror you hit with our car! You kept driving on, oblivious, and it was only when I voiced it that we stopped to tape our mirror back so that the rental people wouldn't notice! They *did* notice, by the way, and you owe me the deposit they took for it!"

The words, Cameron could hear. Words that painted a story; a story that was lived in the past, but which was clear in his mind like it happened only yesterday.

Another bolt of pain to the head as he felt pressure on the side; the cloth he sensed being pressed there again to stem the flow of his own blood.

"Do you remember what I said, darling? I said I never wanted this dream to end. You ignored my words. Well, that is what I thought at the time. We drove back toward the hotel that night after dinner. The dark roads, windy and deserted at the time. We followed the west coast road back towards the town of Oia, as we knew we would recognize where the hotel was on our way. We spotted the grand, blue domed architecture and the bell tower. We sat in the courtyard of that church watching the deep, calm, mysterious Aegean Sea for hours, in silence. You turned to me and said 'This is our dream. This is our safe spot. This is us'. That moment, like this – now, here – at the same spot, the same courtyard; the Anastasis Church in Oia."

"You came for me, Cameron. You came. But I am not what you needed to come for. You need to know and to understand what this was all about. You need to see that your path here was not an accident. Our story was not made by chance. Siena – she is the one that needs protecting. She holds the key, the secrets. What you will hear from me now is where this all has been leading."

Cameron's pupils dilated; his neurons fired upon hearing the revelations Emilie was telling him. Siena. Their daughter. The person he yet still needed to hold, to tell stories to and to keep safe. Emilie placed her soft hands on his forehead, fingers interlinked through his hair. The sound... the ringing continued. He tried to scream to make the deafening noise stop. It reached a peak; he was unsure if it was in his head or surrounding him. He found the strength to open his eyes. Gradually, weak eyelids, heavy like the stone he lay on. He could just make out a halo of a person walking in the distance, away from him. The legs, the white dress floating like the sheets he remembered in the bazaar in the streets of Oia. The hair lying gracefully on her shoulders and back. *Turn back, don't leave.* Then darkness and silence. The ringing ends as Emilie walked away.

CHAPTER SIX

Now

A television glowed in the far end of the room. It must have been muted as Cameron was unable to hear anything from it. As he adjusted his eyes to the brightness of the television, he could make out a news programme playing. He blinked a few times to remove the blurring of the tears sitting in his eyes, to focus on a smartly dressed news presenter with a blue tie and white shirt, who sat behind a desk speaking. Across the bottom of the screen, Cameron read the text: 'BBC Breaking News. Local outbreak of virus in village in China kills hundreds in days.' Cameron blinked once more as his eyes went out of focus again to adjust to the opposite side of the room. He took time to focus on a figure in the corner of the room. He could see the familiar frame of a woman standing, looking away from him out of the window to the day outside.

"Sofia, where is she? Emilie?" His voice was harsh and breaking in sound. He felt razors in his throat as he spoke. His tongue was swollen and dry like concrete.

"Hey, there you are; I didn't think you would be awake until later. How is the pain? Stupid question, I know." Sofia turned slowly and gently walked over to the bed. "I am so glad you are OK; well, as OK as you *could* be, of course."

It was difficult for Cameron to think straight. Certain flashbacks of the last few memories came and went in his mind like a French Renaissance film noir. He shuffled to sit up slightly in the hospital bed, but a machine bleeped at his side as he moved. Then the pain of a memory from before he'd ended up in that bed. "Sofia, my daughter, Siena – I will not get to see her, will I?" Cameron could tell of Sofia's uneasiness as he spoke.

At that moment, he understood that she had known for a long time that this would be the outcome. That Siena would not be able to meet her father – he would never be able to tell stories or be there for her homework or do any other normal fatherly activities he so wished he could do. He was stripped of the one pure thing he had always craved for. To provide belonging.

"What was all this about, Sofia? You knew, didn't you? Why did you let me find Emilie if you knew we couldn't be together? If I had no chance of holding my daughter? Why, Sofia?" Straining his voice, it came out with great effort.

Sofia looked past him as she spoke. "We... we had no other means or ways to be sure. There was just no other way around it, Cameron. Believe me, we tried – we looked at every angle we could, but there was just no other way we could guarantee that this would succeed. We all lost important aspects of ourselves in this and we all risked a great number of personal things."

She glanced back at Cameron at that moment.

"When Emilie told me she was pregnant, it was an unexpected turn and a complication." Sofia bit her lip at the realization of the poor choice of words. "I'm sorry... not a complication – that's the wrong choice of words – just something we hadn't factored into our planning."

Another bleeping sound from one of the monitors threatened to divert the concentration on Cameron's face. But he did not alter his resolve, to focus on Sofia.

"We had to make sure we altered our thinking – not only to protect Emilie, but Siena too, for the future. And, as much as you will hate us for doing this, we then also had another way to ensure you would help us. To use Siena as leverage."

"I can understand you using my daughter to get me to do what you needed. I would have done the same in your shoes. But never did I think Siena would be part of a bigger plan with you. You kept that from the organisations; you shielded Siena from Heather, too. This has all become about her now!"

Sofia sighed. "It became the perfect plan without anyone knowing. Siena made you more determined in your task. It made you more focused, hungrier. We needed to protect Emilie – not only for her to complete her work and for you to gain trust in us, but we also knew Siena needed to be hidden from the world, from the organisations, as she–"

Cameron finished Sofia's sentence for her, "She will now carry on and complete the work that both her mother and father started. Siena carries the secrets of both. That's why her identity cannot be known, that's why I will never meet her and that's why she will never know her true father." He turned toward his pillow, looking away from Sofia.

"I am sorry, Cameron. It has given us another way to protect everything for humanity, and Siena, with time, with the right learning and teaching, will be able to have your discoveries and Emilie's work completed. She will be able to truly save us from ourselves."

"They will never stop hunting us, Sofia; they will find out

about Siena. Look at how powerful they are. Look at what they've done to me!" Sofia turned away from Cameron; she took a few steps as if to leave the room. Then the pain returned to Cameron. The pain of the memories. They echoed loud in his head like a drum beating, repeatedly. "They didn't do this, did they? *You* did! You were there, at the restaurant!"

Sofia sighed. "It was the only way. Just like they now think my father is no more – he can stay hidden and carry on with his life in the shadows. We have done the same with you. They needed to think I had killed you. It took all this time, all these years to be able to get to the point where they would be satisfied with the narrative that I had created for them. That I had learnt all I could get from you and that my hatred and anger towards you were enough to drive me to kill you. And we succeeded. You may have escaped near death by me, but it was all calculated. They needed to see you fall, to see you die. But only with careful precision could we keep you alive. The woman you met, Friday, is totally trusted by the organisations, but she is on our side too. We have worked together for all these years and, in time, we will take them down from within. She has helped with you and my father."

"And you? I suppose you want me to believe that the organisations are just going to let you walk away from them, just like that?"

"I have proved my loyalty to them – over my father, over you and over Emilie. I delivered what I was charged to do. I am not a fool, Cameron; I know they will keep eyes on me forever. That's the price I have paid for this. But I also know that the time will come when we are once again strong enough to bring them all down. But now is not that time. Now we all need to go into the dark. Become shadows."

"And where is Emilie? What becomes of her?"

"She is safe, for now. With the organisations thinking you are dead, the link and answer to her work is now missing in you. There is no reason, at present, for them to focus any longer on Emilie's research. They have a defective copy of her work that she was clever enough to alter. And thanks to Heather's own selfish demise, she provided the perfect opportunity to get Emilie and Siena away from the eyes of the organisation."

Silence followed. Cameron shifted his head on the pillow. The bandage was causing him to itch again.

"So, they think all the individuals who could have an answer to all this are now dead? Is that what you are telling me?" Cameron managed to say eventually.

"Yes, Cameron. They were worried that Emilie's research and your discoveries would one day come out into the open and destroy them and everything they stood for. Now, with you both gone, they feel that is not a possibility. But..." she paused again.

"What?" Cameron tried to raise his voice but lacked the strength to get it to its true volume.

"They are using Emilie's defective work to experiment with and to try to complete it. This is causing more concerns and issues for us all, but they see it as an acceptable risk and collateral damage." She turned her head to the television in the corner, which was still showing the news about the virus, and Cameron followed her line of vision, immediately understanding what she meant.

With that, he closed his eyes and muttered, "No."

The light faded outside the window as a cloud moved

across the sky, covering the sun like a blanket. Cameron turned his head away from Sofia and the television. He felt torn, hurt and even betrayed. Not by anyone but himself. Thinking that he was one step ahead of everyone and would get to be with Emilie and Siena – yet all along, he was the one who was being pulled along in this game. He thought to himself, *How could I have been so blind, so foolish?*

"Who will ensure her safety? Who will bring her up?" he asked.

"She will be well looked after and protected; you have my word on that. When the time is right, perhaps you will meet her. But that is a long way away. She will need to grow and become a woman who can tie all this together on her own, with our guidance from afar. Only then will she be able to understand."

Cameron closed his eyes. Even now he couldn't command tears to come. Now even he had doubts as to whether Emilie was also a victim in this or if she'd been party to the plan. Now he understood that he would never have the chance to know.

"Cameron, I'm sorry."

When he made no reply, she started towards the door, placing her hand on the door handle.

"Sofia?"

She turned slightly, keeping her hand on the handle. "Yes, Cameron?"

"They know Siena is out there, don't they?"

Sofia sighed. She closed her eyes, took a deep breath and answered. "The list. *Acta Sanctorum*." She hesitated. "They have made an addition to it. I'm so sorry, Cameron."

PART FOUR

Dearest Siena,

My dear daughter. It won't be long now until we can be together in the real world. You are thirty-eight weeks. The creation of life is such a beautiful mystery of life, Siena. The more I allow myself to fall into the comfort of having you in this life with me, the more I feel impatient to want to share with you and show you everything there is to see. You will, no doubt, want to know how I chose your name. Well, Siena, one of the most beautiful cities in the world, is in Tuscany with its romantic, haunting, medieval brick buildings. I write this letter from there. I have been in Siena for a while now. This vast area of hills is encased by valleys and has the most perfect Mediterranean climate.

The old streets of Siena have the quaintest houses and the people here have so much love and kindness within them. The families have so much time and respect for each other and they really embrace togetherness. I often sit for hours in the shade of the towering Siena Cathedral. The façade is such a sight to witness – one of the most fascinating features in all of Italy. I sit tracing over the gargoyles and saints on the façade and each time I visit, I find new aspects of characters to them all.

I remember the first time your father and I visited this city.

How I miss him dearly. How I am sure you will have an abundance of questions surrounding your father. I only hope that you will one day be able to ask him face to face yourself. How I hope I will be able to do the same also! To see his face, to be able to hold his hand and to have his embrace once again.

I miss him so much it hurts. But don't let that make you sad. We must be strong, little one.

Now, more than ever, I need to be focused and strong to make everything safe and clear for your arrival. You will need to be protected from all this – from the game your parents are involved in.

You will come to realize that life can never be planned. Perhaps that is the beauty of time and life or perhaps that is its curse. I guess I was at fault for making that mistake also – thinking I could work out all the answers and be in control of my own destiny. But you see, to be able to control one's destiny, you must understand that there is no such thing as destiny in the first place. If I told you the future, then just by you knowing it, the future would change its path in that instance. Think of the colour green. Now, if you had free choice, knowing I told you to think of the colour green, would you have changed it because it was your own destiny to change it or because you knew I wanted you to think of that colour?

I didn't have the chance to tell your father of your creation. Of the miracle that you are. As I write this, he does not know of you and probably will not know of you for quite some time yet. That tears me apart more than anything, but also that you have been robbed of the chance to have your father holding you, kissing your head and marvelling in your smile and cry.

Your father and I had not planned on having a family yet, but that does not mean it was ever a mistake. You, if anything, have become the pinnacle and saviour of us having a new vision, a new horizon to aim for. Your importance will grow as time passes and as you grow into a strong adult, you will discover, I hope, the wonder of everything that surrounds your birthright from me and your father.

When the time is right, you will read this letter to remind you that although you didn't have a normal childhood, with how you perhaps imagined a family unit would be, it is imperative for you to know and to believe that we both love you so much, in a way that even words on this page are too primitive to try to explain with. I cannot define what a soul is, but I suppose it would encapsulate the spiritual aspect of a person. The emotional and intellectual inner energy of one's self. You are that, to your father and me. The mere thought of it is so delicate that it will fade away if you linger too long in order to capture it.

You will come to learn that the beauty and purest aspects of this world and life are not what we bring as people – they are what we already have at our disposal. We are so blind to see this at first, because it comes to us with no sacrifice. I hope that you start to see this early on and I will do all I can as a mother to help guide you in that manner. To help you wonder at the sky, which races on forever and ever with no end in sight. Creating a life of its own, with the emotions and moods it brings. The vast oceans that swallow themselves whole and never get tired of wanting to explore the earth, no matter which way the land takes them. The marvel of thousands of species, even just the ones we know of, how they interact and how all seem to know their places. This is all the beauty and innocence that even I was blind to. This is what I never want you to miss out on, my love.

Please know that certain decisions, which were made for you, were made to help protect you. I know you had no choice in these decisions and there will be nothing I can do to take that back or to right the wrongs. Those choices and decisions were made long before your father and I even met. As you will learn, it was the past that your father and I had that caused a collision in each other's worlds without us knowing it. I suppose you are paying for our blindness. But what I can try to provide you with is safe passage until you are strong enough to face the decisions you want to make.

I will help you focus and grow into a strong, magnificent woman. I will show you how science and humanity are, at present, all mixed with emotion and a lack of clarity. You will see how powerful these things are and how that power is craved by the evil within us all. We hold so many secrets as a species and so much pain and destruction come with that. We are foolish and selfish, yet feel we are so superior. I trust that you will discover my work and your father's work in time. You will learn that my work will not be finished by me alone and that only those of the purest souls can carry on the work to its full potential. But with that comes great danger. That danger emanates from the fact that people are blinded by greed and by the need to harbour power for their own gains. They want power, so they can feel that they have something over others. The imperious demands of us all are of our own kind. But in reality, we all are equal and it's our own inner demons that tell us otherwise. I am sorry that you will be the one to carry this burden of hope. But, your guidance will be critical for others – just like how you are guiding me right now.

Goodnight and sweet dreams, my dear child.

CHAPTER ONE

Later

Siena

She had felt his eyes watching her for the past few minutes from across the room. Although she was no stranger to people noticing her in public due to the looks she'd inherited from her parents, she felt this stare was more than just the simple interest of a stranger. Not one to be paranoid; perhaps it was just someone who wanted to experience the freedom of being out in the open again since the recent years. After all, the last few years had been a situation the likes of which had never been experienced before, for the planet and for everyone on it. To live in total isolation for so long, going against every aspect and right of what it meant to be human, to try to unite and fight against a common enemy that had killed so many millions across the globe. It was just nothing anyone could have prepared for. So as Siena stood there, in the great hall, taking in the breath-taking works of art, trying to experience and remember again what it was to have such freedom to learn and communicate again, she wondered if the eyes looking her way now were those of a friend or foe.

The dimple on her left cheek was always the first thing

that caught the attention of others. The way she smiled always enhanced the beauty of the dimple. The softness of her voice, yet with the gentle pressure of command and assertiveness. She always made movement seem so carefree and effortless. The way she bounced every time, taking steps like springs were part of her natural skeletal anatomy. The perfect balance of being humble and courteous, yet also setting an atmosphere for respect and admiration to be given to her.

Although it was a cold, autumn Sunday, with a grey heaviness to the air, Siena felt alive more than ever, being out and pottering around the city, visiting some of her favourite coffee houses and art galleries. After deciding to settle and complete her studies in London, she felt a sense of belonging here and an attachment due to her untold past. Although she didn't get to visit London with her mother, she was always told stories of London, with the delights and history surrounding it, by her mother, when she was growing up and travelling around various European cities. Perhaps knowing her mother and father had met in London was the aspect of attachment she felt now. Her father remained a force in her life that she hadn't met. How she kept that dream of meeting him alive within her and imagined the various things they would talk about and discuss when they finally met. Her mother would remind her of him every day when growing up and Siena had a mental and emotional picture of this man. But the more she thought of this image, the more it frustrated her with her longing to meet him.

The drizzle of rain started to fall. Siena was reminded of the letter her mother wrote to her, while she was still in her womb. How the letter explained that humans took for granted the simple wonders of this world.

Siena left The National Gallery, which was situated just on the steps of Trafalgar Square. Today it was a total contrast to the footage on television of this area when the great lockdown had started in the latter part of 2020, with the deadly spread of the coronavirus spanning the world. Families pulled apart, with members coming down suddenly with the illness, many unable to survive. Medical services around the world, under stress and strain, were pulling together to save the unfortunate. Governments imposed social isolation and total lockdown of cities and country borders were closed. All aircrafts were grounded. The normal hustle and bustle of daily life ground to a halt. Outdoor spaces became eerie, empty abysses of a vacuum. They weren't ghost towns, they became ghost worlds. Never would humanity think that rows and rows of bodies would be buried in containers on islands due to the sheer numbers of deaths; most families being unable to afford funerals or even to attend to say goodbye to their loved ones due to the deadly contagion of the virus. Leaders around the world stood and confirmed to the public that only a few people died from contracting the virus. How they also asked people to stay indoors, claiming that they could contain the virus and that a 'good outcome' would be deaths around twenty thousand. How that figure spun out of control to rise like a balloon with no sign of losing its hot air to elevate it. How thousands turned into hundreds of thousands, into millions, into entire cities, regions, countries and civilizations.

Now Siena walked through a busy, crowded Trafalgar Square. People were laughing, shouting and speaking. Others were holding hands; a couple kissed while standing on the steps and children threw balls to each other. How all this was now normal daily life again, yet knowing there was a time when all of this had ceased to occur. Just empty, hollow, painful, deafening silences everywhere.

This was the destruction that the virus named COVID-19 had caused. The deadly and highly contagious virus, which was the invisible enemy that ripped through the world. Siena was all too well-versed into the pathology of the virus – after all, her parents were part of the cause and cure without knowing it at the time.

She glanced at her watch and smiled, as she knew she had time to visit where she felt a strong attachment to her father. The place where she could hear her father's whispers, his voice in her head telling her, teaching her and comforting her.

As she weaved through the pedestrians on the pavement, she watched how families and friends were out, many holding hands and wrapped up warm, ready for the afternoon or evening performances they may be going to see. The theatre district hid behind the streets of Covent Garden, bordering the Strand. The dullness to the afternoon created the perfect backdrop like a stage, for the warm lights of shopfronts and stores to radiate out around everyone, creating the illusion of warmth for them. A blanket wrapped around everyone tightly.

Approaching on the right is Waterloo Bridge and standing on the corner is the eighteenth-century neoclassical grand building of Somerset House – a magnificent building with its central, open courtyard that had been used for various exhibitions and concert venues. It was also used for the traditional open-air cinemas and the annual ice-skating rink, complete with a towering Christmas tree every December. Within the grounds, to the east wing, is the Courtauld Gallery, which has an acclaimed collection of masterpieces. Names that can be traced back over time, which have taught us so much for today. Artists such as Botticelli, Cézanne, Degas, Monet and Renoir. They all sit on the wall of Somerset House, while fountains play outside in the courtyard in a splendour of elegance. As Siena made her way past, she moved her slightly damp hair to the side, away from her face, and breathed in the air. She stopped to look under the arches into the courtyard. She closed her eyes and pictured her parents spending endless hours here. Sitting, reading, holding hands, walking through the fountains discussing the merits of each artist's work and what message lay beneath. The sounds around her faded into the background and she was awoken again to the sound of a child's scream and laughter as they ran and jumped at the fountains.

She looked down the road, in the direction of her travel, sighing at the thought of her father once walking those very streets, that very route. She continued down the Strand toward Fleet Street and Ludgate Hill.

She approached the busy intersection of Fleet Street, crossing over to get onto Ludgate Hill with Farringdon Street running in front of her path. She could feel her heartbeat quicken slightly as she knew she would see the dome appearing in the distance. No matter how many times her eyes fell on it, it always had the same influence on her. She held her eyes steadfast to the pavement in front of her for as long as she could. But the pull, the attraction, the calling of the dome was too great. She hesitated for a second and stopped walking. Then looked ahead and up. There it stood.

Waiting for her, just as it did for her father. Breathing its deep meaningful breath to assert its imposing presence – St Paul's Cathedral.

She knew it was nonsensical to think that the cathedral could sense her every time she walked by, calling her to come in and to visit the Whispering Gallery, the crypts, the hidden passages and the dormant room. Her logical sense knew that bricks and mortar couldn't feel or retain events and pass them on to her over many years, but she had always been unnerved by this place because of the history that her mother explained to her. The tiny hairs on her neck and arms stood to attention as she continued to walk past the churchyard of St Paul's, heading towards Cannon Street. She wished she could be invisible to the world at this point, as she felt like everyone was conspiring against her under the instructions of the cathedral. She shook her head and thought, *It is nonsense.* She quickened her pace, reminded herself of the perfect day so far and allowed the raindrops to soak into her thoughts to dampen any residual trauma.

A further ten minutes' walk and she had arrived to take a left onto Walbrook and stood outside the modern, tall, glass Bloomberg Building. The building used light and shapes to create the illusion and spatial awareness of deformity within light. The design won several accolades and awards for architecture by incorporating structures such as a vortex ramp inside the building and using six hundred tonnes of bronze imported from Japan and granite from India.

As Siena entered, she made her way to the far end where the escalators took her seven metres underground to arrive at the opening of several rooms, which housed over fourteen thousand artefacts, including the first written mention of the name 'London'.

Siena walked into the great main chamber of the Temple of Mithras. As with all places, this had remained closed off due to the virus outbreak. It remained hidden from the outside world once again, just as it did for centuries before its initial discovery.

She stood by the central atrium, looking across the remnants of stone wall structures. The air had a dry but cool presence to it. She walked slowly up the aisle; arms folded across her chest. With a deep breath, she inhaled the memories of this place, filling her lungs with the saturated history full of secrets and mysteries that this place held. Her eyes calmed at the stage that unfolded in front of her. She stopped to take in, with deep concentration, the magnificent display of stone carvings. The same display she had visited many times repeatedly, of late. Her eyes traced over the delicate markings on the stone walls. She had memorized these markings to such a degree that she would be able to recreate them – from the exact dimensions down to the minuscule detail. Such detail would include the most important aspect of what was missing in the display: the spaces for the missing symbols from the carvings. Symbols, which to this day, had never been recovered or documented in any surviving manuscript. She smiled, moved her hand delicately to her neck and pulled out her necklace from underneath her shirt. A ring reclined on the chain. Resting there, like it owned its position on the neck of Siena. This very necklace and ring, which were mysteriously delivered to her on a sunny afternoon one spring day, with nothing but a note with the words: *'From Goram'*. The name that she knew was once her father's trusted driver and confidant in London. She ran her fingers around the circumference of the ring, feeling the delicate symbols of it and tracing her eyes at the same time to the missing segments of the stone carvings in front of her. *How convenient that those key aspects of coded symbols are missing from the stone slabs,* she thought to herself, and turned to walk away while pulling from her pocket what seemed to be a scrap piece of paper. She slowly unfolded it, so gentle with her touch so as not to disturb the ink on it, as though the text written on the paper would jump off and float away if discovered. The text read:

Acta Sanctorum

Maynard
Cameron
Emilie
Siena

Aleksandr lives in London, UK. Having a passion and fascination of history and how that is reflected in culture around the world, he focuses his writing on that view point.

His career has spanned many backgrounds that he encompasses in his writing. Having being involved in the medical world, creative industries of film and music and also balancing his real passion of humanitarian work, he finds all those aspects as inspiration for his writing.

Focusing now on bringing all that his inner passion and reflection has taught him to share in his writing with others. He is embarking on writing a series of novels with a narrative of meaning and thought.

He is a keen health advocate and exercise enthusiast with an addiction to all things that taste like coffee!

"Writing gave me the door to help unravel the aspects that our brain cortex locks away, deep within us, to alter how we interact with others and the world around us. Fearful events, trauma and hurt that we do not process correctly can cause pain for those around us that care. It is very easy to project pain in others and our surroundings if we do not look within us first. It has now become a lifelong mission for me to become a better version of me and continue to value important lessons to always be learnt. Human interaction needs to always make us reflect and better ourselves."

Please scan the QR code below
to take you to more books by Aleksandr
and to leave any comments or reviews

Also available from Alexsandr Jarid

SUNFLOWER

Burnt out, broke, obsessive freelance journalist Hugo Janson sees his world closing in all around him. Feeling suffocated with simple daily tasks, he struggles to maintain functioning in today's society. He has lost the woman that loved him unconditionally, lost respect professionally from his colleagues and has debt mounting all around him. Just when he felt all was lost, a stranger called Femi befriends him and takes his hand on a quest to redeem himself on every aspect of his life. Hugo and Femi chase the lost Sunflower of Vincent Van Gogh to prove his obsession was not futile in nature. A new friendship brings Hugo validation in himself and seeks to settles the monsters within him. But what is unleashed instead, is far worse than he could have ever imagined.

Coming soon from Alexsandr Jarid

NEW HOPE

Intelligent, independent, focused and with a passion for life. Siena has everything going for her. Surrounded by friends who are her only family and together they are working on ground breaking research that could change the face of humanity. What is there not to love about her life?

But, all is not settled under her surface. The darkness that has cursed her parents now hunts her. The shadows rise and Siena now faces the greatest test of her life. Pushing her mental, emotional and physical attributes to her breaking point. A guardian from the past arrives to protect her against an evil that is not what it seems. Siena soon realises there is no present state, only that of the past and what lays ahead in the future.

Printed in Great Britain
by Amazon